A HERO'S WELCOME

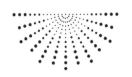

ALSO BY DANIEL KELLY

Heroes of Troy:

The Fall of The Phoenix

A HERO'S WELCOME

PART II: HEROES OF TROY

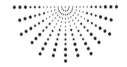

DANIEL KELLY

CONTENTS

THE STORY SO FAR   xi

Chapter 1   1
Chapter 2   5
Chapter 3   9
Chapter 4   14
Chapter 5   17
Chapter 6   25
Chapter 7   29
Chapter 8   32
Chapter 9   36
Chapter 10   42
Chapter 11   50
Chapter 12   57
Chapter 13   61
Chapter 14   69
Chapter 15   74
Chapter 16   83
Chapter 17   88
Chapter 18   92
Chapter 19   100
Chapter 20   107
Chapter 21   111
Chapter 22   115
Chapter 23   119
Chapter 24   130
Chapter 25   134
Chapter 26   148
Chapter 27   156
Chapter 28   160
Chapter 29   172
Chapter 30   178

Chapter 31   182
Chapter 32   191
Chapter 33   196
Chapter 34   200
Chapter 35   205
Chapter 36   212
Chapter 37   222
Chapter 38   236
Chapter 39   251
Epilogue   258

Acknowledgments   261

For my parents
Who believed even when I didn't

"If history were taught in the form of stories,
It would never be forgotten"- Rudyard Kipling

THE STORY SO FAR

Troy Has Fallen

Twelve hundred years before the term was penned, Agamemnon has achieved a pyrrhic victory, his army reduced to almost nothing.

A traitor in the Greek army had warned Priam of the wooden horse, and rather than destroy it on the beach Priam turned it into an opportunity: he sacrificed his city as a distraction while a group of refugees led by Aeneas, including his only remaining son, escaped the slaughter.

Agamemnon, the tyrant, has had his manpower so reduced that he must return to his stronghold of Mycenae.

CHAPTER ONE

THE AXE CRASHED DOWN BESIDE HIS HAND, SPLINTERING WOOD. Any closer and he would have lost fingers. His first inclination was to pull his hand away and he flinched, but a second later he was gripping tightly again as the ship listed to the other side, nearly floundering.

"I said, cut that damn rope," called the captain. "The loose sail is going to pull us over!" This time Agamemnon did move away as the sailor took another swing at the offending rope, which sailed away into the storm like a ghost disappearing into the night.

The captain had wanted Agamemnon to stay in his cabin below deck, but the idea of being trapped below if the ship sank terrified him.

It had been blowing a gale for two days now, having sprung up suddenly at dusk just a week out of Troy and scattering his remaining fleet over the wide ocean. His captain had not yet been able to find a safe place to beach on the rocky coastline, and was trying instead to stay a little further out to avoid the risk of being broken against the shore.

But two days of a storm was too much for any ship; using the oars only to correct the course and keep them away from rocks was still too much for the exhausted crew. It was time to find somewhere to beach or lack the strength when an easier option arose.

Agamemnon was losing hope, accepting the irony that he had fought a ten-year war to destroy Troy only to die in a freak storm. Then a shout came from the prow. The words were impossible to make out over the scream of the storm, but the noise of someone shouting drew the eye and the lookout was pointing at the coast to starboard.

He couldn't believe it, was reluctant to believe it, having finally accepted his fate after all they had gone through. Agamemnon looked, straining to see as he leant from the railing in the direction the lookout had pointed, while the ship once again tried to throw him overboard. He could see nothing but the crash of waves and sea spray competing for dominance over the thundering rain that was determined to be wetter than the ocean.

As he strained his eyes and wiped another wave from his face, only for it to be replaced by rain, he saw it; or rather, he saw something.

It was impossible to make out, with no discernible shape or colour. He was relying completely on the knowledge and experience of his captain and crew to identify the smudge on the horizon: a lighter shadow in a world of them, one that didn't move with the storm, didn't blow with the clouds or erupt with the waves. Suddenly the helmsman was struggling against the rudder, trying to push the boat against the waves, while the captain was screaming orders for the men at oars to make one final effort.

Agamemnon experienced a relief he had never felt in the heat of battle and he ran to the struggling helmsman, throwing his weight against the rudder as it fought the waves to turn the gigantic bireme towards shore. Slowly, with feet slipping on the wet wood, the rudder started to move until they had brought it to the limit of its capacity. Muscles straining, they held it against the strength of the ocean. It felt like an age before they could feel the prow of the vessel pulling to the right, and then all at once a wave struck them side on and the ship tilted alarmingly from the impact.

Forcing the rudder back to a straight course towards their smudge of hope, it took almost as much effort to avoid over-steering. Once they had the course set, however, between the oars and the waves hitting the stern to drive them forward, holding her steady became hard but they could feel her moving forward. The smudge slowly became an outline, and a hope he hadn't dared harbour bloomed in Agamemnon's chest.

Through the years of war, as he had expanded his empire and united the armies of all the cities of his Greece, the Greece he had created, Agamemnon had always been focused forward to the next battle, the next city, the next war. Always pushing onward, he was driven by insatiable ambition.

For three days now he had accepted that he was going to die in a storm, in a sea he couldn't fight or conquer, and all that had motivated him for so long now seemed a waste of time. He would have given up his dreams of conquest just to be home, to raise his children and make love to his wife. As with every other dream of his life, that now seemed possible; he had survived, the beach was close by.

Not close enough, it seemed, as a horrible crash sounded and wood splintered and shattered. Rocks were suddenly visible where, seconds before, oarsmen had struggled. Where the oarsmen were now Agamemnon couldn't tell, only that the side of the ship had been all but ripped apart and water was now flooding in.

As rocks halted their forward momentum, the ship lurched forward and listed horribly as Agamemnon's feet left the deck for the last time and the sea rushed to meet him, taking him into its embrace.

CHAPTER TWO

Days dragged into weeks sitting on the shore. Nestor had managed to beach his ship and two others had also, the morning after the storm had broken over the Aegean. Five ships had left Troy together, heading for Mycenae; now two were missing and Agamemnon was among their passengers.

To have survived ten years of war in Troy for this - to die at sea while travelling home? No, it was impossible; Agamemnon had to be out there somewhere. Thoughts swirled in Nestor's head, which felt too small for all that was going on inside it. He looked back out to sea, scanning the horizon. It was a big ocean, and only luck had brought the three ships on to this beach after the storm had scattered the fleet. Agamemnon had to be out there somewhere; anything else was unthinkable.

He'd had his last sighting of the sleek bireme when the light had failed on the night of the storm. The lamps hanging from prow and stern, by which to steer at night, had remained inter-mittently visible for nearly an hour after dark as it bobbed up and down behind the huge waves. Nestor had done all he could to follow, whipping the men into a frenzy and even jumping down to add his own considerable strength to the oars, but it had been no good.

Soon his own ship was bobbing alone like a cork in the ocean and the decision was taken from his hands. Finding somewhere to beach the stricken ship became the only option, as the alternative was to be knocked around blind in the dark sea until it inevitably managed to capsize his ship.

It had been almost dawn when the mast had snapped; the men, exhausted from trying to add some little direction to their torment in Poseidon's domain, were slow to react as it came down. No sail was attached in this weather but, as another colossal wave lurched the body of the ship upwards, it came into its path with the weight of a falling tree; the weight had crushed at least ten men but fortunately had formed only a small crack in the hull. More men had been caught in the path of the rigging and dragged overboard to a watery grave.

It was impossible to tell exactly how many had been crushed instantly and how many dragged overboard while alive, but all told there were twenty-three men missing from his boat with another six walking wounded. It was hard to tell which of the dead were luckier, the crushed or the drowned, thought Nestor grimly. The storm had washed most of the blood away before dawn, but splinters of bone embedded in the bench stood testament to the devastation it had caused.

Frustrated, Nestor turned away from the sea to the beach full of men. Spits hung over fires, hunting and fishing parties had been doing their jobs and the beach was a busy camp, running efficiently, but he couldn't take any satisfaction in it while they were stuck there. He knew he had no choice; he couldn't just cut down a tree and stick it into his boat, since they wouldn't last very long when they went back to sea, but they were far from any big town and the timber had to be cut fresh before treating it.

And this beach was running efficiently, just as bloody Troy had. Ten years he had spent stuck there; even if he hadn't been worried about Agamemnon and the other ship, he sorely missed his own wife and family. He longed for his little house up in the hills, with his sheep and goats, well away from the bloody beach and sea. After ten years in Troy, if he never saw another beach again, that would be just fine by him.

Absentmindedly his hand went up and rubbed over the rough skin on the side of his face where the burning sand had left its mark. He'd been lucky to have been under the arch of the gates when it had fallen so that only the drifting particles had been carried drifting in the air onto his face.

He had seen it coming down of the wall and remembered clearly the confusion before he had seen the men it touched screaming in agony, ripping at their armour trying to get it off. He had just managed to turn his head and close his eyes in time to be saved the worst of it. The less fortunate were left blind and hideously scarred, and would never fight again.

Those even less fortunate had suffered in terrible agony for days, until the order had been given for them to be put out of their misery. Tents had been filled with men screaming in agony and begging to die. Some who had managed to obtain weapons had done the deed themselves.

It was a vision which still haunted his dreams; an experience he would never forget. Some things couldn't be excused by war.

Nestor walked with purpose up the beach to where the carpenters were working on the wood for the new mast and replacement planks where his hull had taken the crack. He barked at them, "Is that bloody mast not ready yet?"

They exchanged nervous glances, frustrating him more, before one spoke up. "Nearly," he piped. "It's having the final treatment now, but the pitch for the side with the new planks will take a couple of days yet."

"A couple of days!" repeated Nestor.

"It's necessary if we're to stay afloat," said the man, a little more confidently.

"Huh!" was Nestor's response as he turned away. There was nothing he could do except wait.

CHAPTER THREE

CLYTEMNESTRA LAY IN BED, HER LONG, THIN MUSCLE-CORDED body immodestly covered with the white Egyptian cotton sheets which had been a gift from her lover Aegisthus. Through the window the room was washed red from the rising sun, a welcome relief after the storm which had battered the coast over the previous week.

Her red curls spilled over Aegisthus's toned stomach as her head rested on his chest. She watched the rising of the sun while her lover slept on, tired from the trading trip he had just made to Athens, and from the welcome she had given him on his return. She blushed slightly, remembering the night before, and stroked his belly.

Agamemnon had never deserved her, this she knew. Her father had bartered her to the exiled prince to forge an alliance between Mycenae and Sparta. Her sister Helen had been part of the same bargain, but at least she had been able to remain in Sparta as queen while Clytemnestra had been shipped to Mycenae.

After six years of marriage, during which she had provided Agamemnon with an heir and three strong daughters, he had deserted her - chasing off with his brother Menelaus after that slut Helen when she'd run off with the young prince of Troy. He had left her alone, waiting, for nearly ten years.

Worse, he had sacrificed their eldest daughter to Artemis. That was what had almost broken Clytemnestra: her baby girl, Iphigenia, murdered for the favour of the gods in the quest to find Clytemnestra's little sister.

No, she wouldn't wait around for him like some faithful dog. Aegisthus was only too willing to accommodate her. He wanted all that Agamemnon had, after losing the throne of Mycenae to him. He wanted to insult him by claiming not only the throne in his absence, but also his beautiful wife. Although Clytemnestra knew she was part of a prize to Aegisthus, it was also obvious how much he wanted her in her own right and that was a thrill she had never felt with Agamemnon. He lusted to have her in a way she had never experienced before, always fading into the shade around her little sister Helen when by rights she was the equal of almost any woman.

Aegisthus gave a contented groan as the morning light woke him and stroked her neck with his hand but she climbed out from the bed and covered herself with a gown before walking over to the table in her room. She poured two cups of water and brought them over, handing him one.

She could feel his eyes caressing her throughout and enjoyed the teasing. "Time to get up," she told him, though she could see he had other ideas in mind and held herself just out of reach. "There's work to be done."

He had been all but living in the palace for three years now, living like he was the king of Mycenae while maintaining his own villa further east along the coast. His own men guarded the palace, training and recruiting for the Mycenaen army to replace those whom Agamemnon had taken to Troy and to ensure a powerbase of loyal men in the event that Agamemnon should ever return. He intended to hold Mycenae.

Reluctantly he dragged himself from bed and began to don his leather armour. "Any new recruits while I was away?" he asked. Clytemnestra had been keeping his records for him and using the city funds for recruiting since they had first discussed the possibility of holding the city and refusing Agamemnon. It hadn't been difficult to plant the idea in his head and easier still to convince him that it had been his idea all along.

"A few shepherds wanting to escape the life their fathers had planned for them," she said, shrugging. "They look as if they wouldn't be able to hold a sword without cutting themselves."

"They all have to start somewhere," Aegisthus countered. "Give them three months and we might be able to make something of them. They don't get paid until they are trained, anyway. And we can send any who are truly useless to Agamemnon in Troy, to help with the war effort!" He winked at her.

For nearly three years now, they had been sending the absolute worst of the recruits to Troy in six-month dispatches. They were probably more of a hindrance than a help to Agamemnon, but it looked as if Clytemnestra was actively recruiting for him while actually weakening his army. Any who showed potential were trained personally by Aegisthus for their private army, in expectation of Agamemnon's return; another year and they might have the equal of the army he had originally brought to Troy.

Hopefully Agamemnon wouldn't bring all the armies of Greece back to Mycenae, but there was no reason why he should; they would all be anxious to see their own homes after so long. Aegisthus and Clytemnestra should be able to dispatch him before he could send a call for support. Well, a little luck and surprise would help along the way.

He drew her into an embrace, crushing her to his chest to kiss her, while she placed her hands flat against the tough armour on his chest and pushed him towards the door. "Go!"

she insisted, a smile curling the corners of her lips as he opened the door and slipped silently into the hall.

She was left in the quiet of early dawn, alone in her room with the taste of his lips on her mouth. It tasted like a promise for the future, for their future. The quiet would not last long; soon the yard below her window would come alive to the sound of Aegisthus training their soldiers, and the sounds of servants coming and going in the palace. She herself would have to deal with a stream of petitioners in her audience hall.

Her mood was soon soured as a thought crept back into her mind. One of her petitioners ten days ago had actually been a messenger. She went again to her jewellery box and took out the missive he had brought. Opening it, she could easily recognise the scrawled handwriting of her husband even if it hadn't borne his seal on the outside. Writing had never been his strong point, her warrior king, and even their twelve-year-old daughter's style far outclassed him.

Agamemnon would instruct his scribe to write out anything official in order to impress a foreign dignitary, but he had always tried to send anything personal to her in his own handwriting. It was about the only personal touch he brought to their life together, but showed some degree of effort.

The message was a simple one, just four short lines. He probably wanted to save the details for his glorious arrival back to Mycenae, so she had had the messenger silenced and had so far not told anyone about the contents of the missive.

The war is over.
Troy has fallen.
Expect us back within the month.
Agamemnon.

After so long: ten years of war, the biggest war in history, bringing hundreds of thousands of Greeks across the sea. A war that would change everything in Greece for hundreds of years to come, it had ended a little too soon for Clytemnestra. One more year would have given her enough time to feel comfortable of victory when he returned, but now it felt as if the walls were closing in around her.

She told herself that she hadn't told Aegisthus yesterday so that they could spend the night together before the reality of their situation was forced upon them, but the truth was that she was fearful. Agamemnon had not come by his reputation accidentally. When Menelaus had inherited Sparta through his marriage to Clytemnestra's sister, they had acquired an army with which to take back Mycenae from Thyestes.

Aegisthus had been too young at the time to fight; no doubt, even if he had been of fighting age, he would have ended as one more bloodstain from Agamemnon's mighty hammer. The stories said he had cleared the palace almost single-handedly that day, laying about him with wild abandon in his thirst for vengeance against his father's murderer.

The floor of his audience chamber had since been replaced, but when Clytemnestra had first arrived in Mycenae there had been a large gouge in the floor; she had been told that it was there that Thyestes had made his final stand against a much younger Agamemnon. When he had fallen Agamemnon had just kept swinging, kept hitting him as if he were felling a tree, until there was nothing left but a pool of blood and pulp staining the stones of the floor.

Agamemnon had never told her about it. Now, though the master of the house was different, a lot of the servants and slaves in the household remained the same people who had served Thyestes before him.

Aegisthus would have to be told this to give them time to prepare. They must decide what to do. Should they still go ahead with the plan? Could they hold the city with the men they had?

CHAPTER FOUR

Orestes sat up on the hill overlooking Mycenae. He had been sent up early the previous evening to check on the sheep and goats for his mother. Slaves were up here almost constantly watching over them; there were twelve of them, so that they could relieve one another. They took turns travelling up and down to their families, to give them a break from sleeping up here in the shepherd's hut surrounded by livestock.

It was birthing season and, because of the storms of early spring, Clytemnestra wanted the stock counted. Some sheep would be lost to birthing, and he would collect the carcases for the kitchens and find out how many lambs had been born.

Usually Orestes enjoyed going up into the hills, away from the watchful eyes of his mother and the servants who reported everything he did. He would bring a few of his friends, steal a few skins of wine and spend up to a week here with a big fire and lots of roasted meat every evening.

Today, though, he sat holding the wineskin to his chest, his back to the fire where his friends were drinking. They were cooking a carcase with a few of the slaves who shared some of the rough spirit they sometimes distilled while they were sitting up the hills for weeks at a time. His friend Castor had tried to drag him into the festivities, but he had barely moved from his spot looking down on the city, a blanket over his shoulders.

His eyes were focused on one area of the city, though nobody would have noticed. It was the walls of the palace that drew his eye.

He knew why his mother had been in such a hurry to get him up this hill yesterday. The livestock were important, but they could have waited. No, it was because Aegisthus had arrived back from Athens late yesterday. Orestes had seen some of his wagons come in the western gate as they were ascending the hill.

Orestes hated Aegisthus and made no attempt to hide the fact. He was now fifteen, having been only five when his father had set out to wage his war on Troy, but he well remembered the big man. With his ringletted hair and his oiled beard, he would bounce Orestes on his knee before setting the child gently to the ground, then picking up his mighty hammer and smashing it into a foreign emissary in a fit of rage at some demand in the space of seconds. On setting the hammer down, however, he would always turn back to his son as a gentle father.

He had only begun to teach Orestes weapon-craft before he had left to take Troy, but had ensured that the best tutors in both academic fields and warfare had been sent to the boy while he was away. Now Orestes almost matched his father's size, having grown to well over six foot tall with the same broad shoulders that he remembered. He still had some filling-out to do, but already he was easily able to handle the spare war hammer his father had left leaning against his throne, a reminder to any who might try to sit there while he was away.

His mother didn't even try to hide her infidelity with Aegisthus, flaunting herself in front of him. Orestes loved his mother as any fifteen-year-old does, and knew what would happen to her when his father returned to find his oldest of enemies sharing her bed. But Orestes knew it was something he would gladly see to watch that hammer find a new home in Aegisthus's skull. He would have done it himself but for the fact that the guards his father had left there had been replaced by men loyal to Aegisthus from his own estates up the coast.

Where the old guards had gone, he didn't know. He knew they were as loyal to his father as he was to them and he would never have let them go with nothing; but ten years is a long time to leave a throne vacant and men's memories were short. His father's men, his men, would have gone to seek what employment they could find to keep themselves fed till their lord and master returned.

Orestes didn't worry too much about the number of men Aegisthus had brought in who were loyal to him: when his father returned, all the armies of Greece would be in his wake and the pitiful few hundred Aegisthus had gathered around him would quickly fall away, abandoning him in the face of the overwhelming odds arrayed against them. Then he would see what the loyalty of his men was truly worth. Still, it rankled that his mother had handed everything to Aegisthus on a plate over the last few years. It showed the difference between the two men: Agamemnon had had nothing handed to him; he had taken it.

His friend called to Orestes that the sheep was ready, and he stopped brooding for a while as he joined them to eat and gulp down some wine, yet he couldn't keep his eyes and thoughts from drifting back down the hill to the palace of his father. His time would come soon enough.

CHAPTER FIVE

PAIN, PAIN EVERYWHERE, AND WATER, SALT AND SAND BELOW it all.

The sting of the salt on Agamemnon's head brought consciousness slowly. The pale light of dawn was leaching into the sky and his eyes sprang open with fear and shock. The gulls, who had been investigating his supine body much too closely, took to the air while calling out their disappointment at their breakfast having moved.

Rolling slowly onto his front, he pushed himself up onto his hands and knees. It took an immense effort to lift up his head and look around the beach on which he'd washed up. Splintered boards, ropes and netting lay all around, sailcloth rose and fell at the water's edge and bodies were scattered everywhere. Some were lying in the water, tangled in the ropes, and bobbing with the current, obviously dead, but others were scattered across the sand as he had been, carried in on the high storm waves to be abandoned as the storm calmed and retreated down the beach.

Water! Water had caused this, and now it was all he could think about. He had to find something to drink. Even the other bodies scattered across the sand would have to wait or he would be no use to them. Looking around, he saw a small stream flowing down from the grassy hills above the beach towards the sea. There must be a natural spring further up.

Stumbling to his feet, he could barely stand. Sand seemed to have got in everywhere, filling his mouth and nose; he could feel it crusted around his eyes and in his hair, but for now comfort must be forgotten to concentrate on survival. He didn't seem to be badly injured, with the exception of a lump on his head, but that didn't stop him hurting all over from a hundred bruises and he limped towards the sound of running water.

The beach was a mess, littered with the bodies of his men, dead or unconscious. One had been impaled on debris, and another had been skewered by one of the weapons thrown ashore with force when the ship hit the rocks at full speed. He could now see in the cold light of day that those rocks were only a handful of yards from shore with the tide out full. Another body lay with a crate buried in the sand where his head should be.

It made him wonder at the capricious nature of the gods, that these men should survive ten years of war only to be killed by a freak storm on their way home.

The smell of death rose with the sun and made him gag. With a mouthful of salt and sand and more crystallising on his skin in the warming rays of the sun, he stumbled over the bodies. Some moaned as his trailing foot hit them when he limped past in search of water, wine - anything to clear the taste out of his mouth.

A scrap of sail had ripped free of the rest and wrapped itself around what was left of the main mast; as he passed it, a piece of rope tangled his legs and brought him tumbling to the ground for another mouthful of sand. The fall accentuated the pains all through his body, screaming in a blaze of fire right through him; frustration and anger got the better of him as he lashed out with his foot at the offending mast, realising too late that kicking a two-foot-thick piece of mast was likely to hurt.

The pain never came as the mast gave way below his foot and rolled away. The sail which had lain over it fell to the side, and he saw long straight hair on a beautiful face that couldn't have been more than twenty-three. The severity of his mistake hit him like a wave.

In an instant the great and powerful Agamemnon, the king of all Greeks, was scrabbling round on his hands and knees pulling at the sail to free her from its clutches and desperately trying to work out where his angry kick might have landed. He was suddenly very glad to have been so badly weakened when he'd kicked out.

There was no apparent injury and his hands moved up to her face, pulling her wet, gritty hair back as gently as he could, desperately hoping that she was still alive. This was the one prize he had thought worthy of bringing home from Troy: Cassandra, once the daughter of Priam. She was no longer recognised as a princess of Troy, since she had left the palace for the life of a priestess of Apollo before the Greeks had landed and the temple had been ransacked.

Contrary to popular opinion, it was not her looks or her body that Agamemnon wanted. As far as he knew the girl was still a virgin, since his men all knew he would kill anyone who touched his property. Agamemnon had heard the rumours years before about the girl, she had predicted that Paris would bring about the destruction of troy but nobody believed in her gift. Agamemnon was not everyone else. And there were those who believed that these, gifts, were lost with a girls virginity.

No, if Agamemnon had had his way the temple wouldn't have been ransacked but it had happened on arrival, before he had even known the temple was outside the walls of Troy; by the time he knew, this girl was the only one left alive.

Angering the gods was never a good idea, a hard fact that

had cost him a beloved daughter, Iphigenia, to appease the fickle Artemis before he had left for Troy. He was certainly in need of the favour of Apollo now.

Struggling to his feet, he looked around and could see the stream running down the beach towards the sea only a few yards away; those yards might as well have been miles while he felt like this, every step an agony. Again he looked down at Cassandra.

He couldn't lift her, he hadn't the strength, but he needed whatever favour the gods would allow him so, before the last of his strength and will gave out, he reached down a huge meaty hand and gripped her by the wrist. With stumbling steps he dragged her along, trailing sand behind and rubbing her roughly till he could fall to his knees by the stream. He dropped her hand and cupped water with his hands into his mouth.

The first couple of mouthfuls he spat out, the liquid doing little more than moving the sand around in his mouth before it cleared enough to make him feel safe swallowing a few mouthfuls. He could feel the improvement in him almost immediately as he gulped down the liquid before reaching back to grip Cassandra's arm again and drag her the last few feet. Rolling her over, he held her head above the water and splashed some onto her face and into her mouth.

He was still trying to feel a pulse, breathing, any sign of life from her as he did this, when finally he splashed water into her mouth and brought on a bout of coughing. He stopped splashing the water long enough for her to cough it out of her lungs before rolling her onto her back again, a little back from the water so that she wouldn't drown. This done, he rolled onto his back and dropped his head on the sand.

It might have been only minutes or it could have been hours later, he couldn't tell, when a cough followed by a low groan brought him out of the semi-oblivion he had let himself slip into. The water he had drunk had helped restore him; although the pain still lanced through him at every movement it was now just pain, no worse than he had felt in the aftermath of a hundred battles. Coherent thought once again seemed possible and he found he could function.

Rolling onto his front, he scooped some more water into his mouth before looking around at the wreckage that surrounded him. Cassandra was still lying within arm's reach where he had left her, but her chest was now rising and falling visibly. He climbed to his feet and heard the groaning again.

Looking around at the bodies of his men, he moved towards the source of the noise. If he could find a few men alive, he would have help checking everyone else. Shambling forward, he found Alkon trapped under one of the beams broken away from the ship. He reached down and tried to lift the beam, gripping the broken section closest to Alkon and groaning through gritted teeth at the pain lancing through him as he tensed every muscle in his body for the lift.

Seconds stretched as they do when you are in such pain, then the beam gave a shuddering movement as broken debris leaning against it tumbled away. The beam itself was still in position and he couldn't lift more than a few precious finger-breadths above Alkon's chest, but he could feel the light sigh of release and laboured breathing coming from the man. Veins bulging in his neck as he strained against the weight, he hated the sure knowledge that he was going to have to set the beam back on Alkon. Closing his eyes, he gritted his teeth and suddenly it felt lighter; he could feel movement coming from it. His back slowly straightened till he was once again upright and he opened his eyes. Polybius stood opposite him, with blood trickling from a cut to his head and more dried on his leg, lifting from the other side.

Slowly they managed to manhandle the beam down past Alkon's feet and drop it onto the sand, where they both lay down to recover themselves. Agamemnon looked up and reached out a hand to grip Polybius' forearm. "Am I glad to see you," he finally managed to utter, in a voice still coarse and dry.

Polybius slowly got to his feet and went to check on Alkon. "A few broken ribs, but I don't think the lungs are punctured so he should survive. And you?" he looked directly at Agamemnon as he spoke.

Agamemnon stood up slowly and looked down at himself as if it were something he had forgotten to do. Bruising stood out brightly on the parts he could see but there was no visible blood, perhaps because he had woken up on his back with half of him still in the water. "Better than you I think," he replied and Polybius raised a hand to gently touch the source of the dried blood on his forehead.

"This seems to be just a scratch," he replied. "A little bruising; the leg is worse, but I was just tying off a bandage to stop it bleeding when I heard you trying to lift that." He indicated the beam. "Have you found anyone else alive?"

"Only Cassandra; she's over by the stream, still unconscious." He indicated the direction with a vague wave of his hand, "It's fresh water, by the way; you'll probably be needing a drink." Polybius nodded his appreciation and Agamemnon continued. "His moaning drew me to him. We have to find a few more capable of helping us search, or we'll never manage to check everyone in time."

"I can help with that," said Cassandra, walking towards them. She was obviously shaken from her ordeal, but she was of royal blood and didn't let her fears and discomfort show. Carrying the bottom half of a broken amphora which she had filled with water, she went first to Agamemnon with it.

"Let them have some," said the king. "I can get more later." So she brought water to Polybius, who took a couple of long drinks before kneeling down to try to dribble some into the mouth of the unconscious Alkon, who coughed most of it out on the sand.

"If you could refill that and bring it back, then try to find something we can use for bandages and bind his chest," said Polybius, indicating the injured man, "then Agamemnon and I will start checking the bodies." He looked to his king for confirmation, and Agamemnon nodded.

So began the longest day of Cassandra's life. Ten years a prisoner of Agamemnon and she had never before seen a dead body, having been kept in Agamemnon's tent during all the battles. Today there was nowhere to hide her.

She did not consider herself soft; as a priestess of Apollo she had worked long hard hours in the temple, and while Agamemnon's prisoner in Troy she had treated many of his men after battle for many wounds, but she found herself glad of Polybius's decision. She wrapped the wounds of those alive, those who could still be healed, while Agamemnon and Polybius sorted through the living and the dead.

The living they carried up the beach, one by one, as gently as they could so as to avoid worsening their injuries. They laid them on the softer, drier sands at the head of the beach. Some of the least injured were still in the water, held aloft by floating debris or in the shallows, and many of the dead had little more than scratches but floated face down in the calm waters with necks at unnatural angles after being thrown from the ship.

The dead they moved over to the rocks bordering the beach. Although they were still as respectful of their dead as possible, they knew that it was the living who needed them now; so the pile of the dead grew and they kept them separate from the living in order not to waste time on what they could not save. When Cassandra asked Polybius, he couldn't say for sure how long they were going to be stuck there or how long it would take to organise such a big pyre with very few able-bodied men, so the bodies had to be kept separate in an attempt to keep disease from spreading through the survivors.

The brutal practicality in how they thought of and dealt with their dead shocked Cassandra, but these were men who had spent their lives in the trade of death. Polybius explained that it wasn't that they didn't care or wouldn't mourn their dead, but that they wanted to save as many as possible.

'As many as possible' turned out to be fifty-seven of the two hundred souls who had been on board. Of those, ten had woken up well enough to help Agamemnon and Polybius sort through the rest of the bodies and wreckage. Some bodies were missing when Agamemnon counted, lost to the waves or dragged away in a current. Agamemnon counted them as part of the dead.

Polybius had set two men apart from the others. When they had finished, he took Cassandra aside to explain that those two would not see the following morning; she should make them as comfortable as possible before he set out with the rest to scour the wreckage for anything they could use for supplies while they were stuck here.

Agamemnon sat with the sick, now that everyone had been checked. Cassandra watched him, surprised at how gentle the big war leader was in dealing with his injured men. She was less surprised to find him well versed in wrapping and binding cuts and breaks; such things were common in battle, requiring every soldier to have some basic knowledge of healing.

As the sun arched across the sky, the small pile of surviving foodstuff down by the rocks grew larger. It was mostly cured meats in wooden barrels, almost all the amphorae and ceramic containers having been badly smashed in the wreck. A small group of injured men lay groaning in their makeshift hospital. The huge pile of dead men, which Polybius and the other walking wounded had dragged as far as possible across the beach, smoked in the warm spring sun as the dried brush and wood they had piled around the corpses began to take the flame.

Guilt ate at Cassandra's stomach at the relief she felt, knowing that if everyone had survived, the little food they had would not have lasted more than a few days.

CHAPTER SIX

ODYSSEUS WOULD BE THE LAST TO LEAVE. AGAMEMNON SHOULD be almost home by now, he thought, as he sat and watched the morning rise over the sea - that is, if Poseidon had permitted it. The storm that had torn through the Aegean over the last two days had left Odysseus with no doubt that he had been right to offer to stay back and search for any survivors of Troy.

He grinned inside his beard: hunting survivors indeed! He was glad that Agamemnon still trusted him so much now that the war had ended; it kept his home safe, but he had no more intention of hunting survivors than he had of mimicking Icarus and building himself a set of wings to fly home. If his plan had worked, the survivors of Troy were somewhere outside the Aegean and hopefully beyond Agamemnon's spiteful grasp by now, on the ships he had hidden up the Hellespont for them.

Achilles had entered Troy knowing the plan, with enough information to get as many people to safety as the seven ships would hold, and Aeneas should have met them there. He was not certain what would happen after that.

He harboured a hope that Achilles had left with the ships, but the man was stubborn on a good day and Troy had been the greatest battle the world had ever known. Maybe he was somewhere in the charred ruin of the city he could smell even here. It had finally stopped smoking only when drenched by the rain of the passing storm, and blackened timbers still poked up out of rock which had cracked and fallen in the heat.

The horrendous fires which had burned for days had done to the walls of Troy what no army ever could; now only a stretch of wall remained standing around the fabled gates, testimony to the greatness that had been. All the building had been cleared from inside that stretch so the fire had nothing to burn, but without the surrounding wall it would collapse within a generation and the rubble would be carried away by the locals to be recycled for the walls of their own homes. It saddened him to know he'd had a hand in the fall of Troy and that, in a few short years, the greatest of cities would be but a story told to children and dismissed as a fairytale.

A call from his men recalled him from his brooding thoughts. They were pointing out to sea, gesturing frantically and running towards him. Isadore came pounding down the beach towards him, with warning of a ship which Odysseus was now able to see on the horizon.

The vessel making its way towards them was wallowing low in the water, its sail hanging limply, trying in vain to catch a breeze in the still morning air with oars rising and falling irregularly. This ship had weathered the storm of the previous nights at sea, that much was clear. The fact that it still had a mast at all stood testament to both the sturdiness of the ship and the skill of the captain who had survived the waves which, even here in the shallows, had battered the beach.

A single ship riding so low in the water with no sail gave him no way to recognise it. One of Agamemnon's, returned? It seemed unlikely. A Trojan ally? If so, it was coming late to the party and posed no threat to Odysseus's fourteen ships. Still, if it were a Trojan ally there might be more survivors of a fleet making their way there even now.

Nobody ever died from being too prepared, he thought as Isadore arrived beside him still babbling and gesturing, out of breath. These kids were as panicky as any he had seen but they were children; the first of those born of the men's Trojan slaves were now reaching a useful age.

Odysseus let him struggle for breath for a second before frustration took over and he cut the lad off. "Tell the men to form up in full armour. It's probably nothing; the ship's half-sinking from the storm, lad."

Isadore took off towards the main camp and soon men in armour were approaching across the beach. Odysseus was still sitting there when they arrived. He didn't think this was going to require him to be armed when all his men were, whatever this one ship held.

As it came closer, he could see why it seemed to be struggling: they were in worse shape than he had first thought. Only half the oars were out, with water coming over the side, and the other half of the oarsmen were emptying buckets, trying to get enough water out to stop her sinking completely. It was a fruitless task, as she was sitting so low that water was coming in around the oars as fast as they could pail it back out. Nobody on board was going to have enough energy to cause trouble when they arrived.

Still he didn't stand his men down, turning his head briefly to see their shining ranks standing ready, their curious eyes also on the struggling vessel. It was another fifteen minutes before the ship was close enough to hear the captain bellow orders and encouragement. There was no telling how long the ship had been floundering in the water, and there was only so long the men could struggle to keep her afloat and moving, but there was nothing Odysseus could do but watch as their fate hung in the hands of the gods.

It was impossible not to feel sympathy for them and Odysseus leant forward, silently cheering them on, as they neared a point where they might be able to swim to shore. Drowning was the great fear of armed men at sea: being dragged down to the watery depth by the weight of their armour.

As the minutes slowly dragged on, his men were no longer silently urging them on but beginning to vocalise it. The noise began to rise behind him, taking on the feel of a sporting event. It felt as if there should have been two ships racing, that the men were watching chariots race around a circuit, but it was only one ship and the ocean that were racing.

Those on board must have heard the cheering and taken heart, because Odysseus could have sworn that the oars redoubled their efforts in a last burst till the noise of the hull scraping on stone mixed with that of an oar shattering and the screams of at least two men on board as an oar fouled the line.

Whatever was happening on board was drowned out by the shouting and cheering of his own men, as ropes were thrown ashore and they rushed forward to take them and drag the ship up the beach.

It was only when the vessel was finally settled on sand that exhausted, dirty faces began to rise over the sides of the ship.

The first one he saw was little more than a child, maybe twelve, with a head of tight red curls so unusual that they caught the eye. Odysseus didn't recognise the boy, but there was something familiar in the face. Then another face appeared and Odysseus felt his heart rise in his chest. Philoctetes, one of the most famed archers in all Greece, had been left behind and thought dead almost ten years ago when a snake had bitten him in Lemnos on the way to Troy. Though looking considerably older, that was certainly him staring back over the side of the ship.

CHAPTER SEVEN

AEGISTHUS SNATCHED UP AN AMPHORA OF WINE AND HURLED IT across the room, smashing it against the wall behind Clytemnestra in a fury. "Now!" he bellowed. "You have known this for two fucking weeks and you're only telling me now?"

"You were in Athens; what was I to do?" she replied calmly. She knew he hadn't meant to hit her with the amphora; he was just letting off steam. She had seen him throw and he didn't often miss. Besides which, she was a princess of Sparta; she had trained as hard as any of the men and worried little about getting hit. She might have a slight frame but the muscle wrapping her bones was plain for all to see, and even after having four children she exercised and fought daily.

Still, she stared with disdain at the wine running down the wall like blood. Someone would have to clean it up later, but the red drops irked her, playing on her mind like a premonition of the blood that would flow before this was over.

He was still pacing on the far side of the room, stopping every time he passed the balcony and looking out as if he might see ships appear on the horizon at any minute. Much as it amused her to see him stressed, she felt much the same way as he did and his reaction only confirmed that they were not ready for Agamemnon's return.

"I have already sent men east to your estates," she said, pulling her eyes from the puddle of wine. "They may be able to get word of his arrival before he gets here." Turning to pick up her own goblet of water, as it was still ten in the morning, she took a slow sip before continuing. "They have orders to have all of your men mobilised and ready if needed, and that also leaves the palace looking undermanned, as if we were sending all the men we could to him in Troy and not as if we're preparing for a siege here."

"Undermanned?" he asked, confused. "How many of the men did you send?" The annoyance was clear in his tone.

"Enough," she said in the same tone, right back at him. "Around half the garrison you had here. Enough to prevent it from looking as if we're preparing for a siege when he gets here." Hands on her hips, the Spartan strength was clear to see and Aegisthus knew she was annoyed with him for pressing her, but having replaced all the men loyal to Agamemnon it was a bit late to start backing out of the coup now. When they had replaced his house troops, that would have raised some awkward questions; when they had packed off Arimnis, his steward, a retired veteran, maybe death could have explained that; but removing his captain, Markus - that had been a point of no return.

Even if Clytemnestra tried to back out now, Aegisthus doubted if she could manage it. Agamemnon would know something was wrong.

"So, what now? Do we just accept him back? You are finished with me, so I can just shuffle back to my villa and hide until he decides he wants another war?"

"Have you always thought with your dick and I've only just noticed?" she said icily. "He has returned before we are ready, even if he only has half of his men with him. Yes, we welcome him back; we throw a feast and we use our brains where brute force won't win."

"So that's it, then. We wait," Aegisthus growled. Although he wanted Mycenae, he was sickened by the idea of Agamemnon pawing Clytemnestra when he returned as a conquering hero.

"Yes, Aegisthus," she replied, "we wait." Softening her voice, she moved closer to him as he brooded like a petulant child. "We wait. Your men have orders to hang back but to shadow his approach, careful to keep out of sight." She was all but purring in his ear now, with one hand on his chest.

"We organise the biggest festival Mycenae has ever seen to welcome back the conquering hero." She could see the muscles tensing in his jaw, could feel his rage at the situation radiate off him. "And then, when he and his men are all drunk and exhausted, we strike from the shadows."

Instantly his eyes shot up to meet hers, the rage and insult gone from them to be replaced by the eager excitement of a child hearing he was to get a new pony. It surprised her that it had taken him so long to see it. Sometimes he could be quite dense. Maybe that was what she liked; his innocence made him easier to bend to her wishes.

CHAPTER EIGHT

ARESTUS WATCHED FROM HIGH ON A HILLTOP OVERLOOKING THE beach, while Salonius and Alexi waited further back over the slope of the hill. They had seen the smoke billowing over the hilltop two days ago while scouting the coast.

There was no hiding the fact that Salonius and Alexi were soldiers, with their scarred arms, cropped hair and the tip of Alexi's nose having been removed by a sword blow years before, so Arestus had to take the last stretch over the hill by himself.

Although he also had the build of a soldier, he added a slouch to his rounded shoulders, tousled his dark brown hair with some straw and dirtied his face. He had added a slight lurch to his walk, and the clothing taken from an unfortunate shepherd they'd killed earlier completed his disguise. The tunic was ill-fitting and itchy. That was the worst thing about this bloody assignment, the filthy, itchy tunic he was forced to wear so he could hide in plain sight.

Well, that and twenty noisy, smelly, bleating sheep that stood grazing around him as he sat on a rock overlooking the beach several hundred yards away, where the remains of a crashed bireme lay in the sheltered lee of the rocks leading into the cove.

———

ALMOST A LEAGUE below Polybius was finishing his meal, ignorant of being watched. It was amazing how quickly you could get used to anything, he thought, as he looked across at the still-smouldering pile of corpses. They had been burning for almost two days now. At first the smell of the burning hair and flesh of their former comrades and friends was enough to put them all off their food, but as one day bled into the next and the pyre continued to burn, hunger and exhaustion won out.

It amazed him how long the fire burned without need of the huge amounts of wood that were usually used for a single pyre, but as they had begun to burn the melting fat from the corpses had caught and fed the flames. This was enough by itself to keep the fire burning; as the flames ate into the flesh, more fat from the bodies deeper in the pile was free to join the fire.

By the second day, the flames were so hot that nobody could approach closer than twenty yards and the cliff face throwing the heat back in their direction had begun to take on an ominous glow; parts of it were now flaking, in danger of separating from the cliff itself.

To Polybius, the worst thing was that by the second day, after the revulsion of the smell of his friends burning had abated, he realised that they had made him think about roast pork. While busy checking armour and weapons, his mind was distracted and his mouth watered at the smell of roast flesh.

When the tide had gone out and the wreck had been sitting almost at the waterline, finding most of their equipment had turned out to be a simple task as the heavy bronze had quickly sunk to the bottom, and there it had stayed. Although it was simple, the task had also proven hazardous as two men had badly cut their feet on sharp edges of wreckage and weapons hidden under thin layers of sand as they went about retrieving their gear.

But that was the worst of it. The cuts had been deep, going almost to the bone but had been well cleaned with the sea water, so it was just a case of binding the injury as best they could in the circumstances and proceeding with considerably more caution.

He himself had found Agamemnon's hammer, but it had taken all the strength he had to pull its great weight out of the sucking depth of wet sand. Not many men had the strength to wield such a weapon in battle, but Agamemnon had always been a larger-than-life figure.

Ajax Telamon would have been another such figure, but he had died holding the gates in the final push that toppled Troy. He would be remembered as a hero as long as there were Greeks to remember him. Agamemnon had promised that a statue would be built to him in Athens to remind all that he had given everything for the people of Greece.

While some of the others had treated the injured, Polybius had sat near the freshwater stream they had found washing the salt from weapons and armour. If they were needed, they had to be cared for and the salt would destroy them. The oil with which all bronze was treated and polished had been completely washed off between the salt water and the grit of the sand, and the oils they had brought with them, both for eating and work, were floating in an oily scum on the water from the broken amphorae; so Thesis was scraping the thin layer of fat from the carcasses of the horses who had died in the wreck.

It was labour-intensive but it kept the men's minds off the fire smouldering down by the rocks.

After a week recovering here on the beach, both the meagre supplies which could be salvaged from the ship and the horse-meat salvaged from the sea were beginning to run low; they would have to go hunting soon or people were going to go hungry.

Thankfully, most of the injured were on the mend and

already on their feet so Polybius looked forward to moving their camp up the hill from the beach quite soon; probably in the next two or three days, though it was hard to tell with the injuries.

Although very few would be stupid enough to attack such a large group, if they knew how many were injured and how few could put up a fight, they might well be encouraged. And given that none of Mycenae's other ships had yet been spotted off the coast, they had to assume they were on their own for the time being if anything did happen.

He would feel much better when they were off this exposed beach, with nowhere to run if anything did happen. Their only advantage was that they couldn't be flanked but, with so few fighting men, if a group of twenty riders happened to pass this way they probably wouldn't have too much trouble finishing them off.

Getting off the beach would also allow them to send out a few hunting parties into the surrounding hills and forests to try to stretch their meagre supplies. At the minute, though, as low as they were on stock and everyone's stomachs rumbling on short rations, he was really hoping for deer or game birds - anything but pork. Looking across the beach at the smoking pyre, Polybius thought that he would probably be sick at the smell of boar roasting.

CHAPTER NINE

Six years earlier ...

ARIMNIS STUMBLED OVER SOME ROCKS, HIS CANE SUPPORTING HIM. How had it come to this? Hadn't he been loyal? Hadn't he fought in every war Agamemnon had dragged him to across Greece for ten years, until he had injured his leg in battle in the northern Peloponnese?

A spear through the leg had seen him retired, though in truth he didn't think he would have had many years left in the phalanx anyway. But Agamemnon had seen him taken care of. Arimnis remembered that much; Agamemnon had always taken care of the men retired in his service.

Usually he found them a little plot of land, and maybe a wife for those not already wed, to raise the next generation of Mycenae warriors.

Arimnis's injury had come from getting between the general himself and a spear-wielding barbarian straight out of the Carpathians, and in return Agamemnon had brought him into his own home and made him steward. Ah, ten good years ...

Then this: begging to eat with some shepherds in their hut in the hill.

They were slaves of Agamemnon's own house so he knew them all well enough, having been in charge all that time. He was thought well of among them, well enough that they didn't begrudge sharing what little they had, which had become even less since Arimnis's replacement had taken over six long weeks ago. The occasional confused look when a different shepherd arrived was the only noticeable reaction he had received here.

Still, it wasn't fair to ask them to share what little they had, so he had already decided to move on when he arrived limping to the shepherds' hut this evening. It was one last visit to say his goodbyes and explain that he was going to Athens, in case anyone cared. He also wanted one last meal before he set off.

He had contemplated ending it himself. He still had his weapons and armour from when he'd served Agamemnon but little else. Most of what he had acquired over the years was presumably still in the little room he had lived in in Agamemnon's complex. Even the money he had saved over his lifetime was there, but Clytemnestra had not allowed him back in to collect it after accusing him of being a spy and kicking him out. He shook his head sadly at the memory.

On the last bend before the hut, the path crested a small rise before levelling out for forty yards where the hut and pen stood before the slope carried on up the hill. As he reached the top of the rise, he saw Markus sitting in front of the hut talking quietly with the shepherd. As he saw Arimnis, he rose and moved towards him. An awkward silence filled the air between them and Markus looked down at his feet uncomfortably.

Markus had fought alongside Arimnis even before Agamemnon had taken power back from his uncle and was of an age with him, but still a warrior and chief of Agamemnon's, he wore his hair in a long black plait of wiry tight curls halfway down his back and carried himself well, so it was especially disconcerting to see him so uncomfortable.

"Has she sent you to finish me off?" he asked, noting that Markus was fully armoured and armed, his shield lying against the wall of the hut. Markus's head shot up and his eyes widened. "I suppose that's good in a way. I hadn't the stomach to do it myself and, if it has to happen, then I'm glad it's at least someone I know."

Markus sputtered with indignation and hurt. "What? No, that's not it at all!"

"Just make it quick and clean, please, Markus." Arimnis carried on talking over him, glad at the prospect of finally ending it rather than living as a crippled beggar after the honours he had won in battle over his lifetime.

Markus, still the warrior, had not let himself go over the years that he had acted as the house guard, drilling the men hard and training the new recruits personally before sending all he could with the return boats headed for Troy as reinforcements for Agamemnon's war. Now he was walking towards Arimnis purposefully and, despite himself, Arimnis dropped his own head in anticipation of the blow to come and barely realised what was happening when Markus gripped his shoulders.

"No, Arimnis," he said again. "Well, yes, in fact she had told me to find you and kill you but that was nearly a week ago, and I told her what I tell you now." Arimnis's head lifted to look Markus in the eyes, "No," he repeated.

Silence reigned between them for a moment, as Arimnis searched Markus's eyes for the truth behind his words, then it was broken by Markus. "I'm sorry. I knew that you were no spy, and I should have spoken up earlier when she was accusing you. But I was torn between the order Agamemnon had left me with, to obey Clytemnestra, and what I believe he would have wanted and believed himself, and they were not the same."

"Thank you, Markus," Arimnis replied, at a loss as to what else to say or how to convey how much the gesture meant. "What now? She won't like you refusing to obey her orders, Markus; you have probably made life a lot more difficult for yourself. I don't want to cause you trouble, and she will probably send someone else after me, anyway," he said at last.

"It won't cause me any more trouble," said Markus with a sardonic smirk. "She fired me as soon as I had refused her, though I would have to be a complete fool not to have seen through the ruse. She knew I would refuse; it was all a pretext to get rid of me. Most of the house guard have been changed in the past few weeks, since that Aegisthus started to stay over. She's replacing them with his men, and the new recruits coming in now barely remember Agamemnon."

He shook his head sadly and walked back over to the hut. The shepherds were busy making themselves scarce, probably anxious that this meant another mouth for dinner and having to go to sleep hungry. They need not have worried. Markus, it seemed, was a better dinner guest than Arimnis had been, producing a pound of lean veal and a few vegetables to add to the pot. The man's face lit up at the sight of the meat and he disappeared over towards the fire again.

Markus then produced a skin of wine, pulling the stopper out with his teeth and taking a long pull on the skin before passing it across to Arimnis. Together they drank in companionable silence as they watched darkness settle over Mycenae, and it felt ominous as if there were a darkness falling over the land. There was a shift in power happening in the city below, and Agamemnon wasn't even aware of the risk he was taking by being away from his seat of power for so long.

As with all darkness, lights began to kindle in the windows of the houses and while there was that slim light, there was hope.

Eventually Arimnis broke the silence. "What now?"

Markus took another drink from the skin and set it down. He reached behind his shield and took out a small leather sack, tossing it to Arimnis who caught it to the sound of coins clinking inside. "I got that from your room before I left, and a few of your other personal possessions which are waiting for you downtown. You didn't hide it very well!" He winked as the shepherd came around the corner with steaming bowls of whatever stew he had managed to put together.

"Now we eat," he said, nodding toward the approaching shepherd. "After that – well, you've been out of work longer than I have and had more time to think about it, so I was hoping you would have had some ideas by now."

Arimnis put the string of the purse around his neck, dropping it into the neck of his chiton quickly, took the steaming wooden bowl and a hunk of bread from the shepherd and nodded his thanks. He sank into deep thought for a few minutes. "I was just getting ready to leave for Athens," he said then. "I thought I might find work as a bookkeeper or something similar in one of the houses there."

Markus thought for a minute, chewing on the hunk of bread he had dunked in his bowl before answering. "Yes, Athens sounds good. It's just a few days up the road, so we can keep an ear out for Agamemnon coming back. We could get some work protecting a few caravans, or maybe some rich merchants."

Arimnis laughed around his mouthful of stew, finally managing to answer. "Positive as always, eh!" He tapped his lame leg, saying, "I don't think I'll be much use protecting anything with this."

Markus looked him over slowly, as if seeing him for the first time, and eventually nodded. "Another seven men have been let go from Agamemnon's service; all men who served with him, all the men who were loyal to him." He took another mouthful of stew and bread as he thought before continuing. "If we pool our resources, we can get a small house near Athens and work from there. You run the house and take care of the business side of our service as well as bookkeeping. As far as anyone else is concerned, you will own the business and we are in your employ, so you can talk to the merchants and organise work and prices for us."

"Hold on, Markus! How long have you been planning this? You seem to have everything worked out." The bowl forgotten in his lap, he looked sideways at his friend and asked, "Do you really need me for this?"

"Every business needs a front man, Arimnis," responded Markus. "It's not charity; we would all have equal shares and more may join us as she gradually gets rid of them. It will keep us together and fed, ready for Agamemnon's return if – when he comes back. And if something happens while we are away guarding a caravan, you will still be around to hear and round us up quickly."

Silence settled over them as they finished their meal, broken only by the incessant chirping of cicadas and the occasional bleat of a sheep. Arimnis's mind was in a whirl with the speed of recent events. Being fired had been a surprise, but this was a bigger one; could life be getting better?

He was so lost in his own thoughts that he barely noticed when Markus mumbled contentedly as he lazed against the hut wall, working his way through the skin of wine. "Yes, Athens will do nicely for a while. I had been meaning to see it anyway; they say Telamon has made a beautiful city."

CHAPTER TEN

THE STORMS HAD PASSED, AND WITH THEM THE DANGERS OF landing. The winter storms had come early this year. Eudoros had expected them, but the ferocity had taken him by surprise. Poseidon was angry, and Eudorus did not think he was the only god to feel that emotion. The Greeks loved their trickery in war, but he did not think any but Athena could truly appreciate what they had done in Troy. All laws of hospitality had been broken; they had given gifts of peace hiding poison, and they had been accepted into the city in friendship disguised as a horse, only to slaughter the recipients.

The gods will have their due, he thought ruefully; not even Athena could protect them now.

For his part, he had followed his master's orders.

His master, yes, but all among the Myrmidons were equal. Achilles was their lord, but even he treated them as equals. In battle, however, a leader was needed and who better than the greatest blade who had ever lived? It still grieved Eudoros to have had to follow the order which had sent him from Achilles' side, but standing before the great fortress of Phthia he could not claim Achilles was wrong.

Still, visiting the temples of Poseidon and Apollo, *en route* to the city, had seemed wise. He had not simply been putting off his arrival at Phthia; after all, he was the senior officer of the Myrmidons.

The stories Achilles had told him about Peleus came back to him: how he had forced Achilles into exile; the beatings Patroclus had received at his hand, forcing the boy to join Achilles in Troy; the drunkenness fuelled by Thetis having left him. He now surrounded himself with sycophants who spent their days reminiscing about his time with Jason and the Argonauts. Surely the stories surrounding the man were fantasy, the raving boasts of a drunkard. Jason had been a legend when Eudoros had been a young man, but even then, they had spoken of a young Peleus ... another man, surely.

Against his better judgement, the march towards Phthia was spent inside Eudoros' head, counting years. He was not much older than Achilles. Could this Peleus be the same?

It was dark on their arrival. The gates had been shut against the dark: creatures of the dark, come to attack his city. Even knowing this was superstition, every city closed their gates at dusk. Still Eudoros marched on. Drawing his kopis at the gate, he hammered the pommel on the thick wood. The town was still active; he could hear the sounds of taverns and revelry beyond. No response.

He hammered again.

This time a hatch opened in the wall adjacent to the gate. "We are closed for the day," said a sentry, obviously already in his cups. "Come back tomorrow," The hatch shut with a finality that left Eudoros speechless.

Thump, thump, thump, went the pommel of his kopis.

Again, the hatch shot open. "I told you ..." The sentence was never finished as Eurodos' arm shot through the hatch, grabbing his throat and pulling him forward.

Indicating the black armoured shadows in the night, he said,

"We are the Myrmidons. We bear news of your lord's sons. You will open the gate now, or we can come through it; either way we are not waiting until morning." Choking was the only answer he received, but he held on for a few more seconds. The Myrmidon reputation, carried with them through half of Asia Minor, left no doubt of their ability to carry out the threat, and through coughing and spluttering, as the hatch snapped shut they could hear the bolts moving on the other side of the gate. Whether it was from fear of the Myrmidons or fear of what their own king would do if they tried to stop his son's men, they could not tell.

Slowly the gates swung inwards, opening the city to returning heroes, almost as if the Argonauts themselves were returning with the golden fleece. While those warriors had worn golden bronze, however, these warriors of legend, soaked in the light, seemed to dim the city in their passage as they marched in file up the narrow claustrophobic street, five abreast.

Years of war, of marching, of travel by ship had left them completely unused to the civilised towns of Greece. The hard-cobbled streets echoed against the walls with the ring of their sandaled feet striking in unison. The civilians and even the armed men of the city turning out, hanging from windows, watching as rank upon rank of sun-darkened soldiers in black, soul-eating armour marched by torchlight in the dusk, and the whole town became darker.

On to the agora they marched. One of the guards from the gate had obviously run to warn them of the coming men. The sight of the armour and their legend was enough to send many people back to their homes with their doors locked, their curiosity unsatisfied and only their prayers to keep them company. The palace made up one side of the agora and the barracks another; as they arrived men were pouring from the latter, still doing up their armour. On the steps in front of the palace stood a man who could only be Peleus.

Red-rimmed eyes indicated how he was spending his evening. A long white chiton, thrown over one shoulder, was spattered with both food and wine, and yet the apple had not landed far from the tree. With long muscled limbs and grace of movement, the stories of his travels with the Argonauts were not so difficult to believe when looking at him.

Eudoros dropped to one knee, aspis on the ground in front of him. Those behind him did not but he had not expected they would; these were Myrmidons, not his household guard. Their loyalty and oath were to the Myrmidons alone, to one another.

"Greetings, my lord!" called Eudoros.

"Greetings, indeed." Peleus looked down, eyes scanning the massed ranks filling his agora. "I hear the dog, but see no sign of the master. Is my son still too much of a coward to come forward and greet his father himself?"

Eudoros felt men shuffle behind him. That sort of comment about Achilles was not welcome among the Myrmidons, who had all worked, Achilles as much as any, to make the Myrmidons the most feared warband in all the Aegean - loyal only to the black shield.

He gave them a moment to steady themselves. They all knew of the animosity between father and son; Eudoros had given a speech on what to expect as they left the boats, stressing the behaviour he required of them.

He rose, all signs of deference to Peleus disappearing. "Your son is not among our number, lord."

"Dead, then. That would mean the end of the Myrmidons, I suppose." Peleus did not look in the least perturbed at the thought of the death of his own flesh and blood. "Then you have come to return Patroclus to his home before you disband?"

"You are mistaken, lord. I bring news of the death of one of your sons, but not as you assume," Eudoros answered, uncomfortable at bringing this news to a father. "Patroclus died in battle." He looked down at his feet, wondering how to go on, "Know that he died with honour, leading a charge which stopped a Trojan advance. He fell to mighty Hector's blade. Know also that Achilles avenged the death." It felt hollow, even to him.

"Avenged!" shouted Peleus. "Avenged! Better Achilles had died." His red-rimmed eyes were leaking onto his cheeks. "And he couldn't even be bothered to bring the news himself."

"My lord, in truth, we do not know if Achilles lives or not." Eudoros hesitated, not sure how much to reveal. Achilles had made it clear that Peleus' loyalty would not be to him or to them, but the hero still wanted his people protected.

Peleus' head shot up, eyes searching Eudoros' face. "Explain!" he barked.

Over the next half-hour they stood there while Eurodos explained the war, the battles, how Patroclus had died and Hector. He told of the plan Odysseus had hatched with Agamemnon involving the horse, and how Achilles and Ajax were to lead the attack and hold the gates. Despite the bitterness Peleus felt towards Achilles, he was clearly proud that his son should take such honour in battle. Eurodos kept back only what Achilles had told him to hold back: his real plan upon entering the city.

"So Troy has fallen. Where then is my Achilles? Is he in Argos, being honoured among Agamemnon's heroes of the war, seated at his right hand, or did he die holding the gates?" Peleus asked, making it clear to all which outcome he would prefer, though largely indifferent.

"The war may be over, my lord," answered Eurodos hesitantly, "but your son, Achilles, ordered us to return here with all haste when Agamemnon returned to Troy, under cover of darkness. Our orders were to be at your disposal should things go awry."

"He said what?" bellowed Peleus.

"He said that, if things did not go as planned, Agamemnon might take out his temper on allies, lord. He sent us to fight for you, should the need arise."

"Should the need arise!" growled Peleus, grinding his teeth. "You, the Myrmidons, were formed for his protection. Not only have you failed to keep his younger brother alive, a mere child, you then abandoned Achilles in a nest of enemies." His voice rose as he went on. "Pah!" he spat. "I should have expected no less from a filthy band of mercenaries."

Eurodos hand involuntarily rose to wipe at his eye, the missing one with the patch over it; the hole still wept occasionally. "With respect, my lord, this band was formed by your son and the first ships financed by your late wife. We joined as your son's comrades. Achilles has no need of protection, and his last command was to come to your aid."

"Achilles has no need of protection?" Peleus made a show of looking round the agora. "Well, I don't see him safely returned."

"Achilles will return when the time is right. All we need to do is trust his ability and follow his orders," Eurodos replied. "We did not abandon him, and it was not we who exiled him in the first place."

"You arrogant whelp!" screamed Peleus pulling his xiphos from his hip and advancing on Eurodos. "I should cut you down."

Eurodos made no move as Peleus advanced on him, but as one the Myrmidons at his back locked shields and adjusted their spears to point straight at Peleus, moving forward a step till they were almost in line with Eurodos. Tensions rose several notches as Peleus' own men took up their own defensive stance, but their nervousness was obvious for all to see. When any threat to Phthia materialised, they would have expected to have the wall as their first line of defence, not to have an enemy inside the walls and already formed up.

"So he sent you to defend me but you would draw on me instead!" he thundered. "He thinks Peleus, who served with Jason and the Argonauts, who fought alongside Hercules himself, needs your protection!" The man he had been, before bitterness ate him up, was still hidden there somewhere; the man who had existed before the night terrors from the things he had seen and done. Achilles had told Eudoros about some of them, which had kept Peleus awake drinking all night and ruined a good man. He had driven his wife away from him, and both his sons also, because he could not forget.

"Not you." Eudoros still hadn't moved, and now looked slowly around the square. "Achilles worried about your people."

"I can look after my people," Peleus snarled, "without mercenary scum who left both my sons to die."

Eurodos looked around at the soldiers crowding the street around the agora. He had no doubt that the Myrmidons would leave victorious; but at what cost?

"Then it seems that the best way for us to defend your people is to leave before your city turns into a battleground." He dropped his head and shook it sadly. "I suppose that is still following his orders to protect them from harm." Looking back at the massed ranks, he gave the signal to withdraw.

He could hear the audible intake of breath from the surrounding warriors as his men began backing out of the agora and down the street towards the main gate. "Remember this if Agamemnon comes," he said. "You have sealed your own fate."

The gates of Phthia slammed shut behind Eudoros, the last Myrmidon to leave. He could still hear Peleus laughing as they backed away, but his loyalty was to Achilles' last orders and a fight would have seen too many deaths.

"What now?" asked Phillopos. He had taken the position of Eurodos' second.

Eudoros thought a moment. "East again, I think. There is land near the Dorics, and from there we will hear any news of Achilles' survival. Let's go there for the present. Achilles gave us all a home in the Myrmidons; maybe we can win a home for him there if he ever returns."

CHAPTER ELEVEN

BLOODY STINKING SHEEP. ITCHY SHEPHERD'S CLOTHING. ROCKY hills under his arse with nothing but bloody rocks to lie down on. This was not why Arestus had joined the army. In fact, this was specifically why Arestus had run away from home at fourteen - to get away from his family and their bloody goats, constantly bleating on a different bloody hill. Everything else you could get used to, but trying to sleep every night on hard, pointed bloody rocks was the worst of it.

Still, at least he knew this was only temporary. Arestus had confirmed the arrival the night before, creeping down in the twilight when men's sight was at its weakest, and even then he had almost been caught.

Agamemnon's men were sharp-eyed, but he was better. Old Cam had taught him as they stole sheep from right under a shepherd's nose. Cam's death was what had decided him that the army was the life for him. The excitement, the adrenaline, drove him; he would have a more adventurous life than his father.

He had placed each of their sentries before he made his move down the hill to the beach, marking the rocks they used to shelter and rest against; but somewhere on the climb down one had moved, blast him! Doing a circuit between the other two, apparently.

Arestus threw himself flat against a rock, blade whispering half an inch from the fine leather sheath at his waist as every muscle tensed. He held his breath as the steps came closer, burning in his lungs as a shadow passed only feet from him.

His calm arrogance shattered, he peeled himself from the rock as the footsteps receded into the darkness. Checking his background, Arestus looked for anything he could be highlighted against, any light-coloured rock against which his movement could be spotted. He checked the position of the sentries again before he moved a few steps closer.

Breath rasping in his lungs, he argued with himself. He had to get closer, but this was a risk to the whole mission; confirmation against caution. Breathe. Take a few more steps.

Suddenly he saw him, sitting around a campfire with his men. Arestus had only one memory of the man from his early childhood. The hair was greyer now, the face a little more lined and scarred, but even in Greece there were only so many men with that commanding presence, who exuded power while sitting in rags on a beach.

Agamemnon was back.

Silent as a wraith, Arestus slipped back up through the sentry lines and disappeared into the black night.

Agamemnon had started moving his men off the beach that morning. The pace was so slow that he knew they had to be carrying a significant number of injured, but with enough able-bodied men to do it, so there would be too many to ambush with Arestus' little scouting party.

Solonius was already on his way to Mycenae to report, while Alexi was returning to Aegisthus's estate in the hills to make sure all the men were ready. With a little luck they might be given the go-ahead to attack before they even reached Mycenae;

the sooner Arestus could get out of this itchy woollen garment the better.

Alexi should be back in three days. A straight run there to relay the message and back, Solonius would probably take a whole week, going flat out. From the looks of Agamemnon's group, though, they probably had three weeks travel ahead of them with the injured, so Arestus wasn't holding out much hope of getting back into his own clothes any time soon.

———

"GET your lazy asses up that hill!" Agamemnon bellowed at his men, "A full ten days you have spent taking your ease on the beach." The hobbling continued slowly with men limping, holding their chests where their ribs had been broken or with arms in splints. Blood and bandages were the only thing in abundance among the steady stream of men. Any worry he had about pushing them while they were still injured was offset by the knowledge that lying unmoving for much longer meant that their joints would begin to fuse. They needed the exercise.

He watched them come up the dune from the beach, wincing time and again when he saw someone slip or overbalance, knowing the pain it must be causing them. They needed his strength as a leader more so now, or else they would lie there till they ran out of food on the beach and by then their joints would be too slow to be of any use for hunting. They would slowly starve.

Agamemnon was painfully aware of what a nice target they made. Anyone attacking would be completely unaware that they were carrying nothing more valuable than their weapons. And of course, there was always the chance that they were still in enemy territory.

The ship's captain was dead, and Agamemnon could only read the stars well enough to give a rough direction without the proper tools; who knew how far off the storm had thrown them? Thrace had sided with Troy in the war, to have their revenge against Agamemnon; they were not likely to worry about gaining any treasure. Landing on any of the islands would probably not end much better for them; they had nothing but pig farmers there, but enough of them could spell trouble.

The other consideration that had kept Agamemnon from having pushed them harder before now was that he was painfully aware that these men with him were the only soldiers he could be sure were still alive, since the storm had driven them apart from the rest of his ship.

They had been lucky to survive. He couldn't rely on his prayers that the others were still alive.

Polybius was the most senior man still standing. Agamemnon had to admit that he hadn't a lot of time for the man, but he was proving himself to be a very capable officer. It begged the question of why he had never been promoted before; there was obviously something about him that had worked against him. He brushed the thought from his mind as Polybius marched down the dune towards him, but he forgot to brush away the scowl until the man was almost on top of him.

"Is something the matter?" asked Polybius, seeing the scowl.

"What?" said Agamemnon, realising how he had been looking at the other man. He quickly continued, "No, no, it's nothing; I'm just worried about the men pushing over this type of ground with their injuries." He waved a hand in the general direction of the column of men and the area.

Polybius grunted an acknowledgement of his words, so Agamemnon went on. "How does the ground look up ahead? Do we know where we are yet, at least?"

"Not yet," replied Polybius. "We have sent out scouts, but they haven't yet returned with anything substantial. They have orders to hunt while they're out, if they get a chance, so that could be delaying them but we need the food. It will probably be another couple of hours before we hear."

Agamemnon nodded; Polybius was right, he supposed. Cassandra had taken him aside to show him the state of their food supplies; even the bread they had been able to make had required quite a lot of fresh water to drink, given the amount of salt water that had got into the grain. He just hoped it wasn't going to make them sick or they would be delayed yet again.

"Fair enough. Tell me as soon as they get back. If you have no news yet, why are you here?"

"There is a sighting, but the man who reported it was not sure you would want him to approach yet, since we would be announcing our presence, so to speak."

"A sighting of whom?"

"See the edge of that hill up there?" Polybius pointed to a hill a couple of miles away. "Just below the peak there is a single shepherd with a flock, and perhaps ten miles further on the other side of the hill there are three villages, only a few miles apart from each other."

"And the shepherd has not seen him?" Agamemnon asked sceptically

Polybius spoke as if talking to a child; Agamemnon could feel it getting under his skin. "Whether he has seen him or not, he would need to be the only blind shepherd across the Aegean not to have noticed this many men camped on the beach for the last ten days."

He had a point: they did stick out like a sore thumb. "Is this going to be a problem? If I knew where we were, it would be easier to decide what to do with him."

"So far, no," replied Polybius. "He hasn't left his flock since we noticed him. I sent Vasilik back to keep an eye on him; if he looks like making a move to inform others of where we are," he shrugged, "well, one shepherd should not be too difficult to deal with."

Agamemnon sat deep in thought for a few minutes, sparing a glance up the hill where he could just make out the motion of white on the hillside; he felt that his eyesight hadn't been as good over the last few years, but now he knew what to look for he could see white movement. "Any dogs with the shepherd?" he asked eventually.

'None were seen or heard," replied Polybius. They both knew that wasn't confirmation, as they could have been mixed in with the sheep, but for now it would have to do.

Again silence fell as Agamemnon thought. If they had made it to Greece then in all likelihood these sheep belonged to someone owing him fealty, and killing his own people without proper cause would not be the best start of his glorious return home. The sheep would make it easier to feed his little band, but if they had been dropped in dacia, or worse still Thrace, then stealing livestock would be a sure way to bring trouble down on their heads. And they did not know how many miles they had yet to cover, with enemies possibly following them. He had no idea how far or in what direction the storm had blown them during those days at sea, and since the navigator had burned with the other bodies, there was as yet no way to find out.

"Avoid them until we know more," he said eventually. "The men will just have to hunt for the time being."

"As you say." Polybius went away to relay the orders and Agamemnon looked down the group, seeing Casandra near the back helping one of the last men who was healing from a fractured leg. The girl had impressed him: most priestesses of Greece whom he had seen did little but attend the holy flame and commit sacrifices, with the obvious exception of priestesses of Asclepius, but she had been working all day with them and kept going without complaint, often leaving only when the others were settling in for the night, to wash herself and offer her nightly prayers to Apollo.

She had warned him before leaving Troy that, had she not

travelled on the ship with him, they would both die before arriving in Greece. It left Agamemnon wondering about the other ships again the other women, his army. Had her premonition meant they were all now gone beyond the waves?

Many wars he had waged, fighting from the front ranks while he build his empire, and never had he felt a fear like that he had harboured during the storm. In any battle the strength of your arm, your courage and skill, may carry you through; in the vast sea, all that counted for nothing. He had watched his brave, skilled seamen climbing the mast to take in the sail and being swept away by a freak wave, and there was nothing he nor any of the others could do about it.

Again his eyes were drawn back to Cassandra. He had often let his eyes roam over the girl as she got ready for sleep in the tent they had managed to construct from the salvaged sail which he shared with her.

CHAPTER TWELVE

Odysseus sat by the campfire, listening to Philoctetes recount his story. It was already late in the night and thankfully the child had fallen asleep. The young man's arrogance was astounding, even knowing who he was.

Philoctetes had introduced him as Neoptolemus, but everyone referred to him as Pyrrhus. Odysseus had assumed this to be merely a reference to the boy's red hair, in itself almost as unusual as his father's golden blond, but soon found it more accurately described the lad's fiery temper.

He was the illegitimate son of Achilles. The news had stunned Odysseus. It had been enough of a surprise to learn that Philoctetes was still alive and that Agamemnon had sent a ship to retrieve him, but he had not realised that Achilles had a child and apparently neither had the man himself.

Philoctetes explained how Achilles had had a brief affair with King Lycomedes' daughter before the war. "She called the boy 'his farewell gift to me'," he explained. The child had grown up on the rocky island of Skyros, raised on his mother's stories about his amazing father and whichever other tales from the war had reached them.

Odysseus sat in stunned silence as Philoctetes related how his grandfather, King Lycomedes, doted on the boy, humouring his every whim. The boy trained every day, wanting to be as good a warrior as his father. Lycomedes had even spent gods alone knew how much to buy the child his own matching black Myrmidon armour, half the size of his father's, when the boy had pestered him constantly about joining his father in Troy.

"Agamemnon had heard about the boy through traders," said Philoctetes, looking up at the sky with a faraway look in his eyes. "The day his ship arrived, I thought they had come for me." He took a long pull from a wineskin and shook his head. "I was merely a passing thought."

Odysseus looked across at his friend, whose bitterness was plain to see. "Lemnos was on the way to Skyros," snorted Philoctetes.

"Philoctetes, I'm sure it wasn't like that." Odysseus reached across to put a hand on his friend's shoulder, which Philoctetes shrugged off.

"Oh, yes, Odysseus. It was exactly like that. Oh, he wanted me as well, but only because he had begun to question you. Pyrrhus was the prize; I was merely conveniently placed along the route."

Odysseus was confused now. He had obviously had too much wine, because none of this was making sense to him. The more Philoctetes explained, the more confused Odysseus became. "If that were true, why would he leave before you got here? He hadn't even told me to expect you, Philoctetes. None of this makes sense."

"It makes perfect sense, Odysseus; you are just losing your cynicism in your old age." He snorted again as if he had made a brilliant joke, and took another pull from the wineskin while he watched Odysseus sort through the thoughts in his head to try to make sense of what he was hearing. Eventually Philoctetes went on to explain.

"It wasn't Pyrrhus he needed, exactly. He wanted to control Achilles. Pyrrhus wasn't being brought here to fight," again a snort of laughter, "though the gods help whoever tried to stop him. He wouldn't have been allowed to put himself at risk like that. No, he was a hostage against Achilles' good behaviour." Odysseus' eyes widened as he finally connected the loose ends.

With a slight smirk of pleasure that for once he knew what Odysseus did not, Philoctetes continued. "Achilles didn't know that the boy existed, true enough, but even so - can you imagine him letting anyone hurt his blood kin? Agamemnon kept it from you, Odysseus, because he didn't trust you anymore as much as you like to think. He thought you had grown too close to Achilles in your time here."

Odysseus was catching up fast now and the realisation of what he had missed stunned him. It could have cost him his life, had things gone differently. Agamemnon had grown more and more paranoid, erratic and unpredictable during his time in Troy; that the army had looked with awe at Achilles had only fed the fires of his paranoia.

"Once Troy had fallen, he didn't need the boy anymore. That's probably why he wanted me to stay behind when he left." It all added up. "How did you find out about all this?"

"The captain he sent for us told me." A grin split his face as he went on. "He seemed to enjoy taunting me with it; the old bastard had a mean streak. An awful shame that he slipped and fell over the rail during the storm, with only me there to see." The way he was smiling sideways at Odysseus told him all he needed to know about the captain slipping; no doubt he'd had a knife in his ribs before the 'accident'.

Odysseus patted Philoctetes' shoulder, which he allowed this time. Remembering the captain's unfortunate fate seemed to have eased his mood somewhat. "You did the right thing." Nothing more needed to be said. Together they sat in silence looking into the flames as they thought about what they had learned since the ship had scraped up on the beach: Philoctetes had discovered that the war had been over before he'd even arrived, and Odysseus had realised that his return home could be more dangerous to him than the war had ever been.

CHAPTER THIRTEEN

ARESTUS HUDDLED DOWN ON THE HILLSIDE, HAVING PASSED another miserable night. Not wet, not cold; in fact, this morning was brightening up nicely with an early sea mist burning off. He wasn't hungry. His rations were holding out well and he had even supplemented them, gorging on a lamb which had annoyed him in the night.

No, he was just miserable and bored, annoyed that he had to sit here in these itchy clothes on this hard ground, watching these bloody sheep, while Solonius and Alexi were having a fine time riding back and forth to the villa and Mycenae. He was stuck here with these damned bleating sheep, with nothing more to occupy him than watching a desolate group of refugees from the ship hobble their way away from the beach to the south. That had to be the worst of it, the tedium, all the while knowing that his comrades were probably living it up on the town with wine and women while he was stuck on this bleak, rocky mountain.

Agamemnon's scouts were making their avoidance of him very obvious. They clearly felt no threat from a lone shepherd, and he watched them wend their circuitous ways past his position. This had worried him the first few times, thinking that they might attempt to encircle and catch him. With no weapons bar his little utility belt knife, he would have no chance to defend himself and would be completely reliant on his acting skills to keep him alive.

Those fears were unfounded, though, as they circled back with whatever they had managed to forage and hunt during their scouting. He had moved his camp and the flock across hills, keeping them in sight but doing his best to move the sheep onto good grazing areas as a real shepherd might do, making it look as if it was they who had moved after him, and even then they gave him a wide berth.

He heard Solonius well before he saw him, yet another reason why he was left on the hillside while the others rode errands. Those city boys would never make it as scouts or survive unsuspected on the hillside, and if they were questioned, their city accents would be a dead giveaway. Still he sat there as Solonius made his way to him, attempting to conceal himself among the rocks and shrubs.

"Good morning, Solonius," he said over his shoulder when the other man was still twenty yards away.

"Ye gods, Arestus, how do you always manage to do that?" Solonius gave up all pretence of attempting to sneak up on Arestus and scurried down the rocks to where he waited.

"You sneak around like a cow with a bell around its neck, Solonius," he told his friend mockingly. "So, what news from Aegisthus? Are we to gather the men from the estate and try to ambush him on the way?"

"You need to come with me right away." Solonius hadn't even asked for a drink or sat down properly. Agitation was coming off him in waves and his eyes were feverish; not in a sickly way, he seemed perfectly healthy, but adrenalin produced its own heat.

"What's wrong?"

"The orders were to set up an ambush since it's just this ship alone, but things have changed," he replied, looking around nervously.

"Don't worry, Solonius, the nearest of them are almost a league away." He pointed to the main camp. "He sent out scouts this morning, the same as always, but they should be miles away by now."

"Should be, perhaps," mumbled Solonius. "The nearest is about two hundred paces beyond that outcrop," and he pointed to the way he had come. "Alexi is covering the body as we speak."

"Another?" Arestus' eyes widened. "A single scout going missing is one thing, Solonius, but that's two now, counting the one on the first day. That's going to draw attention."

"Actually, it's three." Arestus nearly choked but Solonius went on. "We came across two of them this morning looking for you. The first one we took by surprise, but the second one was drawing an arrow on Alexi when I cut him down. That's why you have to come, now."

———

POLYBIUS CAME RUNNING down the hillside towards Agamemnon and he knew already that the news wasn't good. The sun would soon be going down behind the hills to the west and the camp was just settling down after supper. A lot of the injured were beginning to look better, even while being dragged along with the camp, but the wreck had been nearly three weeks ago now; though they were still slow and in a lot of pain, the column of men were beginning to pick up speed as they made their way north.

Polybius slid to a halt by Agamemnon and dropped his hands to his knees as he caught his breath. "What's wrong?" asked Agamemnon, trying his best to keep calm.

"Another two scouts have gone missing," replied Polybius, still puffing.

"What? Are you sure they aren't just late reporting in? It's only just dusk now." The words felt hollow as he said them and he could feel his stomach begin to knot. The look Polybius directed at him confirmed the bad news even as he said it.

"Since the first disappearance, they've been under orders to be back an hour before dusk." He kept his voice low so that the other men wouldn't hear him, but it didn't stop him answering with exaggerated patience as if he were lecturing a child. "An accident or injury might account for one, but not two."

Agamemnon felt that old anger, which had been missing since the wreck, bubble inside him but he squashed it down. Until they knew where they were and what they were facing he needed all the men he had here, and he needed them loyal. That did not stop him from making a mental note to make an example of Polybius when they got back to Mycenae.

That was his priority right now: to get back to Mycenae, back to his centre of power. It was the one saving grace he could take from that disaster at Troy. He had lost most of his army, but the Greeks had mostly been unwilling subjects at best, held together through the force of his will and the threat of his retribution. They were seen as weak, but if the truth about Troy made it back some might finally have found the backbone to have turned against him. But it had been them he had sent in first.

Achilles and Ajax, gone; Ajax Locrian too, but he was little loss. His biggest threat had been removed when Troy had fallen and, by holding his Mycenae back, he had avoided the loss of his core. The addition of the Spartans had been a welcome boon when his brother fell; leaderless, they had accepted his authority. Menelaus was his brother, and for all he loved him, the man had been a fool if he'd thought they were going to go back to Greece upon the return of Helen.

Now all he had to do was to get back to Mycenae, and hope his other ships had survived. That would leave him with the single largest surviving force in Greece. Nobody would dare try to leave his newly-forged country.

"Okay", he said, stroking his beard. "How many men do we have on their feet?"

It was Polybius's turn to stop and think. "Most," he answered eventually. "If they have to fight, they won't lie down if we're attacked and will sell their lives dearly." That was the warriors' way. "But about five should still be resting injuries and legs if we can manage it."

"Good enough," said Agamemnon, looking around. "We'll pitch camp here. Those five will have a day's rest, but at first light everyone else breaks up into groups of four to search the area. If they were attacked, I want to know for sure and I want the bodies brought back." He waved a hand at his surroundings. "I can't imagine this area being able to hide more than four men can handle, but if I am wrong have every group warned to shout out if they come across anything and record what direction each group takes."

"Very good, sir," replied Polybius. "I will organise the groups tonight so they will be ready at dawn."

"And have them rotate so that there's always one group here resting with the injured, in case enemies try for an easy target."

———

It was the nicest part of the evening. Cassandra had taken on all the cooking for the camp, but it was simple when there was only one big pot: stew all round, with whatever meat happened to have been caught that day and whatever vegetables they had managed to salvage or steal, and she had been quite proud of what she had managed to do with some of the herbs she'd foraged in the forest during her evening walks.

One of the men had to clean up after eating, giving her a little while before it got dark every evening.

Foraging here was easy; this land was so wet compared to her home across the Aegean. Life just sprouted naturally from the ground. Even the rocky hills were covered in a tough green grass with sprouts of herbs, but this little forest they were passing with a stream running through it was like a treasure trove, providing herbs she did not recognise from home. The smells of the place were alive and damp.

Mushrooms were her personal victory. Pockets of them nestled in the shelter amidst moss at the base of the trees, which amazed her, but she still had to let some of the local men check them every time she brought some back. She loved how they tasted, but the men had all panicked the first time they had seen her about to add them to the pot. It was all very strange; she had eaten some raw in the forest to check they were good, but the men had thrown away nearly half of that first batch. Apparently, there were some that could kill a man with a single bite. Maybe it was Apollo who had saved her; she was still his priestess, after all.

———

IT HAD NOT TAKEN long to organise the men into groups. Agamemnon sat on a high rock overlooking the camp, cleaning his own armour and weapons in preparation for the morning. Nobody was going out there unarmed, knowing they were being slowly hunted. He would take first watch tonight himself. Not knowing where they had landed, he had set a watch every night; now, until whatever was happening could be stopped, he had decided to double it and take a more personal role.

The sound of others doing likewise drifted up to him as he pulled on his pteruges, the layers of leather lying comfortably over his thighs as he began again to polish his bronze cuirass.

He rubbed yet another layer of fat into the metal, paying special attention to the clasps, in the hope that he could save it from corroding after its little swim in the ocean. As things were, all he had was the fat he had managed to scrape from the animals the scouts had brought down. He hoped it would be enough.

Alkon came up to the rock he was sitting on and sat at the edge, looking down with Agamemnon. "The men are all organised. Polybius has turned in already. He's taking second watch, so I'll wake him at around midnight." He took out a stone as he spoke and began sharpening his xiphos.

Agamemnon nodded, looking around as his hands continued their work. Years of taking care of his own equipment had made it second nature. Cloth rubbed fat over a smudge in the polished bronze; it would be streaky but it was better than corrosion. "I'll be staying awake as well," he replied. "At least until I'm sure we don't need to worry about tonight." Alkon thought about telling him it wouldn't be necessary, but he had been serving with Agamemnon since before the great war and knew there was no point in arguing; when his mind was made up, there was no chance of changing it.

He settled himself on the rock and fell into the slow rhythm of drawing stone down the length of his knife. The gentle swishing noise created an almost hypnotic pattern. Time passed slowly as the camp below settled down for the night. He could make out the dark shapes of the other sentries in the shadows surrounding the camp. Others were settling into their blankets, as close to one of the camp fires as they could get.

"Where is Cassandra?" asked Alkon, looking around.

Agamemnon froze, eyes frantically searching the camp. The cuirass dropped from his fingers, clattering against the rock as he hopped down. "She was in the forest, where she goes every night," he called back, already stalking towards the tent he shared with the woman.

"Did anyone see her return?" he called over his shoulder as

he walked away. He'd been inside less than ten seconds when he remerged, carrying his hammer as if it were as light as a spear, and shouted to the camp, "Has anyone seen Cassandra?"

Heads shot up from blankets all around the camp with murmurs of "No," and "Not since dinner," but Agamemnon was already moving.

CHAPTER FOURTEEN

THREE DAYS THEY HAD BEEN GONE, THREE DAYS, AND IN THAT time Odysseus had had his men scrubbing the ships down, checking the wood, tarring the hull. The sails had been checked and mended where they needed repair.

The hulls had been packed with amphorae of wine and water, sides of fresh meat from the last of the stock animals he had been keeping during the siege, and more packed in salt barrels, smoked and pickled. He had included wheels of cheese which had been maturing nicely; he had even had a few smoked when the meat was being done. There was enough to keep them alive during their impending voyage.

But where were Pyrrhus and Philoctetes with their men? That's what was delaying him. They had been out hunting refugees almost every day since they'd arrived. Too late for the war, Pyrrhus still wanted to be able to say he had fought for Greece against Troy; if that meant doing Agamemnon's dirty work for him, the boy was only too pleased as long he could say he had fought in the war where his famous father had died.

Odysseus could understand it to some degree. It was the biggest war the world had ever known or likely ever would.

Well over five hundred thousand souls had departed, including the women and children caught up in the slaughter that had followed the fall of Troy, not to mention the huge number of Greeks Priam had decided to take with him when he died. However, Odysseus had no stomach for hunting any who had escaped the butcher's block.

Odysseus had never thought to see anything like the slaughter of that day. Even the armour of the dead was irretrievable, mostly mashed together underfoot of the Greeks trying to get at the Trojans; any who had survived as far as the palace … he could still hear the screams. The flames which had consumed them, bathed in naphtha, had burned hot enough to melt bronze. As the floors of the palace burned away, creating a chimney, the air drawn in had heated it to a smelting furnace until it became too hot and the stones had cracked; then it had all come crashing down, sending a jet of fire into the sky with its last groan.

Besides which he had, he hoped, helped some of those refugees to escape, providing ships and food, and even finding Aeneas to captain the ships and guide them to somewhere safe from Agamemnon's wrath. Aeneas had been an arrogant ass who didn't want to leave the 'glorious' battle, but Odysseus had convinced him that he could find more honour as the hero who had saved the last remnant of Troy than as another body on the fire.

Dragged back from his thoughts by the pounding of hooves on sand, Odysseus looked up to see Pyrrhus and Philoctetes riding into camp, the boy jumping nimbly from his horse with all the grace of Achilles in his long limbs. Philoctetes, age and old injuries slowly creeping up on him, set a much more sedate pace, bringing his horse to a complete stop before swinging his leg over and sliding down the animal's flank. Philoctetes stood and arched his back after an obviously arduous ride, but

Pyrrhus was already taking a long pull from a waiting waterskin.

Odysseus made his way over to them, trying to conceal his annoyance at having to wait around on this spoiled child who was attempting to make a name for himself by tracking down and killing unfortunate refugees, just looking for a place to survive in a world which had cast them out. He could do nothing for them, he knew. Pyrrhus was following Agamemnon's orders; in fact, he was doing what Odysseus himself had been told to do. But ignoring the order was one thing, acting against it ... well, that could mean the end of Ithaca if word ever reached Agamemnon. No, he must continue to play this game a little longer if they were to survive the storm.

"Philoctetes, Pyrrhus, greetings. What news?" Odysseus sounded as jovial as he could. He had consciously named Philoctetes first and directed his question to him, giving him seniority over the boy, still trying to instil a little humility in the lad and let him know he wasn't in charge here. If Pyrrhus had noticed he gave no sign, overriding his older companion before he'd had a chance to answer.

"A great day's hunting," he beamed. "I don't know what you have been doing here all this time, Odysseus, that you haven't hunted down all these Trojans already. The countryside is ripe with them. We are only back because our men are weighed down with the spoils."

Odysseus groaned inwardly. These people had seen their city and their homes destroyed mere weeks earlier; with nothing but the clothes on their backs and the few weapons they had managed to hold onto, they had run into the countryside to hide. Most had probably had little or nothing to eat since. Demoralised, beaten, starving, they were now being hunted by probably the most dangerous 'boy' they could ever have imagined, and he was imagining this to be his great victory.

Outwardly, however, he gave no indication of his thoughts. "Excellent news, Pyrrhus, excellent. They must only now be crawling out of whatever hole they had been hiding in. It is fortunate that you were here to find them before we sailed for home."

The flush of excitement was bright on Pyrrhus' face as he laughed. "Sail for home? Not a chance, Odysseus. We were hunting these Trojans down for Agamemnon, which is only right, but he has left. Troy may have been destroyed, but that leaves this whole land open to anyone with the strength to seize it." He had a manic gleam in his eye that Odysseus didn't think would have been there had he been around for the last days of Troy. Odysseus looked pleadingly toward Philoctetes, but Pyrrhus went on. "I will rule this land, answerable to none but Agamemnon."

"But Agamemnon has gone," said Odysseus.

"Exactly," replied Pyrrhus, and Odysseus knew the boy was lost in his dream.

"We leave as soon as we can get the tide to return to Greece," Odysseus said, trying a different tack. "I will send messengers to Agamemnon as soon as we arrive, informing him of your decision to stay here and rule for him. Where should I tell him he can find you?"

Without missing a beat, Pyrrhus answered, "We have taken a town a day's ride south along the coast, Epirus. I will make that my home for now, but there may be little point in looking for me there for I intend to travel as far as I must, tracking down any last remnant of the Trojans and their allies."

"Very well." Odysseus nodded, knowing that if the son took after the father even to a small degree there would be no changing his mind. He turned his head to the other man. "And you, Philoctetes?" he asked. "Will you be accompanying us back to Greece?"

The older man spread his arms wide in a hopeless gesture, "I missed the war and so the spoils," he said in a disappointed tone. "Yet I too have been away from what home I had for ten years too." He looked down, as if still coming to terms with his own decision. "I will stay," he said eventually, looking up at Odysseus. "There is a chance for me to make something of myself here; there is nothing for me back in Greece."

Odysseus was disappointed but he understood and nodded. "Then this shall probably be our last night together. Will you stay and join me in a farewell dinner and some wine?"

"We would be honoured," said Philoctetes, before Pyrrhus had a chance to say anything that might cause offence. Looking pointedly at Pyrrhus, he said, "It may be some time before we have the opportunity to avail of Greek wine and hospitality again."

CHAPTER FIFTEEN

Aretus followed Solonius over the hill behind him, keeping carefully to the falling shadows of early dusk. Alexi was down the opposite slope with the two horses. They had not expected to bring Arestus back with them, so the two horses would have to split the burden by taking turns to be double-mounted.

As they came down the slope Solonius became more and more agitated, casting nervous glances around in search of Alexi. "Where is he?" he muttered. "I left him right here." Calling out was not an option; Agamemnon and his men were far too close.

Arestus saw the shapes first and grabbed Solonius' sleeve, pulling him to a halt. They crouched down. Arestus could just make out movement at the edge of the forest; gesturing for Solonius to stay low, he started making his way towards the shapes in the gloom as quietly as possible.

"Alexi!" called Arestus when they were only twenty paces away and could clearly make out the shapes of horses.

Scuffling ensued and the whisper of bronze being drawn from sheath. Arestus was convinced he had made a grave error, and Solonius was tugging his sleeve to move him back when he was answered. "Arestus?" Alexi asked in his gravelly voice.

Rising and striding forward, he approached the voice until he could make out Alexi standing in the shade of the trees sheltering between the two horses. "You had us worried for a second there."

"Well, I thought that if any of their other scouts were coming back this way, I should try to stay out of sight," replied Alexi.

"You did that, all right," Solonius said, finally coming forward. "You hid so well that I couldn't find you with the light failing either, you fool!"

Arestus decided it was time to calm things down before they started raising their voices. "We've found him now, so everything is fine." He was used to being out in the country at night, but even in the early dusk the way Solonius shifted about indicated that his nerves were twitching at every owl hoot and animal movement at the edge of the forest. "Did you see any other scouts?"

Alexi was nervous, but not of their surroundings; he at least wasn't spooked by the forest and being away from the city he'd grown up in; he was nervous at having been alone after killing two of Agamemnon's men, with another fifty only a league away. "Nothing came by this way that I saw." Arestus didn't doubt he would have spotted any scouts; he almost expected the man's nerves to have conjured up a phantom army while he waited.

"Good. Well, it's unlikely that any of them will leave camp now till dawn. They would be likely to break a leg stumbling around when darkness fell. We would be well advised to do the same thing and leave before dawn. Agreed?"

Solonius still looked as if he wanted to make a run for it but he wasn't going to say so in front of the others, and Alexi was much more relaxed now that the three of them were back together. Both gave a resigned nod and they moved the horses inside the treeline.

They had just settled inside the treeline on a slight clearing, tethered the horses and lain down on a grassy mound when they heard a stick crack. They all started at the sound but only Solonius looked worried. "Settle down," said Arestus, barely loud enough to hear. "It's just a fox or something looking for its dinner."

"As long as we're not it," joked Alexi as he lay back in the bowl of a tree.

They were just settling down again when Alexi and Arestus heard more sounds and looked at each other, eyebrows climbing. Was that music? Solonius heard it too and almost jumped but, before he had uttered whatever he was going to say, Arestus forestalled him with a raised hand, listening intently to the night.

There it was again, carried to them on some stray breeze: a gentle humming.

Signalling the others to stay where they were and keep quiet, Arestus crept between the trees, silent in the hazy dusk. After he had disappeared from view, the silence stretched on. Solonius and Alexi sat watching the trees where Arestus had vanished, straining to hear any sound. Silence reigned, as if even the animals of the night had abandoned them. The minutes drew out and Alexi could see Solonius growing more agitated as time went on.

Eventually he stood up, quietly looking around, then hunched down a little and crept over to where Arestus had disappeared. Looking back at Alexi, he motioned him forward. Alexi stayed where he was, sitting upright against the tree, motioning frantically for Solonius not to go but the bigger man disappeared and there was nothing left for Alexi to do but follow. Arriving at the treeline just in time to see Solonius disappear into the gloom, Alexi followed as best he could until the humming became clearer.

Distracted, watching his footing, he almost walked into Solonius' back before realising that the other man had stopped. As his eyes adjusted to the gloom in the trees he could see Arestus up ahead, crouched down behind a tree, watching something. Solonius had started to move forward when there was a loud crack as a stick broke beneath his foot. Arestus' head spun around and saw them as both Solonius and Alexi froze, but a yelp behind him indicated that whoever he had been watching had just spotted them also.

Suddenly everything seemed to happen at once. The yelp drew Arestus's attention back to the forest and the sound of more wood cracking, then Arestus was on his feet running after whoever had been there. Alexi and Solonius took off as well and painfully crashed through the trees, trying to catch up with Arestus.

A squeal sounded up ahead and Solonius stopped suddenly, then Alexi slammed into his back, causing them both to stumble. Alexi stretched up on his toes to look over Solonius's shoulder and saw Arestus on his knees on the ground astride a young woman.

Twisting and struggling under Arestus, the girl fought with ferocious abandon, punching and scratching Arestus' face until he managed to pin her arms to the ground. His bleeding face had already taken a battering while chasing her through the forest with branches and briars tugging at him. Even after he had pinned her down she continued to twist and struggle beneath him, but with his considerably heavier weight bearing down on her, this didn't bother him much.

Alexi pushed out to the side of Solonius to get a better look. She was pretty, very pretty; Alexi was captivated by her dark, slightly tilted eyes and skin darker than the local girls, the colour of good rosewood. Her black hair hung in messy loose curls from her dash through the forest. Even with the snarl on her face, she seemed to brighten her surroundings . He was so captivated that he took a second to notice that she too was badly scratched and bloody from her headlong flight through the woods.

She was shouting something at them but it made no sense; some foreign barbarian tongue.

"What are you doing, Arestus?" asked Solonius at the same time as the words dripped from Alexi's mouth. "Who is she?"

Arestus answered both questions at once. "It's Agamemnon's little whore. I saw her with them at the beach, and thanks to you two following me she had seen us, we cant let her go back to him or it'll all be over"

Again she shouted something at them, but this time they made out the word 'Agamemnon' among the jumble of words.

Arestus was furious and released her just long enough to backhand her across the face, shouting, "Shut up!" at the girl as he pinned her arm again.

Alexi felt an almost uncontrollable desire to protect the girl, but was also the youngest of the three with all the insecurities and need for acceptance that came with adolescence, all he managed to say was, "Hey, easy on, Arestus. There's no need for that."

"No?" snarled Arestus with a raised eyebrow, fury dripping from his mouth as he spoke. "There would have been no need for that if you had just done as you were told. What part of 'Wait here' didn't you understand?"

"We just ... " Solonius got no further as Arestus' rant went on.

"No, you had to barge into the forest after me like a blind bull and draw the girl's attention. And now what?"

Solonius was looking down at his feet but Alexi kept looking between the girl and Arestus with a silent pleading in his eyes.

The girl guessed where this was going and, in heavily

accented greek around a rapidly swelling jaw, the obviously foreign words came to her. "Please ... " she stammered, tears flowing freely from her eyes. "Please don't hurt me. I won't tell."

Arestus didn't even acknowledge her words, but stubbornly refused to look down at the girl he was holding. They were soldiers; raping and pillaging were part of war, but this wasn't a war and killing unarmed women didn't come naturally.

"Which one of you is doing it?" he asked.

Solonius and Alexi looked at each other in shock and chorused "Us?"

"You got caught, not me. This is your mess to clean up."

"Couldn't we just ... tie her up or something?" Alexi was still trying to find a way to save the girl.

"No. She could escape and get their attention, or someone could come looking for her. It's unlikely they would take the risk in the dark but the chance is there. Either way, she can't make it back to them now so the only alternative would be to leave her tied up in the hope that she would starve to death. Doing it now is merciful."

Solonius raised his eyes, looking the girl over. A look Alexi had seen on his face in the darker streets of Mycenae gleamed in his eyes. "So she has to die." Alexi felt that something inside himself was dying too. Then Solonius went on. "If she is going to die anyway ..." he licked his lips, leering at her legs where her skirts had moved up her thighs in the struggle, "it would be a waste not to make use of her." His eyes were darting between Arestus and Alexi as if seeking permission or agreement.

———

THE DARKNESS WAS PRESSING in under the canopy of trees but it wasn't pitch dark yet, thank the gods, and she seemed to be keeping to an animal trail through the woods. She should have been back before now; even in safe times, the woods were not a place to go wandering at night. Unseen branches whipped Agamemnon's face and briars pulled at his clothes, tearing at his arms and legs as he ran through the forest, his eyes swivelling constantly to seek signs of her passing. It had been a long time since he'd been hunting, but the long-engrained practice of childhood assisted him as he saw a broken branch here and a tuft of hair there; he pressed on, legs pumping, lungs working like a bellows as he thanked the gods for her lack of woodcraft, she left a trail like a herd of cows.

He could hear men following but didn't stop to wait for them; gripping his hammer near the head, he charged on through the undergrowth. Running had never been his favourite activity; it was his immense strength and brutality that men revered. Put him in battle with his hammer and nobody could stand before him, but after fifteen minutes his thighs were screaming at him to stop. He kept going.

He began to slow, thinking that he must be almost through this little forest, then a glint of light off to his right caught his eye and he changed direction. Through another bush, he found himself standing at the edge of a tiny clearing. On the other side he saw what he had feared: three men, two holding Cassandra's arms out to the side while another lay above her, one hand over her mouth, the other pulling at her himation; arse bare.

The sound of him bursting through the bushes brought their attention rapidly back to their surroundings. As Agamemnon stepped forward the man on her right was the first to react, releasing her arm and rising in one movement as he reached for the sword he wore. His spatha had barely left its sheath when Agamemnon struck, the hammer catching him under the jaw in a huge upward swing. The sound of his bones cracking was followed immediately by the wet slap of his crushed head emptying against the tree it hit.

The man on top of her had rolled off and the sound of Cassandra's screams filled the forest, setting birds to flight.

Caught in a struggle to reach his own weapon in the tangle made of his chiton, Agamemnon's downward return of the hammer caught his lower jaw. It was only a glancing blow but enough to crack the jaw as the hammer continued down with all of his strength and anger, crushing ribs, lungs and spine, driving him into the unyielding tree root underneath.

By the time Agamemnon was lifting the hammer to deflect the blow from the third man, it never came. Shock had frozen the man still holding Cassandra's arm. The same could not be said of Cassandra: at some stage during the death of the first two men, she had pulled the knife from the second man's belt and now the last man was looking down in shock as it protruded from his chest. He managed only one word, "Sorry". Blood began to drip from his mouth as his hand finally slipped from her arm and he fell on his side, followed by a snarling Cassandra who screamed as she stabbed his chest over and over again till at last she fell to the ground, covered in his blood and crying.

Noise in the trees behind him made Agamemnon spin, hammer raised, with a snarl on his face only to recognise his own men arriving at the gory scene. As he turned back to Cassandra, his face softened. She had backed up against the bole of a tree clutching the knife and staring in terror at the men like a cornered wolf, ready to sell her life dearly.

Agamemnon dropped his hammer to the ground with a dull thud and moved towards her as blood and flesh splattered the ground where the weapon had landed. Her eyes were flickering between him and the other men and she flinched when he touched her arm gently, swinging the knife round towards him but his warrior's reflex caught the hand holding the knife before the blade touched him.

Holding her hand in a strong but gentle grip, he slowly took the knife from her hand and set it on the ground, putting his big arms around her and holding her head to his chest. He whispered in her ear, "Don't worry, they are dead. We killed them. Nobody is going to hurt you," as she wept against his chest.

He could feel the eyes of his men on his back as he held her and they looked over the scene of slaughter, nobody moving or saying a word until her sobs calmed and her body ceased to shake. Putting an arm under her legs, he lifted her against his chest and stood up, ready to bring her back to camp. To those watching, he looked like a man of normal size holding a child.

Looking at the group of men who stood there, he reasserted his authority. Adopting a stern look, he called out, "Polybius, you and Cletus search the bodies for anything of interest, and take their weapons too. Alkon, you and Leukos take my hammer and her basket and whatever she was carrying. The rest of you, cut a path back to the camp; my arms are already torn to pieces."

Nobody questioned his orders and a path immediately opened through the forest as the remaining ten soldiers hacked as quickly as he was walking through the underbrush. Twenty minutes later he brought her into the tent they shared. When he laid her down on the bed gently, she still hadn't said a word, not replying when he asked if she wanted anything, so Agamemnon went back to the tent flaps and pulled them aside. He could just see her weary eyes watching him in silence. He wanted to say something, anything that might help, but could think of nothing. In the end he left and the tent flaps closed on the silence.

CHAPTER SIXTEEN

ORESTES SAT IN HIS MOTHER'S ROOMS WITH CLYTEMNESTRA herself sitting behind him, running her fine-toothed comb through his hair. Washed and groomed, he felt as if he were being sent to the market to be sold as she gently combed back his hair. He was wearing his finest tunic and a new travel cloak lay on the bed.

"But, Mother," he repeated for maybe the tenth time, "I don't want to go. I want to be here when father returns."

Clytemnestra turned him roughly to face her. "You may still be back before your father returns." She rolled her eyes skyward. "The gods know he takes his time returning after ten years, but until he comes you are to follow the orders he sent, and those are that you must go to Sparta right away and meet your betrothed."

Turning him around once again to run the comb through his hair, she went on. "You are lucky. Hermione is said to be an exquisite beauty …" she hesitated, the bitterness coming out in her voice, "and without her mother's arrogance and sense of superiority." Her hatred of her sister was well known. "The marriage will seal the union of our two cities now that

Menelaus and Helen are dead. We need to build our strength if your father's dream of an empire is to be realised. And you will one day inherit the land he has built."

Orestes still did not want to go. He had no interest in marriage, and certainly not to the cousin he had not met since they were both babies, but to argue with his mother was a waste of time. He set his jaw and determined to do as she wished and just get it over with as quickly as possible, in the hope of getting back in time for Agamemnon's return to Mycenae.

He was excited by the thought of his father finally ending Aegisthus' time here. He knew his mother thought that she had been awfully clever in hiding their relationship from him, but he was well aware of it and determined to let his father know how faithless she had been in his absence.

"Pylades and Castor are going with you, along with the escort of your father's guards, but this isn't a holiday Orestes, I expect you to look after your sisters while you are there. There may be some fine suitors in Sparta, though a prince of Corinth or some other power would bring us more strength" said his mother. Orestes grimaced at the thought of chaperoning his sisters, and From looking around the palace recently Orestes guessed that they were really Aegisthus' guards, which worried him a little. Still, his little group would also be equipped with their finest armour and weapons so they were hardly helpless, having had better tutors than the guards, and he would have his two best friends watching his back.

"Your horses are being made ready in the yard, and your bridal gift is ready on the cart which will accompany you. Orestes, are you listening to me?" Orestes snapped back to the conversation they were having, or rather the instructions his mother was giving him.

"What? Yes, yes, the gifts are on the cart. Of course I'm listening, Mother," he replied irritably.

"Good. Now there will be games to celebrate your visit, as is only right. Don't embarrass me or your father; those boys in Sparta train all their lives, but so do you and you have the blood of Atreus flowing in your veins." She continued to instruct him on Spartan custom and protocol. Who better to do so? After all, she was herself a Spartan princess.

Orestes strapped on his cloak and kissed his mother goodbye, then made his way down to the stables where the rest of his company were already waiting for him.

———

"IT'S THREE DAYS' work, Philip; the rest will be spent relaxing," Arimnis said again, exasperated. Philip was the last of the men needed for this trip but they had been doing so well around Athens that he had become too relaxed about work.

"Yes, but it's Sparta, Arimnis." Philip leaned back in his chair, shaking his head. "When you say 'relaxing', you really mean two days of boredom; there's no theatre, no entertainment - hell, they barely have a bar worth speaking of. We'll spend our time there locked in a house playing dice."

"Look, Philip, this is an important contract; so much so that even I am going, to monitor it. And if the rumours are right and the war in Troy is over, you can expect a lot more competition for these jobs from now on, with thousands of soldiers returning; so suck it up and get your kit ready." Arimnis was standing waving a finger at Philip by then, until he noticed Markus leaning against the doorframe with an amused expression on his face.

"I don't know what you're laughing about. This is the biggest contract we've had," Arimnis said crossly.

"He's messing with you," laughed Markus. "Philip, go and get your stuff ready; we leave in an hour." Philip rose with a smirk and left, squeezing past Markus at the door. When he was gone, Markus came into the room that Arimnis was using as an office and took the seat vacated by Philip. "You don't have to come, you know."

"Yes, I do. He wants the shipment monitored the whole way," Arimnis replied, leaning heavily on the table. His old injury was obviously playing up.

"We can manage that," Markus assured him but Arimnis was already brushing off the offer with a wave of his hand. "Well, at least travel in the cart."

"Very well," said Arimnis. This showed Markus quite how much the leg must be bothering the old bookkeeper, that he would agree to travel in the cart like an invalid or a child, and he shook his head sadly. He remembered the man on campaign with them, the proud warrior. Markus didn't doubt that, if they ran into trouble, Arimnis would still give a good account of himself before he went down.

"Well, I'd better go and make sure the rest of the men are ready to leave." Markus pushed himself up from the chair and was on his way to the door when Arimnis spoke.

"Do you think it's true?" Arimnis sounded almost like a child, nervous and unsure of himself. Markus couldn't fault him over that. It had been more than ten years now. "Do you think it's over and they're coming home?"

Markus paused, giving himself time to gather his own thoughts. He had been avoiding thinking too much about it, keeping busy training the men and going out working since the rumours had started almost a week before. They both knew Arimnis didn't mean 'they'; the question implied was 'Is *he* coming home?'

Even now that they were the most successful and profitable mercenary group in Athens, if not farther afield, Markus knew that all the contracts they had were very short-term so that they hadn't tied themselves to any other master. Arimnis had argued that it was simply more profitable that way. As some of the few professional trained and tested soldiers left in all of Greece, or at least those not tied to a particular ruler, they were in high demand by traders worried about bandits attacking their shipments. But they both knew deep down that they were waiting for their lord's return, in the hope of returning to Mycenae.

"I don't know, Arimnis, that's the truth; but even if it's true, will he want us back?" he asked the question over his shoulder with a sad look in his eyes. "You know what she will tell him, and will he believe us or his *wife?*" The word was filled with all the scorn and hatred they felt for Clytemnestra. He knew that they had done nothing to warrant their treatment, but she was the lady of the house and Agamemnon knew nothing of her treachery. What reason had he to believe two old soldiers?

"Let's just keep our minds on business here until we know more, eh?" he said, carrying on out the door.

Arimnis watched him go, then stared at the papers in front of him with a heavy sigh. He had been trying not to think about that possibility, but now the thought was out there and, as with Pandora's box, once it was out in the open he couldn't put it back. He shook his head, started putting away the papers and got ready for the trip. The fresh air would do him good.

CHAPTER SEVENTEEN

PHILOCTETES WATCHED ODYSSEUS AT THE STERN OF HIS SHIP AS they moved silently out across the bay. A sadness had come over him while saying his farewells. Odysseus was a good man, from all Philoctetes had ever heard, and a big part of him wished he was on board that ship sailing away with Odysseus - sailing back towards Greece and home.

Although he had not participated in the war, Philoctetes might as well have done. It had been ten years and more since he'd seen his home. He had set out, his heart swelling with pride, along with the entire Greek fleet. It had been a beautiful spring morning. It had been a glorious sight: a thousand strong ships, a thousand masts against the horizon; all of Greece united in a single purpose.

Harbouring in Lemnos, taking shelter from the night at sea, had been his undoing. They were due there, of course, to collect men and supplies, food and fresh water for the last stretch at sea before arriving to lay waste to Troy.

Asleep in his blankets a little way up from the shore, he must have rolled over in his sleep that night and startled the night dweller. The ohia had made its nest among the rocks;

when he rolled over near it, the snake had bitten his leg and Philoctetes had woken up screaming. No sign of the snake was ever found, but by the morning his leg had swollen to almost twice its original size with weeping yellow marks from the bite.

In his fevered delirium, he hadn't even seen the boats move off as he writhed in pain in the hut of the healer on Lemnos.

There he had lain for ten days, fighting the fever which racked his body. A month had passed before he was capable of standing again, and for six months he had struggled to regain his strength.

And now, once again, the remainder of the Greek army was sailing away from him as he sat upon the shore. Should he have left with Odysseus? he asked himself for the thousandth time. He could have returned to Greece and worked the family farm. Was there anything left of the farm, though? Were his parents still alive? And what would he be returning to?

No. He would not go home. He would not be remembered as the man who had missed the war, without even the spoils to set up a life for himself. Pyrrhus was right about that much. After the war here, there was nobody left to challenge the men they had brought with them. Here they could be kings.

Pyrrhus was already trying to prove himself a man, having taken three concubines in Epirus.

Philoctetes turned from the sea as the ships became nothing more than dots on the western horizon. Gathering the men from where they had been eating around the breakfast fires, he set out south along the coast, heading for their new home: Epirus.

ODYSSEUS WAS STILL LOST in thought near the stern of his ship. The last in his fleet to leave the shore, they took up the rear of the formation, watching the shoreline they had occupied for a decade slip away.

That place had taken his youth. While he should have been with his beloved Penelope and his children, he had been off fighting Agamemnon's wars. Not that he had had much choice in the matter, but that did not change the fact that Telemachus would by now be almost full-grown, a man in his own right.

It would have been the boy's thirteenth year only a month previously and Odysseus had no memories of him after he'd learned to walk. Was he taking after Odysseus, short, brawny and clever, or was there more of his Spartan mother in the boy? Was he lithe and athletic?

Kimon, his second-in-command, interrupted his thoughts, coming down to join him with two cups of well-watered wine. "Oh, Kimon, thank you," said Odysseus as he accepted the cup.

"There were times when I never thought I would see that sight," said Kimon, staring back at the shore.

"Hmm?" Odysseus was still half a world away.

"The beach of Troy, seen from a boat sailing away," Kimon explained.

"Oh, yes," said Odysseus. "What did you make of the boy, Pyrrhus?"

Kimon thought over the question for a minute before answering. "He is every inch his father in his arrogance, and although he has the training and he is good, he will never be half the warrior his father was." He swirled his cup, looking into it. Odysseus knew him well enough after all these years to know that he wasn't finished. Kimon was a deep thinker, not as shrewd as himself but he saw things clearly.

"The lad is desperate to prove that he is his father's equal, trying to make a dead man proud. It's a task that will consume his whole life, I think," he said eventually. "Now that the great war is over and he does not have that opportunity to prove himself, I think he will do as he said: set up a kingdom at Epirus and use it as a base to hunt down survivors of Troy, even if it takes him to the ends of the world."

"I had the same thoughts," Odysseus replied, finally taking a sip from his cup. "You're not going to like what I have to say next, Kimon."

Kimon nodded. He had been with Odysseus almost since they were children and knew him better than Odysseus liked to admit. "Where are we going?"

Odysseus looked at him. "Am I that easy to read?"

"Only to someone who knows what to look for," said Kimon. "For a man going home to the arms of his wife, you have been brooding constantly these last few days."

Laughing, Odysseus clapped him on the arm. "Spoken as one who has never been married," he said, winking. "And the men?"

"They will follow where you lead, never fear. They may want to return home, but they trust you."

"More fools they," said Odysseus quietly. "As soon as we pass out of sight of land, send the signal to the other ships. We turn south-west."

CHAPTER EIGHTEEN

AENEAS LAY AWAKE STARING AT THE ROUGH STONE CEILING. THE ground lay cold beneath him, the mouth of the cave open to the elements. The warmth of the beautiful Dido curled in the crook of his arm was all he needed, for this land was often too hot during the day.

Through the long hard days fighting the storms at sea, he had not dared to dream of finding such a location for their landing. Carthage seemed too perfect to be true. A city already built for them; a natural harbour cut into the land, protecting their ships from even the harshest of the winter storms. And best of all, the queen of these people lay asleep in his arms.

From the moment they had arrived, from the moment he had met the queen, there had been something between them. His eyes strayed to the beautiful sword she had given him not long after their arrival. It was similar in design to his own kopis, but slightly longer with a completely enclosed hilt that would wrap around his hand; inlaid with swirling silver, it glittered in the light. It was truly a weapon worthy of a king.

She had taken him on a hunting trip today, in order, he suspected, to demonstrate the bounty of the land. Though this was only a tiny fraction of the empire she controlled, Carthage was the jewel in the Phoenician crown. It was from here that they were gaining dominance over the sea. He had already seen some of her navy and it had been a sight to behold, maybe even enough to challenge a united Greece. Where had they been during Troy's great siege? he wondered idly.

The hunting trip had ended abruptly when the skies had suddenly closed in, with dark grey clouds that promised more than a little rain. Aeneas had recommended making a dash for Carthage. Dido had laughed lightly, with a coy knowing smile and a tilt of her long dark neck, and teased him. "Are all men of Troy made of salt, that they would melt in a little rain?"

She had taken his hand and led him along. "Come, there's a small cave over here we can shelter in till the rain passes."

The rain had passed at some point, unknown to them. They had received the first drenching when they were all but thirty heartbeats from the cave mouth, but this wasn't the rain of home; not the gentle start, nor the heavy fall of a winter storm. This was like being thrown overboard at sea. The clouds opened and it fell in bucketfuls.

Had Dido not been leading him by the hand he wouldn't have seen the cave opening ten feet away, so heavily was it falling, then they were through the opening and it was dry; looking outside was like watching a waterfall pass.

"The gods must be angry, though I can't think why," said Aeneas, shaking the water from his head.

"Don't be foolish," Dido answered, giggling, as she too shook off the rain. "This is the rains of our lands - when it's hot it's very hot, then the rains come all at once. This is what gives our land its bounty and keeps the river flowing life into the fields."

She stuck her spears into the ground point first, so that the rounded bases rose into the air a few feet apart, and removed her cloak to hang on the spear. Turning her head to him, she said with a smile, "Hang up your wet clothes to dry while we're waiting."

Aeneas did as she suggested. As he was hanging up his cloak, he felt her hands running over his shoulders, sliding his chiton down. As she pressed her body against his he turned his head, seeing her dress hanging on her second spear. She reached up on her toes to whisper in his ear, "In fact, I think our gods are happy, since they have provided the opportunity for us to get to know each other better." Aeneas couldn't argue as her mouth moved over his in a deep kiss. Suddenly very glad she had insisted on not taking an entourage of guards and servants.

Now he found himself lying awake, staring at the rock ceiling.

Romulus and Remus – Hector and Achilles in their new identities - seemed to be settling in well, too. With the rest of his people, they had taken to relaxing down near the beach, eating and drinking their fill. Remus and his men had suffered only during the voyage; for Romulus and the rest, including Aeneas himself, it had been almost ten years since they had seen such largesse. Food and wine flowed in plenty here. It was perhaps even richer than Troy had been at the height of its power, before the Greeks came. For the hundredth time, Aeneas swore under his breath that the war was not over, that Greece would pay for what they had done to Troy.

Aeneas had carried his father from the city to the boats during their flight, only to see the old man die in Sicily. His bones were interred there but as yet they had had no funeral games; that would be rectified when they found somewhere to call home, somewhere they could build again.

He looked across at Dido. She was beautiful, a true queen, but something about life here didn't feel right. He didn't feel settled, as if this was not where he was destined to stay.

Maybe he could build something himself, somewhere Troy could rise from the ashes. Like the golden bird Romulus had hidden in a cloak in the hull of the she-wolf, the phoenix would rise from the ashes and lead them in battle to avenge Troy.

————

REMUS CAME to Aeneas a few days later. It was late afternoon and he had just left Dido's quarters as she was preparing for her bath. Walking down the hall, Remus casually pulled alongside him as if he just happened to be passing that way himself. In reality, he had been in the royal gardens for almost two hours waiting to see Aeneas.

"You are looking well," Remus commented. "The food and accommodation are obviously agreeing with you."

Aeneas flushed a little at the jibe. Remus chuckled as if he hadn't a care in the world. "The queen has been most welcoming," Aeneas responded, not rising to his bait.

As they passed outside the palace and had no walls around them, Remus's chuckling dried up; the grin was still there, demonstrating that they were playful friends, joking for all the world to see, but his tone became much more serious. This was the man who had helped lead their little party from Troy to the boats. "We need to talk," he said in lower tones. "Romulus is down by the bitch already; he will be waiting for us there."

The bitch was what Romulus had taken to calling the ship which had been carrying him. She was a sleek bireme named the she wolf, but after her rigging had nearly sunk her in the latest storm and they had limped into Carthage, he had used the nickname and, much to the captain's irritation, the name had stuck. Romulus was no sailor and had no love of the water.

"Is something wrong?" Aeneas asked, looking in surprise at his friend, who was still smiling as if he were making fun of him.

"We will talk at the ship," replied Remus as they walked.

Twenty minutes later they were walking down the beach

towards the ships. Romulus rose to meet them as they approached.

"Greetings," he called, moving away from the fire.

Although they had been given quarters in the town, courtesy of the queen, Romulus had made it clear to them all that a guard would be kept on the ships at all times so there were always some men down here and fires burning at night. That meant it was not unusual for them to be seen sitting here around the boats come early evening.

"Greetings, Romulus," replied Aeneas as they gripped each other's arms in greeting. "Remus tells me you've been looking for me." Romulus and Remus exchanged a look that told him something was wrong. "You wanted to talk to me?" he persevered.

Remus shrugged, looking slightly abashed. "I thought you would want to tell him yourself. You heard them, after all."

Romulus shook his head slightly. He had been hoping Remus would have broken some of the news to him by now. Aeneas was already very attached to the queen.

"We think we should move on from here, sooner rather than later." Aeneas looked like he had been slapped. His jaw hung open as he took in what had been said and his eyes swivelled to Remus, who looked uncomfortable.

Romulus quickly tried to fill the gap. "We have been here long enough. Our people have recovered; we are healthy and strong again."

"You have felt it too, then," said Aeneas slowly.

"Felt what?" replied Romulus, confused, but Remus nodded in relief.

"Yes," was his reply.

"We don't belong here; we are destined to be elsewhere." Aeneas looked down at the sand, thinking for a moment. "I had been hoping it was just me." He hesitated. "I like her, Romulus, I really like her, and I think she feels the same. And she has been good to us: opening up the city to us all, feeding us and never asking for anything in return."

Remus was nodding along in both agreement and understanding, but kept his own counsel.

"I have felt nothing, Aeneas; you're right, though, she has been very hospitable." Romulus hesitated but forced himself to continue. "However, I heard something last night at an inn near the docks." He looked at Remus, who nodded encouragingly. "Some of her sailors were talking. They had noticed me earlier, but this was later on; they were quite drunk and speaking in their own tongue. Either they forgot I was there or assumed I didn't speak Phoenician, but I had been trading with their ships for years before the siege started in Troy."

"Well, what did they say that was so interesting?" Aeneas asked, not liking where this seemed to be going.

"Well, at first they were talking about you." Aeneas' eyebrows lifted at that. "Yes, they spoke of how Dido is besotted with you, and one implied that she was neglecting her duties to spend time with you."

"Pah!" Aeneas raised a hand to wave that away but Romulus spoke over him.

"Another said not to worry, that she would get bored with you soon enough." Aeneas' eyebrows jumped up but he didn't interrupt this time. "Then he said something about their fleet, about how they should be on their way back from the east on their latest trading expedition. The journey was expected to be a long one and they were likely to lose a lot of rowers. The other laughed and said it didn't matter; when the navy came back, they would have a fresh supply of rowers lined up like sheep on the beach and even some new vessels."

They watched the confusion on Aeneas's face as he worked through what they were saying. "So you think they want to offer us the chance to join their crews and their merchants?"

"This isn't Troy or Greece, Aeneas," said Romulus in exasperation before visibly controlling himself. He went on more calmly. "I told you I had traded with Phoenician ships back home: well, they don't pay their crews. Their rowers are slaves, chained below deck."

Aeneas was shaking his head. "No, you must be mistaken, Romulus."

"There's no mistake except staying here to find out, Aeneas," said Romulus.

"I'm afraid I have to agree with him, Aeneas," said Remus. "It's a chance I'm not willing to take. Back in Troy, I helped to save you from being enslaved to Agamemnon. I wouldn't want to see you chained here instead."

"I do believe Dido loves you, Aeneas," said Romulus, "but that doesn't protect the rest of us. You can decide to stay if that is what you wish, but we have to leave as soon as possible."

Aeneas shook his head. "No, Romulus. I believe you, though I don't want to. As I've already said, I felt I wasn't destined to be here; I was hoping that feeling meant nothing and would pass." He stared at the sand again, thinking. "When can we be ready to leave?"

Romulus looked at Remus who answered, "We are ready now." Looking at Aeneas, he said, "I have had the same uneasiness that you mentioned for a little while now, so I have been stocking the ships whenever a chance presented itself against the need to make a quick escape."

"So, when do we leave?" asked Aeneas.

Both Romulus and Remus released the breath they had been holding, unsure how Aeneas might have reacted to the news. Again it was Remus who answered, looking at Romulus and Aeneas for confirmation. "There is a high tide around midnight which will aid the ship's launch and carry us out faster. After that, it's at noon tomorrow, growing later every night thereafter. I think we should leave during tonight's turn. It is more dangerous sailing at night, but we can be well away before they realise we are gone."

"So soon?" Aeneas looked stricken.

Romulus nodded. "It is best to do this as soon as possible. Their fleet could be back at any time." Looking intently at Aeneas, he went on. "You should spend the night with Dido and leave when she is asleep. Don't tell even her about this or we may never leave. We will ensure everyone else is here."

Aeneas was nodding. If what Romulus had overheard was correct, then he was right about the need for secrecy. Unconsciously he ran his hand over the hilt of the sword Dido had given him. Thus it was agreed, and a rather subdued Aeneas rose to make his way back to the palace.

CHAPTER NINETEEN

THE FORMER MYRMIDONS WERE NOT A PROBLEM. THEIR discipline and complete devotion to Remus carried them down to the boats in small groups of twos and threes over the course of a few hours after darkness fell.

Some of the others, however, were not so inclined. Following Aeneas' example, some had formed relationships with women from the town and were loth to part with them. The pleasant time they were having here was a major draw for some, which Romulus could easily understand given what they had come from. War and hunger had been all they'd known for years, followed by hunger and storms at sea and the ever-present fear of the unknown. It was a fear they all shared. What they had found in Carthage was luxury such as none of them could have dreamed of a year previously. Romulus knew it would be easier to explain the situation to them, but was worried about the added risk of men talking about it on the streets. They would just have to trust him for now.

Getting word out quietly was the next problem, and ensuring that everyone knew how important it was not to tell anyone what they were doing. Romulus felt fairly sure that some men would be left behind, but there was nothing more they could do. He and Remus sat at their fire near the bitch, looking up the beach at the string of other watchfires in front of the other boats, and every few minutes seeing more bodies moving through their line of light towards the vessels. Had anyone been paying attention, they might have noticed that everyone was moving towards the boats but none returning the other way. All they could do now was hope.

The hours of darkness slowly drifted by. Time felt as if it were moving through honey as they took it in turns to take a stroll along the beach, checking on the other guards but also subtly checking the boats as they did their rounds to see how many were there and how many more to expect.

Nine o'clock became ten, ten o'clock became eleven, and suddenly Remus was watching the tide. It was moving slowly but very surely up the beach towards the high-water mark and there was still no sign of Aeneas. By half past eleven, Remus was just starting to think that Aeneas wasn't coming when he emerged from the darkness. Slightly dishevelled, it was obvious that he had just risen from bed, but he was dressed with the sword glittering at his waist.

"You took your time," said Remus with relief. "We were just thinking of leaving without you."

Aeneas gripped Remus' arm, looking across at Romulus who had remained silent. "She took a while to go to sleep," he answered. Even in the low light cast from the fires burning low, the bright blush of his cheeks was obvious but his wicked smile offset it. Romulus grinned finally.

"She doesn't know you're gone." It was statement and question both. Their entire complement was still only the tiniest fraction of the population of a city this size. If things went wrong they were hugely outnumbered, and they all knew it.

"Not unless she wakes up," replied Aeneas. "Two of her guards saw me leave, but we just exchanged greetings as I passed through. They are used to seeing me about, so it shouldn't be noticed."

Romulus nodded. "Let's hope you're right." Then to Remus, "The tides, Remus, how are they looking?"

Remus had been carefully watching the tides. He had placed sticks in the sand at intervals to help judge it in the poor light and bent to check them now. He looked up as he spoke, golden hair glinting in the glow of embers and eyes bright. "The rise has slowed." He looked across at Aeneas. "You barely made it. It's time to start launching."

Again a nod from Romulus; with the fires burning low little would be visible off the beach from further up the shore. "Remus, you're on the serpent over there," he said, pointing west along the beach. "Aeneas, you have the sprit." He pointed east. "They're both flanking ships. I will take the centre; form a wedge on me. The captain of the bitch will guide us out of the harbour. You need to keep your sides spread until you have dropped far enough back to pull in a little without tangling oars."

Aeneas and Remus were both commanders in their own right, but Romulus had controlled whole armies on the field and any action had to have one man in charge ,in this case the captain of his ship; they accepted this and Romulus' leadership without question in this action since it was his information that had led to the evacuation. They nodded and made to leave but he stopped them.

"Tell the other captains as you pass that we move out now. Make sure they keep it quiet; the curtain walls they're building around the harbour might not be finished, but they could still severely damage us if we get caught between them." Both men nodded. As Aeneas' feet turned in the direction that Romulus had indicated, he stopped and looked down at the sand, one hand running thoughtfully over the silver inlays on the handle of his sword. Then, without a word, he lifted the baldric over his shoulder. Gazing at the beautiful leather scabbard for a moment, he stabbed it into the soft sand.

Barely above a whisper, his friends heard him say, "I will miss her," without looking back at them, as if he were talking to himself, before walking away. They looked at the sword he was leaving behind, sad for their friend, then busied themselves with the task at hand.

As they worked their way across the bay, talking to the captains, each ship disgorged a body of men to begin pushing the ships into the water, scraping their hulls. Sounds from the city reached the ears of Romulus. Everyone else was busy quietly seeing to their tasks, but Romulus had been on edge since the overheard conversation in the tavern and picked out the sounds instantly.

Turning his back on the ship, on the sea and on his men, he strode back past the watchfire, which was almost dead. Windows were lit up in the palace. Only seconds seemed to pass before a stream of moving lights, like sparks from a fire, spewed from one of the entrances easily visible from the hill in the dark. Torches: they could only be torches, and the number of them was increasing as they spread through the streets away from the palace.

He kept watching until he was sure they were moving in the direction of the beach, down what seemed like every street in the city. Other lights joined them as houses were roused by the sounds of their passing, and probably more bodies had been added to the already formidable numbers coming towards them.

The time for silence was over. They had to move now.

He turned back to the ships, shouting, "Quickly, they are almost upon us! Get those ships off the beach, damn you. Move, or look forward to life tied to an oar!" He ran along the beach shouting encouragement and abuse at each ship he passed, first one way and then another, until he was certain that Remus and

Aeneas had seen and were doing the same. His legs pounded on the soft sand as he ran.

When he returned to the centre the bitch was bobbing; the weight was off the sand and the ship free. Men were already clambering aboard, panic setting in as they too saw what looked like a wall of torches coming towards them from the city. The crowd had almost reached the harbour but seemed to be slowing slightly from the run. Still some minutes remained before they arrived, so Romulus grabbed some of the men as they tried to clamber aboard ship and pushed them towards the next, which was still struggling. Around half the ships were now afloat as he shoved bodies towards the struggling vessels.

He turned to see the torches reach the sand. Only a hundred yards separated them now, but even as he looked, the extra manpower had moved the stranded ships into the water. They were all afloat; everyone was clambering on board, with those already in place trying to get their oars into the water.

The churning of oars began, slowly at first, and Romulus still watched the Carthaginians approach. He knew the sound of churning oars. Anyone who had spent time on a boat knew that sound, so physical, and it played out in the oar master's drum-beat and Romulus' heart alike: the rhythmic sloshing of water being pushed around with oars. A ship is a big beast to get moving. The enemy were at seventy metres and coming fast.

A heavy beast, but one hundred and eighty oars working together counted for a lot, and Romulus suspected that some were double-manned with deck crews and marines all below helping, trying to add their considerable strength to getting the ships out into the water. Still Romulus stood on the beach watching the Carthaginians approach, listening to the thrash of water as the oars fought for purchase. Fifty metres away at a run.

He could sense it from the sound, that of oars catching; even a small movement sounded different to the impotent churning of water. The bitch was moving, slowly with that first stroke, but she was moving. She was picking up speed with every stroke of the oar, with every beat of the drum. Thirty metres at a sprint.

Turning on his heel, Romulus made for the stern of his ship and the rope hanging over the edge. Three strides through the water, which was getting deeper with every step, and he jumped as high and far as he could, fingers grasping for the rope which was now moving with the boat. He almost missed and his legs trailed in the water, which was blessedly moving faster now; then he began to haul himself up and over the rail onto the deck.

Sucking in lungfuls of air, he gripped the rail and looked back as the Carthaginians slowed at the water's edge, watching in impotent anger as their prey sailed away. The entire shore-line was brightly lit by all the torches they had carried with them. As Romulus watched, the crowds parted and Dido herself moved to the front to watch the ships sail away.

She saw the sword buried in the beach, and Romulus could have sworn he saw her eyes glittering wetly even from that distance as she plucked it out of its bed in the sand. An eerie silence descended on the beach as she removed the sword from its scabbard, turning it over in her hands, looking at it this way and that in the light as if in doubt.

Romulus felt as if he were present at one of the religious ceremonies in the temples of Apollo that he had attended in Troy as a boy; the silence and the reverence of the crowd who obviously loved their queen. The sword was the centrepiece of some ritual he was not privy to. Then Dido looked out at the ships, halfway to the huge unfinished enclosing walls of the harbour, and her voice carried like a bell, crisp and clear over the waters.

"Men of Troy," she shouted, "it seems I have been betrayed." She slowly turned the sword in a reverse grip facing downwards. "Aeneas!" she shouted, "By my blood and will I curse you. Never will the men of Troy, the sons of the red Mars, find peace." She pointed to the red star which had appeared in the sky as Priam died in Troy. Here they had named that star 'Mars'. "They will travel the world searching for it and find only war, and there will never again be peace between our two peoples." As she finished speaking, she turned the sword tip from the ground back towards her and a collective gasp went up, both on the ships and on shore, as she drove the sword into her body with all her strength.

They watched in horror as she dropped to her knees, hands falling away from the sword and blood dripping from her open mouth, then toppled to one side. The world seemed to freeze, to hold its breath for a second before wails of grief erupted from the host on shore.

In seconds the Carthaginians had surged around their queen and she had disappeared into their number. It was too late to do anything but mourn. In the wailing that followed, Romulus sailed out of Carthage harbour into the still dark waters of the sea.

CHAPTER TWENTY

Agamemnon sat outside his tent. He had paced up and down the embankment of the hill, sat on a rock outcropping at the edge of the camp, and lain down to try to get some sleep near one of the fires; when that failed, he had started sharpening one of the swords they had dragged from the wreckage of the ship. Chipped along the edge from waves knocking it against the shore and tarnished from the salt water, it didn't looked salvageable. Had he been at home it would have been remelted as useless, but options were limited until they reached home and it just might save his life before then. Hammers were great in close combat, but in tight ranks they were more of a hindrance than a help.

As the sun began to rise, the gleam of the blade showed that his work was not in vain, but then he had sat awake for four dark hours, polishing and sharpening it.

There was a solace to be had in the gentle stroking of the blade, the rasping of the stone softly over the edge; it was like therapy for the mind. He had always loved metalwork; as a child, when not training he could often be found sitting with the different smiths, watching them work.

That peace eluded him today, however. He had left Cassandra in the tent he shared with her. The girl had wept unceasingly while he carried her back after the assault the previous evening and had tried to push him away, so that he had to hold her tighter than he would have liked for fear that she would fall from his arms.

He, who had saved her. He had killed those responsible for hurting her, and she would not even meet his eyes, pushed him away when he was trying to protect her. He couldn't understand what he had done wrong.

True, he had done similar things to countless women across the campaigns he had fought and had taken many more as slaves, but that was war.

Why did it bother him? She was, after all, only his slave; he had the right to take her himself if he wanted, but he feared that her foresight was connected to her chastity. That was another worry; she hadn't said anything since the previous night so he had no idea if she was still chaste, or if her gift had been affected.

He was annoyed at himself by how much the situation was bothering him. She was his slave, his property; what did he care for her feelings? As he flung his sword down in frustration, however, he had to admit that he did. It was what had kept him up all night and stopped him from going into the tent. He couldn't stand to see her tear-soaked face, to hear her sobs and feel her push him away.

She had been his from early on in their campaign against Troy, nearly ten years ago, and though he had had many slaves in that time he had never taken her; but he had been away from his wife for ten years and this woman had become close to him in that time.

As he looked down at the sword, he realised that by flinging it down he had just replaced one of the nicks he had spent the night removing. He caught sight of Alkon walking up the hillside towards him, Agamemnon's hammer carried at his side.

"I cleaned the bits off this for you" he said, dropping it at Agamemnon's feet.

"Thank you. I was going to do it this morning when it got bright, much appreciated," replied Agamemnon, leaning back against the rock he had been sitting on.

"No need now," said Alkon as he untied a leather purse from his waist and tossed it to Agamemnon. "We stripped the bodies after you left. Two of them were carrying surprisingly good weapons for common thugs, and they also had this." Agamemnon hefted the purse, feeling the coins rattling around inside, and raised a questioning eyebrow at Alkon.

"It isn't a lot, but that's not what interests me. Take a look inside."

Agamemnon hated playing games but he took a deep breath and upended the bag into his open palm. Three gold pieces and some clipped silvers fell into his hand. Not a lot; it might feed the men for a day, if they found a market. Suddenly he realised why Alkon was interested in the coins; he ran a finger through them, all but one carrying the same markings.

"Argos," he breathed.

"Exactly," replied Alkon, beaming. "The storm must have carried us further than we thought; around the point of Sunium, at least."

"I didn't even see the temple of Poseidon." The disappointment of missing the temple warred on Agamemnon's face with the joy of finding he was in his homeland, mere days from Mycenae.

Alkon's smile faded a little and he looked uncomfortable. Agamemnon eventually picked up on this, asking, "What else, Alkon? Something is obviously bothering you in the face of these good tidings."

"Well," said Alkon awkwardly, "it's just that we searched the bodies thoroughly." Agamemnon gave a grunt so he went on. "We found nothing else. They had nothing else," he corrected himself, "other than their clothes and weapons, and we found their horses tied at the other side of the woodland."

"Well?" said Agamemnon, his patience wearing thin.

Alkon looked down at the ground, thinking of what to say. "They are on your land, sir, close to Mycenae."

Agamemnon thought he understood the man's worry. "We'll be back in Mycenae shortly, Alkon," he said, clapping the man on the shoulder. "With the gods' help, the other ships will be there as well with the rest of the men, or perhaps a few days later. Most of the fighting men have been away with us for so long that it's hardly surprising some banditry has sprung up in the more remote areas. Clytemnestra hardly has the men to patrol the whole of the land."

Alkon was nodding, though he didn't seem completely at ease. "Don't worry, lad. As soon as we're settled back home with the men, we'll send out strong patrols and lick the country into shape."

This answer seemed to satisfy Alkon and he saluted Agamemnon with a crisp, "Yes, sir," turning to leave.

"Alkon!" He sent a questioning look over his shoulder, "Rouse the camp. Now that we know where we are, I intend to make all haste home. We leave within the hour."

CHAPTER TWENTY-ONE

A SMALL DUST CLOUD ROSE TO THE SOUND OF LAUGHTER AS Orestes thumped down onto his back in the sand, Pylades grinning down at him. Orestes laughed too as he struggled to get the air back into his lungs.

They had been readily accepted among the youth in Sparta and this trip was proceeding much better than he had expected. He might even delay his return to Mycenae with the way things were going.

"Mother was right about Hermione," he said as he dusted the sand off his hands and got into position for another grapple.

"It's not surprising that you're so distracted today." Pylades lunged forward as if going for his shoulders but turned his body at the last moment to sweep a leg at Orestes; this time he had been expecting it and he raised his foot just in time, punching down painfully into the flesh of Pylades' thigh. Pylades staggered back a step, the blow having given him a dead leg.

Orestes had hit harder than he had intended. Pylades deserved it, he reasoned; he had only just learned that pivot and leg sweep yesterday from some of their new Spartan friends and he seemed to use it annoyingly frequently. Orestes didn't give him a chance to recover, shouldering into his midsection and driving him to the ground with a whoosh of air from his lungs.

He jumped to his feet again as his friend rolled over, holding his stomach. "You were saying?"

Jeering and laughter had broken out again around the perimeter, but it was all being taken good-naturedly. Orestes reached down, and Pylades took his outstretched hand and got to his feet where he gingerly tested the leg, not yet willing to put his whole weight onto it.

Seeing that they were walking to the edge, a few of the watching Spartan boys took the opportunity to take their place on the sand. At their age the Spartans should already have been in heavier training with the army; these sparring bouts at wrestling and pankration were all but abandoned by adults, except at competitions and funeral games, but on Orestes' arrival a festive atmosphere had suffused the town and the Agoge had been stood down. Everybody seemed to know why the boy was here, and only official rostered guards were on duty.

Last night there had been a huge feast to honour the official betrothal of Orestes and Hermione. Orestes had fallen for the young woman while talking quietly at the fringes of the feast on that first night. Electra had teased him constantly as sisters do.

A year his senior, Hermiones' raven hair fell to her shoulders in soft ringlets, and her eyes were so dark that at times she seemed to have no irises. The rest of her face was hidden behind a light veil until she wed, but she had a strength of limb that showed she also trained in the Agoge. Talking to some of the men today had confirmed this, along with the shocking news that she insisted on fighting with the men as well. A fierce and strong queen she would make, thought Orestes with pride. No meek submissive wife but someone who would challenge and push him, and provide strong children to continue their line.

Pylades rubbed his legs briskly and laughed. "You know I

was joking, don't you?" He playfully clapped Orestes' arm. "I mean, you were distracted, don't get me wrong, but I couldn't blame you. You were chatting with her for an age last night. What have you decided?"

Orestes looked down at his feet with the small private smile of a child. For all his size and maturity, in some ways he was still a shy and awkward youth unused to discussing relationships, even with his closest friend. After a brief pause, he looked across at Pylades and replied quietly. "We are to be wed, that much was decided by our parents before ever we were born, but we are going to wait until Father gets home. With Menelaus dead and Helen missing " - there had been no word of her since the fall of Troy and they had assumed her dead - "my father is her nearest relation and he will present her to me."

Pylades laughed. "How very formal!" He slapped Orestes on the back of the head. "Now tell me, how does my friend Orestes feel about it?"

Again Orestes looked down at the ground considering his answer, and a sidelong look at his friend revealed his nervousness. "I like her, Pylades. I really like her."

There was a momentary pause during which Orestes fretted about what Pylades might say; for years he had heard boys make fun of their companions over girls, but Pylades' face split with a delighted grin and he threw his arm around Orestes. Suddenly the two boys were laughing infectiously. "That's wonderful, Orestes! Too many of these arranged marriages are just for land and power, without any affection."

"She's amazing, Pylades," Orestes told his friend. "I can't wait to introduce you." He looked out across the sand of the Agoge but his eyes were far away and he wasn't seeing the men fighting a few feet away from him. "She's sweet and strong, Pylades, and clever." He shook his head. "People say Spartans only use their heads for fighting, but she could argue rhetoric with the wisest in the land."

"Ah, Orestes, it does my heart good to hear this. Come on, we should toast your future! Let's get some wine." Pylades stood up, grabbing his chiton from where it lay discarded on the bench. Orestes looked up at him.

"A drink at this hour? It's not even midday yet, Pylades."

At this Pylades did tease him. "Well? Are you afraid someone will tell Clytemnestra? Come on, Orestes! It's not every day you meet your future wife; we need to celebrate." Orestes thought about it for a minute before deciding to go with his friend. He had indeed been thinking about his mother's reaction, and his sisters, but they were being safely entertained with the noble ladies of Sparta. But this was his first time away from home alone and he had never known such freedom. He grabbed Pylades' outstretched hand and was pulled to his feet. "This trip could be worth extending for a couple of days," he quipped, and they set off in search of wine.

———

ICARION WATCHED the two boys leaving the Agoge. He sat with two others on the bench opposite amid a group of Spartan youths who were there to practice their wrestling. If you paid attention while watching others train, you learned more than you did while actually participating. But Icarion wasn't there to learn; his eyes had been discreetly hovering near Orestes since they had arrived two hours previously.

The boy was already popular among the young Spartans, which wasn't really surprising. He had been raised in the palace of Mycenae, and although he had his father's charisma, Agamemnon had been absent for so long and Clytemnestra was what she was, so the boy wasn't spoilt and arrogant as were so many of the nobility.

He would have made a good king, thought Icarion as he rose to leave the Agoge, but orders were orders.

CHAPTER TWENTY-TWO

"WHAT DO YOU MEAN, GONE?" THUNDERED AEGISTHUS.

"Missing, my lord. Solonius should have checked in this morning. There's been no word since," replied Pylos.

"Pah! Only this morning, and you tell me there's a problem. He's probably just late; it's only been about five hours." Aegisthus waved the man away and took a swig of his wine, but Pylos stood his ground.

"He is missing, lord," he repeated. "He had ample time to return by this morning. There's been no word from him or the others. I know something has gone wrong."

"Don't be stupid, man. What could have gone wrong? They were sent to watch the progress of Agamemnon's men; even had they been seen, they wouldn't appear to be an enemy or a threat, just three men in the hills. From the last reports we know that Agamemnon's men are lost, wandering around the countryside, so we still have four or five days." Pylos was obviously still not convinced; the self-conscious hunch of his shoulders made that clear. "Clytemnestra, don't you agree?" said Aegisthus over his shoulder to the lady of the house, who was on the balcony, lying back on an ornate cypress couch surrounded by pillows.

"Oh, Aegisthus, just send some men out to check. It's best to be on the safe side. What harm can that do?" Clytemnestra gave a bored wave of her hand to indicate that the conversation was over.

Aegisthus looked at her silently grinding his teeth, before turning back to Pylos. "Very well, send two men. They are to travel together and keep out of sight as much as possible. If they find Solonius, bring him back here right away. Otherwise they are to ride until they catch sight of Agamemnon and come back with his position as quickly as possible. Is that clear?" Pylos gave a quick nod.

"And for the gods' sake, ensure that they don't make any contact."

"my lord." Pylos nodded again and left.

Aegisthus hated being overruled by Clytemnestra and silently fumed but, although he had replaced most of the guards in the palace, he didn't feel comfortable taking the chance of losing men to those who might be loyal to her. There was also the advantage that her presence would make everything so much easier when Agamemnon returned. He would be relaxed, in his own home with his loving wife, unaware that all the guards were just waiting for the signal to end him and the men he would undoubtedly be bringing back with him.

"I have to check on some of the preparations," he said as calmly as he could manage, clenching his fists behind his back.

"Fine," muttered Clytemnestra and turned back to the wax tablet she had been looking over. She was receiving a constant stream of reports about Orestes's trip to Sparta, to ensure the boy was behaving himself. It was important that he should do nothing to jeopardise his marriage and hence their alliance with Sparta and the Lacedaemon lands to their south.

Aegisthus shook his head irritably as he went out the door and heard it click shut behind him. He himself had no such fears for Orestes. He had been laying this trap carefully for the past five years; once he had seen Agamemnon dealt with and Mycenae firmly within his grasp, he would have little use for Clytemnestra and could seal the union with Sparta himself.

Agamemnon had done him a true favour by uniting the land before he left for Troy. Losing the men Agamemnon brought back could have been a blow to the city's manpower if he had still had to worry about fighting the others.

After five years of work and planning, it was all about to pay off. He would take back what Agamemnon and his brother had stolen from him: his city, his land. Agamemnon would die knowing that he had even lost his wife to Aegisthus. It would not bring his father back, but it would be enough; he would be revenged.

Outside, his men were training in the yard. News of Agamemnon's imminent return had spread throughout the fortress and down into the town proper. Aegisthus would have preferred to hold the information back but there had never been much chance of that. He could still only rely totally on only his own loyal house guards; still, it would be good to have trained men after he had done away with Agamemnon and his troops.

Two men on horses were riding down out of the palace grounds, their hooves clattering on the smooth stones and echoing as they passed through the gate into the citadel, heading north towards the lion gate. Pylos was already making his way back from the stables towards him, and Aegisthus swore under his breath. The man was efficient, but he was really getting on his nerves today.

"What now, Pylos?" he barked. The little man had the grace to look embarrassed at least.

"Sorry to disturb you, lord. I just wanted to let you know that they were on their way. They have very clear instructions not to make contact, and at first sighting or contact with our other men to return immediately and report."

"Good", replied Aegisthus "You can go now. I'm going to do some training with the men." Pylos stopped trying to keep pace with him and dropped back as Aegisthus passed into the smaller training yard. He seized one of the training swords and stalked over to where the new men were working with their swords against posts. They wouldn't be doing that for long. Aegisthus intended to give them a proper lesson; he needed to work out his own simmering frustration and hitting the posts wouldn't do. He wanted to hurt someone, and the new recruits looked like a good prospect. It seemed they had just volunteered.

CHAPTER TWENTY-THREE

As the she-wolf's hull dragged itself to a halt with the rough sound of pebbles scoring the timbers all the way up, ripping barnacles from the swollen wood and sending men lurching forward in their benches, Romulus launched himself from the deck, landing with pebbles crunching beneath his feet.

The other ships beached at a more sedate pace moments later, but the bitch was already disgorging people as Remus and Aeneas jumped from the prow of their own ships. After a few words telling the crew to drag their ships out of the water, they made their way over to where Romulus stood, hunched over with his hands on his knees and his head down.

"Was that really necessary?" asked Aeneas. "One large rock on the beach and you'll have punctured the bloody hull."

"Not my biggest concern, Aeneas," Romulus replied in an irritated tone. Twisting his head, he looked up at them without straightening. Then he shook his head and the irritation was gone from his voice. "Have I ever told you how much I hate sailing?"

"Every time we put out to sea," laughed Remus.

Romulus rose up to his full height and turned back to look at his boat. "Those boats are not meant to be in the water for as long as we've had them out."

"Is that your excuse for nearly puncturing your hull?" asked Aeneas in a mildly amused tone.

Romulus wasn't amused and rounded on him, snarling into his face. "No, my excuse is that a board has become waterlogged and swollen, so it was leaking already; half my lower deck of rowers are sitting in water and we were going to go down."

Aeneas took an involuntary step back but, even as Romulus spoke, he deflated and regretted his outburst. Relaxing, he went on in a more jovial tone. "Besides which, it saves us having to do that," pointing at the other crews, who were busy dragging the ships up the pebble-strewn beach. "Or even having the hull scraped of barnacles, most likely!"

He was happy to see that they all laughed with him. Aeneas had understood his momentary fit of temper, or accepted it at least.

"Any idea where we are?" Romulus was looking at Aeneas. Both Romulus and Remus had more experience east of Troy, but Aeneas had grown up sailing the Aegean and beyond.

"I haven't a clue," he said, shrugging. "Somewhere on the coast of Italia, more than that I couldn't say. I have travelled only as far as Sicily before now." He looked out over the rolling dunes above the beach. "I can only offer rumour that I have heard from others."

"Which is?" asked Remus, using a rolling hand gesture for him to continue.

"The Greeks have been colonising Sicily and the southern tip of the Italia peninsula for a few years now, which was fine for trade and such, but lately they have been pushing some of the southern tribes north as they settled the land. That's causing some tension to build between those tribes and the northern natives; battles have been fought to keep the northern lands from the Greeks and from the tribes being pushed north." He spread his hands in a help-less gesture. "We might find ourselves less than welcome."

"Greeks." Romulus ran a hand over his face into his hair as he looked down on their boats. "Well, we're stuck here, at least until the bitch's hull is fixed. She has taken care of us well so far, but she isn't going anywhere without a few new boards."

"We had better set a guard, then. We'll need warning if the natives turn out to be unfriendly." Remus walked off towards the ships to organise the watch.

Romulus stood with Aeneas and an awkward silence followed. Romulus knew he should have said something about the events in Carthage, but the intervening time had mostly been spent separately on the boats, putting as much distance as possible between them and Carthage before stopping. The Phoenician reach was long, but it was obvious that the affair had affected Aeneas deeply.

Eventually Romulus broke the tense silence, looking back from the sand dunes at one of his oldest friends. "I'm sorry about that business with the queen." Aeneas gave a grunt in reply and Romulus went on. "It shouldn't have happened like that. It was a bad ending to a happy time."

"She felt used and rejected," answered Aeneas without looking at Romulus. "She was never going to take it well, but I didn't expect that."

"None of us could have, but you were closer to her than anyone else. Perhaps you could have stayed and had a life with her," Romulus ventured to say.

"No," replied Aeneas, hesitating before he went on. "Those soldiers you heard were right; she would have tired of me. She was fickle by nature and had a temper to boot. If she had woken to find me still there and you gone with all the boats, she would have taken it out on me. I would now be chained in one of their ships." He chewed on his lips for a second. "What do you think about the curse she placed on us?"

"I don't like it, but we'll just have to see what we find here."

"That was a powerful curse," Aeneas said thoughtfully. "A blood sacrifice, and her own at that … she had been a priestess of Astarte, you know." Romulus' eyebrows rose at that and Aeneas nodded.

In minutes Remus had returned, orders having been passed out, and unsurprisingly his ever-present shadow, Diomedes, was following so they ended their conversation about curses. Since finding out that not only had Achilles not killed Hector in Troy when he could have easily done so but also helped them escape, Diomedes had taken to Remus like a loyal dog. Romulus felt a strange pang of jealousy; before they had left Troy, Diomedes had behaved like that with him.

It was all to the good, though. Remus had been feeding the boy well and training him whenever the chance presented itself, and they were starting to form the kind of family bond that soldiers did when they had been fighting together for years. And this was the only family Romulus had left.

Diomedes had visibly grown since Troy. The extra food and training were having dramatic effects on the boy, and Romulus now saw more of his father in him. He wondered if the boy was destined to outgrow the man his father had been.

"Diomedes!" Romulus called and the boy immediately came to his side. "You could use some exercise after the boat journey. Run up that hill over there, and when you get back tell me everything you see: any settlements, people, how the land lies. We need to know where we are."

Nodding in reply, Diomedes took off towards the hill. It wasn't large but it should afford them a good view of the surrounding area. While he was away, the others began setting up camp for the night. Awnings were stretched out over oars to provide some shelter should it happen to rain overnight and dry driftwood was collected along the shore for cooking fires. It was still warm enough in the season to sleep comfortably outdoors, but the recent storms indicated that summer was well over and autumn on its way.

By the time Diomedes returned, breathing heavily with sweat dripping from his nose, pots were already hung over fires with smoke rising in gentle eddies through the calm evening air. The river emptying into the sea here was fresh water, though this close to the shore it would contain some salt from mixing with seawater, so Romulus had sent a group a few hundred metres upriver to collect water. The complaints were audible even from here, but the ships had to be kept provisioned first and foremost.

Diomedes was sucking hard on a waterskin as he got his breath back, but finally managed to speak. "A few farmhouses are scattered around. The land is mostly flat with fields of crops. I didn't see any people, but there was smoke rising from some of the houses so they've probably already gone home from the fields to make their evening meal."

Romulus nodded thoughtfully and looked at Remus, who asked, "Any forests or lakes? Any defended towns?"

Diomedes was getting better at this sort of thing, but he still required coaxing to get answers from him about what he had seen. "There looked to be a forest a little to the north; other than that, just the river and a few small copses scattered across the plains. There were some animals in the fields, but no towns within sight." He gave Remus a look that asked if he thought he, Diomedes, was stupid.

Romulus thought about this. A hunting party should be safe enough as long as they didn't venture too far. Remus and Aeneas gave the barest nods of their heads and it was settled. "Okay, we'll stay here tonight. Tomorrow Remus, Aeneas and I will take a walk upriver and see what sort of welcome we can expect."

They couldn't stay at sea indefinitely; winter would see them destroyed, starved or both. One way or another, they had to try.

———

WITH DAWN CAME a crispness to the air that Romulus felt had not been there the day before. Of course, it had to be his imagination; they hadn't travelled far enough up the coast for the weather to have changed. The most likely explanation was that he liked this place, even if he wasn't ready to relax just yet. He realised that he wanted to stay here; it reminded him of home. The beach was rougher and more pebble-strewn than that of Troy, but for ten years he hadn't seen it and even before that he had been fighting in the east.

The dunes higher up weren't as high as those on Troy's beach, the land beyond was a little greener, perhaps. But in that dim light of dawn, when everything had that faded, washed-out look, with the sun rising behind it that river could easily have been the Scamander, leading up through the low flat plains to the city - his city.

Remus was awake too and came over to him. The disturbance of the pebbles told him that everyone else was still in their blankets. He had woken up a few hours earlier and relieved the sentries, who had gratefully gone back to their blankets for the last few hours of night. Remus had always liked doing the last watch. It was dangerous, since it was the perfect time for a surprise attack when sentries tended to be most tired and least attentive, but if you took the early hours, you could watch the silent world come alive and hear the first birds and animals. It always felt to him like the world being born anew.

"Couldn't sleep?" asked Remus as he sat down beside him, blankets still wrapped around his bare shoulders. It made him wonder if Romulus too had felt the chill in the air, but he didn't mention it. A non-committal grunt was his answer. Romulus had never been a morning person and was in a brooding mood.

Remus looked up over the shore. "Remind you of anything?" he said, gesturing at the view.

"You've noticed that, too?" He looked across at the man he thought of more of a brother than those born by blood brother, who tilted his head a little with a wry smile.

"It's a little smaller," he said, "but yes, in this light I can see what you can."

"What do you make of it?"

Remus took his time answering. That was just his way: he either lost his temper and all decisions were made at once or he liked to think deeply, and Romulus would take the deep thinker over his temper any day. When he finally did answer, it was obvious he had thought it all through.

"I bloody hope it suits us. Another day on that ship would either have killed me or I would have killed someone else!" He laughed. It was a good sound and something Romulus hadn't heard enough of recently. "I'm now almost glad that those savages chased us away from Carthage. They had a good harbour, but the land was dust more than a few miles from the beach. This is like home." He looked around again and shook his head, "We'll just have to see what today brings before we can decide on anything. They could be even more savage and unwelcoming here; we can't afford the loss of men before we even get settled."

He looked across and Romulus nodded; they were of a mind. "Fine," said Romulus. "Let's get a fire going for some breakfast and have the others alert before we go."

Two hours later, as the sun still hugged the skyline, their bellies were full and they left camp with instructions to set a guard and stay alert. They hoped to be back by sunset with news. Two challenges presented themselves while they prepared to leave. The first was getting Aeneas out of his blankets and ready to join them. The navigator had such a flawless sense of direction that Romulus and Remus didn't feel quite safe wandering the countryside without him. The other difficulty was convincing Diomedes that he was not coming with them. While the country looked peaceful enough, they had no idea what was waiting for them and could be returning in one hell of a hurry.

"Besides," said Remus, ruffling his hair playfully, "you need to practice your archery. Go out with the hunting group. I'm hoping you'll have a boar or a deer at the least for dinner when we return." He hesitated and added, "I believe Nisus and Euryalus are leading the hunt."

Diomedes' face split in a grin and he ran off to find his bow and join the hunting party. Nisus was another hero of Diomedes'. The man was famed across Troy for his hunting prowess and this would be Diomedes' first time to watch the expert at work. Of course, the fact that Diomedes was also an expert bowman led to his desperate need for approval from Nisus. Euryalus would keep them safe, he told himself as Diomedes ran off. Since the death of Patroclus Remus had not wanted to form new attachments, but he felt hugely protective of Diomedes.

The combination of the physical exertion of walking and the sun rising from the horizon made the morning chill a hazy dream as they crested the dunes and made their way across the plains, trying to stay parallel to the river without being too close to it. In case they did find trouble, they didn't want to be cornered with their back to a river and no way across.

They carried their swords on their hips and their aspis slung across their backs, just those and two spears per man. Their armour had been left behind, since the weight would be more of a hindrance than a help if they had to run.

At this time of day the few farmers and shepherds were out in their fields; watching them cut the stalks of their crops brought home how late in the season it already was. Even if this was where they stopped running, it was going to be a hungry winter. Some among them would not survive to see the spring in their new home. These worries went unvoiced as they thought about those for whom they cared back on the beach.

Attempts to talk to the local farmers came to nothing; the nervous replies in their bar-bar-bar monotone language brought home how far they were from the civilised lands that they knew. It caused conflicting emotions; they realised it was this that would keep them safe for the time being, but even if they did encounter some form of town or village, they wouldn't be in a position to communicate with the inhabitants and let them know that they meant no harm. Not that they posed much of a threat, three men alone, but they were armed (for self-defence only) and it would only take one nervous scout with a bow, unable to understand their foreign tongue, to cause havoc.

The morning wore on as they moved through the country-side, crops growing high in the fields now turning golden for the harvest. The sun rose high, blinding them as they strained to look ahead. The sound of birds and the gentle lapping of the river a little north of them carried pleasantly on the autumn breeze; but for the tension they felt, they could have been on a summer stroll into the hills.

As the sun reached its zenith, they stopped in the shade of a cypress tree to have some lunch and try to get their bearings. With the sun almost directly overhead, through the shade of the thick branches it was their first opportunity to look east, the direction of their march, without being half blinded by the sun. The countryside remained as it had been, with a few small farmhouses scattered throughout. Few bodies were visible as everyone would be sheltering during the worst of the day's heat, using the break to eat and mend equipment in whatever shelters they had.

Having left before dawn, they had now covered quite a

distance of open land. They were not moving nearly as fast as they might have; with the crops thigh high, keeping track of the course of the river was proving difficult as it tended to veer north as well as east in long meanders. They stopped often on any high ground they could find to track its progress further on, so that they didn't find themselves walking north only to have to turn back south. In this way they were making much greater distance but found themselves uncomfortably close to the river on several occasions.

Just after their lunch, the river began to curve almost directly north with no turn in sight.

"Do we turn back? Maybe we could bring the boats up the river a little this evening and search again in the morning?" Romulus looked at the other two, glancing up at the sky where the relentless sun shone down.

"We don't have time for caution anymore; another month and the weather is going to turn. We will begin the winter with no food and no shelter." Remus was always short on patience and more inclined to take risks. It was why he was such a gifted warrior, always pushing the limits, but he knew that the return trip would be slower as the sun and exertion took their toll on the three men, especially as they had been cooped up on board ship for so long.

It looked as if the deciding vote would belong to Aeneas. Travelling was his speciality. He looked at his companions, who both had valid points. And they weren't just risking their own lives: who knew what those back at the ships would do if they weren't back by nightfall? But they did need to decide if this was a place where they could finally settle.

He glanced at the sky, swollen blue to the horizon, the golden ball only just off its zenith, and looked around the countryside they were in. He could easily mark where they had stopped today by the northward turn of the river if they went back now, but only two or three miles north he could make out hills breaking the horizon. It seemed a logical defensive position if there were a village around here, and if not, it would afford them the best view for miles around.

"Let's make for that hill; it's an hour away at most. If there's nothing to see by then, we'll turn back." He looked at both men and they nodded. Decision made, they set out in silence towards the little cluster of hills to the north.

CHAPTER TWENTY-FOUR

EVEN FROM INSIDE THE PALACE, THE CLATTER OF HOOVES striking stone was unmistakable; they were tearing up the streets of Mycenae, echoing off the stone walls of the surrounding building and coming towards the compound. Aegisthus couldn't have said how he knew, but he already sensed that they would herald trouble.

He had to force himself not to turn and run to the courtyard; instead he maintained his sedate pace and made his way out through the corridor to the yard beyond, where the horses were only now riding under the arch into the stable yard. Banakles rode like a sack of flour and almost fell to the ground as the horse stopped beside a groom to whom he threw the reins. He was followed by Pylos' own son, Hycuse, who reined in more sedately. He was much more the horseman but nowhere near the scout that Banakles was; Banakles always appeared to be on the point of falling off the horse but somehow never did, and he could ride all day like that. It made him a much less threatening figure to the unwary but Aegisthus knew just how dangerous the man could be; that was why he kept him.

Pylos himself was coming out of his office, by way of an

adjoining door to the yard, to meet the riders, so Aegisthus waited in the shadow of a doorway. It showed the importance that Pylos ascribed to the mission that he had risked sending his own son with Banakles. Banakles and Pylos conferred in hushed tones for only seconds before Pylos called Hycuse across, looking agitated, and received a cursory nod in confirmation of the information Banakles had already given him.

As Pylos turned and strode towards the doorway, Aegisthus walked out to meet him. The grim set of the man's face confirmed that the news wasn't good, although the scouts return less than a day after setting out had told him all he needed to know.

"How far away?" asked Aegisthus.

"They are just outside the plains of Argos, my lord," replied Pylos in hushed tones. "They may even be entering it as we speak. We can expect them to arrive tonight at the latest."

Tonight? Aegisthus had expected to have the best part of another week to prepare. What in Hades had happened to those other scouts? he wondered. If they were not dead already, they would wish they were by the time he was finished with them. Solonius, Alexi and Arestus had been with him for years; he could not understand how they would let him down so badly.

"There is some good news, my lord," continued Pylos. "His numbers remain the same, so he has not met up with any of the other ships who came in further up the coast; though there are reports coming in that at least one group are only a day or two behind."

"Very well, Pylos. Start making the preparations we discussed. I must speak with Clytemnestra." He stormed back down the corridor towards her chambers.

Without even knocking he barged into her chambers, where her maid was busy dressing her hair before her large bronze mirror. "Out!" he called to the woman, who looked to her mistress. When Clytemnestra nodded, she picked up her things and scurried towards the door. Aegisthus had already forgotten about the woman and was pacing to and fro past the large open doors onto the balcony where a fresh autumn breeze was blowing back the curtains.

When the door had closed behind her maid with a soft click, Clytemnestra rose from her dressing table and moved behind him, putting her hands on his shoulders to stop him pacing and attempting to calm him. "What is it, my love?" she said soothingly.

"Pylos was right," Aegisthus almost spat out the words. "The scouts we sent out yesterday have just returned."

Clytemnestra looked up into his eyes and saw fear there. It didn't surprise her; Agamemnon put fear into most men. She would have to steel Aegisthus to get him through what was to come. "How long do we have?" she asked

"Till tonight at the latest," he replied.

By the gods, tonight! That was much sooner than she had expected, but she didn't let her own anxiety show. Instead she said, "Then by tomorrow we shall be free of him."

He looked into her eyes and saw the resolve there, and the corner of his mouth quirked up into a tight little sardonic grin. "By tomorrow," he echoed thoughtfully. "Remind me never to get on the wrong side of you," he quipped, while storing away the knowledge of how ruthless she could be.

"You had better not," she laughed. "Now, send away all the new recruits."

"What?" he exclaimed in shock. "Send them away? He is bringing his battle-hardened men here and you want us to stand here at his mercy? We will need every man we can lay our hands on to take him, even by surprise."

"Hush, my love," she cooed at him. "Leave the thinking to me." She gave him a playful pinch. "Even with all the recruits, we can't be sure of victory if they are expecting something, but if the palace is undermanned it will put him at his ease that I was sending everyone I could to him at Troy. And what has he got? Half a ship's complement of injured, half-starved wretches. Even with our reduced numbers, half of those will remain hidden; when they are good and drunk from the party tonight, our men will fall on them in enough numbers to triumph."

Aegisthus could see it all now.

"And Agamemnon won't be with them to lead his men; they won't stand a chance."

"Why won't Agamemnon be with them?" asked Aegisthus, confused.

"It's the duty of a good wife to take care of her war-weary husband," hissed Clytemnestra, all but purring in his ear.

Aegisthus bristled like an angry cat; if he'd had hair on his back, it would have been standing up. Before he could say more, she put a finger delicately on his lips and he paused as she continued. "In my chambers, where you will await him."

It was almost too perfect. Agamemnon unarmed, unsuspecting and vulnerable, his men slaughtered like pigs. Then he would only have the boy to deal with; he was still waiting for his messenger from Sparta to report on that.

Clytemnestra had it all worked out, it seemed. She didn't stop there, either; her next words shocked him. "You will be waiting," she purred, "but he dies by my hand."

CHAPTER TWENTY-FIVE

THE CLIPPING OF ARIMNIS' WALKING STICK WAS STARTING TO annoy even himself as he crossed Sparta. The streets of Sparta were as bad as Mycenae and, although the hillside wasn't as steep as the acropolis, it was a much longer slope so that everywhere you went seemed to be up a cursed hill.

Accommodation for his guard was proving difficult to get. The first two taverns he had visited had been full, and the one he had just tried couldn't take all fifteen men. He wanted to keep them all together, in the vain hope that they might be able to control some of the drinking tonight. After arriving only this morning, he had already secured a possible contract to guard a merchant on the return journey the following day, so hangovers would not do them any favours.

The last time Arimnis had been to Sparta, he had been a much younger man. Travelling in an honour guard with Agamemnon himself, to meet his future wife Clytemnestra, and crossing the town had not seemed such a monumental task. He could remember standing almost where he was now, in the baking heat, with a wineskin in one hand, admiring the view over the valley far below and the orderly rows of vineyards stretching almost to the horizon.

"Cursed vineyards," he grumbled now. "Bloody valley, and cursed scorching sun." His wide-brimmed hat didn't prevent his brain baking and his eyes burning from the constant glare, and he stopped again to rub his eyes and try to ward off the headache he could feel coming on.

Moving his hand to his bleary eyes, he could have sworn he was looking straight at Agamemnon just across the street. "Don't be stupid, old man," he grumbled to himself. "He is still far off in the east. Besides, he would be an old man by now, too." The mirage was obviously a maudlin image conjured up by an old man reminiscing on his younger self.

Yet when he removed his hand for the second time with his eyes clear, he could still see the unmistakable image of a young Agamemnon turning the corner just ahead. Arimnis had to get a closer look, if only to confirm that he wasn't going mad, and shuffled after the young man. By the corner he was sweating and nearly exhausted from trying to catch up, but his luck was in; the young man had stopped halfway up the street at a wine shop. A group of hangers-on were flocking around him, all trying to be heard at once, as they ordered drinks and told jokes.

Arimnis was reminded again how old and beaten he was, as he was forced to lean against the corner for balance after the rush to get there, despite the assistance of his walking stick. Almost lying against the blessedly cool shaded stone to recover his breath, he received dirty looks from the passers-by. Everyone knew what Spartans thought of cripples.

It was only by chance, because he'd had to catch his breath, that he realised he was not the only one watching the young Agamemnon. Then it struck him. He hadn't seen the boy for six years, since Clytemnestra had turned him out of the palace, and he had grown so much in that time. "Orestes!" he whispered almost reverentially.

He stood there, watching the boy enjoy himself, and watching those watching him. Bodyguards? There were three men, keeping a respectful distance from him. Respectful or watchful? One turned his head slightly and the scar from Icarion's mouth back to his jaw was instantly recognisable. Arimnis had been there when he had received that spear thrust, when Agamemnon had retaken Mycenae. It was Aegisthus' man. They were assassins.

Arimnis looked back at Orestes. The boys had obviously been drinking, as boys away from home are wont to do, but they did not look too bad and there were enough of them to prevent the assassins from striking yet, unless they were suicidal. Arimnis turned, looking around. He had to find Markus or Philip, someone to help.

They were delivering the supplies to a barracks near the Agoge, so Arimnis set off in that direction as fast as his crippled leg would allow him, hobbling on the rough uneven flagstones. His cane slipped on the stone, jarring the joint and almost sent him flying on his face. Rushing wasn't helping and he slowed his pace slightly; it was more important to get there safely than to fall and break his neck in the rush, but he knew well that time was of the essence.

Gritting his teeth he kept going, as fast as he safely could, limping quickly, feeling the eyes of the passing Spartans glancing at him and quickly looking away. He didn't care any more; he had bigger things to worry about. Left foot forward, cane forward and he dragged his limp right leg behind. He stopped, hand outstretched against the wall, fat beads of sweat rolling down his face and falling from his nose to splash on the flags, breath burning in his throat while he tried to remember the way to the Agoge. It wasn't the top of the hill, for which he offered thanks, but it had been twenty years and more since he'd roamed these streets with Agamemnon and they all looked the same to him now.

A young boy was walking down the street; a good sign, since they were almost always near the Agoge for school or play, or to watch the older boys train. He must be nearing it. He grabbed the boy's arm as he passed, and wheezed, "Which way to the Agoge?" in a dry rasp. The boy struggled in his grasp, revulsion to a cripple evident even in his young eyes; but it was his leg that was crippled and he held the boy fast, repeating his question. "Which way to the Agoge?"

The child pointed down the street to the left and Arimnis let him go. The boy nearly tripped over himself in his struggle to get away.

Arimnis heaved a deep breath and pushed himself away from the wall, cane clipping down the way that the boy had indicated. At least this street was sheltered a little from the sun, but the effort of walking fast down its length was about as much as he could manage. The street opened out onto a huge square with the Agoge at the opposite side; there was just the huge sand training ground before it now, but even that seemed barely feasible. He pushed on, crossing the street, only to hear his name called from a building he was passing. Turning, he saw Markus sitting at a tavern with a cup in hand, four of his men with him.

"Arimnis!" Markus called again, getting up from his seat. "How are we doing for accommodation?" Realising that Arimnis could barely stand by himself, he dropped his cup to crash on the stone floor and rushed to catch him before he fell.

Markus' strong arms held him by his himation, which was stuck to his skin and drenched through with sweat, his face pale from exertion. "What's wrong?" asked Markus. "What has happened?"

Arimnis tried to speak, but his tongue was thick and dry in his mouth, the only part of him that was even remotely dry. He closed it and tried to work some moisture into his mouth and get his tongue working again. On his next attempt, the words rasped and scraped up his burning throat. "Orestes ... in the ... city."

The confusion on Markus' face didn't lessen. "Orestes? What has that to do with ..."

Arimnis didn't let him finish and wheezed out his next word. "Assassins."

Markus' eyes widened as he grasped what Arimnis was trying to say. "You're sure?" It wasn't really a question; he trusted Arimnis implicitly and they had served together for many years. The older man nodded his weary head, eyes almost glazing over. "Where?"

Arimnis realised with dismay that in his rush he hadn't noted the street name. He pointed down the street he had come from, then to the right at the bottom. The others had realised something was wrong and were getting up.

"Philip!" shouted Markus, then realised that the man was standing only a foot behind him. "Take him a moment," and Philip slipped into the role of holding the almost dead weight of Arimnis. Markus turned to the other men. "Kalliades!"

"Here," was the reply.

"Leave your horse; Arimnis is going to need it. Run and find the others and tell them to follow us as quickly as possible. Orestes is in trouble." He didn't wait for a reply. Kalliades was sprinting up the side of the Agoge, looking for the rest of their party.

Their horses were tied up outside the tavern they had been drinking in, waiting to find quarters for the night where they would be stabled. "Can you ride?" Markus asked Arimnis.

"Do I have a choice?" replied Arimnis with an exhausted wry grin. Philip had given him water from his own skin, hanging from his shoulder, so at least he could talk a little more easily. "It can't be any worse than trying to run." Markus was looking at his lame leg with concern.

"Fine," he said, accepting the inevitable. "Philip, ride on his left and I'll be on his right. Don't let him fall off the bloody horse." Philip was mounted in seconds as Markus bodily lifted Arimnis onto another horse and Philip moved into position on his left. Moments later, Markus was up and they started moving down the street.

They were only managing a light trot for the safety of Arimnis, but it was still a lot faster than Arimnis had managed in the other direction. Even at the more sedate pace, Markus still kept up an almost constant barrage of shouting at pedestrians who were not moving out of his way fast enough. Ten minutes later, Arimnis called them to a halt at the corner where he had first spotted Orestes.

Markus dismounted at the corner, helping Arimnis from the saddle. Horses were not unusual on the streets but the sound of their hooves would draw attention. Throwing the reins to Philip, they stood at the corner and peered around. Arimnis breathed a great sigh of relief to see Orestes still there, though the group with him was now smaller. Markus recognised him immediately.

"Where are the assassins?" asked Markus.

"A few doors away on the right," said Arimnis. "You remember Icarion, Aegisthus' man?"

Markus nodded, placing them with his eyes. "What do we do now?" asked Arimnis.

"We find somewhere to watch and wait," replied Markus.

"Wait?" exclaimed Arimnis, a little too loudly, and Markus squeezed his arm to let him know. "Wait for what?" he demanded more quietly. "To see a knife in Orestes? Do you want to watch him die?"

Markus' voice grew hard and his entire stance stiffened as he dragged Arimnis back and pinned him to the wall. "You're questioning my loyalty, Arimnis? Is that how well you know me after all this time?" Arimnis sagged a little and shook his head. "We wait because we have been away from Mycenae much too long to know what is happening there. For all you know, Icarion could be a bodyguard."

"You don't really believe that, Markus," hissed Arimnis.

"No, I don't, but I also don't know; and killing Orestes' bodyguard isn't going to do us any favours." Markus let Arimnis go and peered around the corner again trying to decide where they could wait.

He barely noticed Arimnis at his elbow, also peering around "Where's the other one gone?"

"What other one?" asked Markus.

"There were three: Icarion and another two I don't know," said Arimnis.

"Shit." Markus scanned the street.

Then everything seemed to happen at once. One of the young Spartans on the other side of Orestes' group screamed, a blood-curdling yell, and all eyes swung to him. Blood was already foaming from his mouth and the laughter around Orestes died away. They stared in horrified silence as the boy, already dying, tottered on his feet for his last few seconds of life. He wore the shocked, wide-eyed stare of someone who knows they are already dead but can't figure out how or why.

Markus pulled his eyes away as he realised that he too had been staring in shock, only to realise that Icarion and the other man were no longer sitting where they had been; they were moving towards Orestes under the distraction of their dying friend, while everyone was looking the other way. "Philip, quickly!" shouted Markus as he broke into a run.

The spell broke on the group around Orestes as, just before the dying boy fell, he was pushed forward off the knife into the group of friends. The man behind with the bloody knife moved forward towards them, and they struggled to get the dead boy off themselves as he advanced, some drawing knives themselves. Among the confusion of the group of half-drunk boys, the veterans' murder skills showed.

The first to get out a knife received a knife across the throat for his trouble while Icarion and his friend moved unseen into the back of the group, knives opening throats and guts as chaos reigned all round.

Other people on the streets saw what was happening but nobody moved in the confusion and half a dozen were down in a heartbeat as screams rent the air.

Markus' feet were pounding the stones as he ran as fast as he could, still thirty strides away and knowing he wouldn't get there in time to prevent the assassination. Two horses passed him at a gallop, and without slowing Philip and Crius launched themselves from horseback through the air at Icarion and his companion, knives outstretched.

Crius' aim was true and took Icarion in the upper back, the man landing hard with Crius on top of him. Philip was less lucky; he managed a killing blow, though a lower one, to Icarion's companion's lower back, the knife tearing him open in a ragged line as Philip's own weight pulled down on it. There was an audible crack as his legs hit the cobbled stone, followed immediately by his scream of pain from the break.

With those two down, the third man was easily overpowered by sheer weight of numbers. Markus arrived just in time to watch him die as one boy gripped his arm, holding the knife at bay above his head with all his strength, while Orestes' companion Pylades plunged his knife repeatedly into the man in a panicked frenzy.

The boys were looking around in fear and confusion, trying to decide who was an enemy and who was a friend. Some of the surviving Spartans were getting ready to advance on Markus, so he held his hands up, empty. "We came to help," he panted, out of breath after the sprint, and pointed to Crius and Philip where they lay on the ground. "See? They killed two of your attackers."

They still looked unsure until he addressed Orestes directly. "Orestes, it's me, Markus," he said, almost pleading. "Arimnis is with me; it was he who spotted these men watching you. He recognised that one," and he pointed at Icarion.

He could see Orestes thinking. The boy had been only nine when they'd been sent away. There was recognition there, but he was nervous after what had just happened and unsure who to trust. Then Orestes' eyes lit up as he looked past Markus. "Arimnis. I remember you!"

Markus turned to see Arimnis hobbling down the street, the reins of the two remaining horses held with his staff. Orestes pushed past his surviving friends, heading towards Arimnis with a trace of a relieved smile on his lips. His expression held terror, relief and confusion all rolled into one as he tried to come to terms with what had just happened and what had nearly happened to him. Markus moved to help Philip, who was still groaning on the ground.

Philip's knee was a mess; blood was pooling underneath and it was badly cracked but the Spartan boys were already dispersing to find medical aid. They may have been thinking about their friends when they sought a medicus, but already Markus could see that most of the injured were beyond help, as was the man moaning and bleeding out his last underneath Philip.

The medicus arrived within a few minutes; after checking him over, he gave him a few drops of the milk of the poppy, which calmed Philip substantially. As he was being lifted on to a stretcher, Markus left him and went to find Orestes and Arimnis.

Arimnis had an arm on Orestes' shoulder; they had tied the

horses outside a tavern and were making their way over to him. "Sorry, Markus," said Orestes awkwardly. "It's been so long since I saw you that I didn't recognise you."

Markus had not really expected him to. Had Orestes not looked so much like Agamemnon, he doubted if he would have recognised him either. He put out his arm and gripped Orestes' forearm, but then pulled him into a hug. "It's good to see you, lad," he said. "When we left, you were barely up to my hip and now, look at you!" He pushed him back and looked him up and down. "Every inch your father."

Orestes blushed shyly, looking at his feet. "I wish I'd known that. I can barely remember what he looked like." The scene before him was one of chaos. "Why did this happen? My friends have been killed. What were they after? And why were you here? I remember you leaving Mycenae, but nobody ever told me why. One day you were just gone." There were tears in his eyes as he spoke. These were men who had watched over him as he grew. Markus himself had taught him the proper grip on a shield after his father had left. Until he was nine, when they had vanished from his life.

Markus dammed the flow of speech. "Slow down," he said gently. "So many questions." He thought for a minute before he went on. "These were Aegisthus' men, and we believe they were after you."

"Me? But why? Are you sure? I don't recognise them from around the palace and nearly all of the house guards are his own men now." Orestes' face was a mask of confusion as he looked at the three attackers lying in a pool of blood on the ground. There was blood all over the place; they had killed seven of his companions before they'd been stopped, and now all their blood was mixed in a big puddle on the ground. The Spartan dead were now being removed, after those injured who had any chance of survival.

Nobody seemed to know what to do with the attackers.

Markus suspected they would end up thrown in a ditch somewhere, as there was nobody to see that they had a funeral, and they certainly would not receive the coin for the ferryman. Markus could almost feel their lost spirits rambling past him as they began their lost wandering of the world, and a chill ran up his spine.

It was Arimnis who answered. "I remember that one from long ago. He is definitely Aegisthus' man. He is probably still keeping a small body of men at his coastal villa, men who would not be recognised, making them ideal for this sort of action." Markus nodded agreement.

"As for why we are here," Markus continued from where Arimnis had stopped, "we have been working as a mercenary band, guarding merchant trains mostly, since we left. It was just luck that had us here in time to help."

"Luck," said Orestes, shaking his head. "Remind me to build an altar to Tyche."

"As for why we left," Markus looked sadly at Arimnis, wondering how to answer that one. "We did not leave by choice, Orestes; more than that it's not our place to say, until we've had a chance to talk to your father."

Orestes nodded his understanding, though it did not brighten his mood.

"Speaking of your father," Arimnis said, head slightly tilted as if trying to hear better. "Rumours are rife but unconfirmed that the Trojan war is over and that Agamemnon will be returning home. Have you heard anything?"

At this Orestes did brighten and was suddenly talking excitedly. "Yes, it's all true! He should be home any day now," he told them. "We received a note to say he was coming. That's why I'm here." He was now smiling. "Mother wanted to have the wedding arranged for his arrival, so we can celebrate his return with my marriage to Hermione."

Neither Arimnis nor Markus were smiling now. Both eyes

were fixed on the other, faces serious and rigid. "So he should be arriving soon?" Markus asked slowly. "Maybe even while you're away?"

"Maybe," said Orestes. "He's already overdue, judging by the note he sent. I wanted to stay and wait for him, but mother insisted that the wedding be organised." He could see that neither man was at all interested in the wedding; they seemed to be having a private conversation without opening their mouths, and both looked unhappy and worried by what they saw in the other. "What is it?" he asked. "What's wrong?"

Again it was Arimnis who answered. "This attack on you by his men, Orestes, then your father's imminent arrival, and you say the palace is full of Aegisthus' house guard?"

Orestes nodded. "Yes."

"He is going to make a move against your father, Orestes." It was Markus who spoke this time. "He was trying to kill you at the same time, to tie up any loose ends."

"No," said Orestes, confused. "No, Father will have men with him; probably most of his army."

"Aegisthus is planning something, I'm telling you; otherwise he would never have risked making a move on you. He was probably hoping that Agamemnon would get himself killed in Troy, but now that he is coming back, Aegisthus is out of time and options." Markus shook his head slowly. "All it would take is a quiet knife somewhere."

The fear was visible in Orestes now, but there was also anger in his face as he thought about it. "We have to get back," he said, looking at the two friends.

"Orestes," said Markus sadly, "your mother exiled us from the city, under pain of death."

Orestes' jaw was clenching and when he spoke there was iron in his voice. "Are you still loyal to Agamemnon?" he asked. "To the house of Atreus?"

The two looked at each other and nodded. "Always."

"Then your lord has need of you now," he said firmly. "Let me deal with my mother. And if Father has any problem with your return, I will be king of Sparta and I will find a place for you here. Now will you come with me?" His voice was rising as he went on and others on the street were watching, including the surviving Spartans from his group.

"Aye," they answered.

"Then get your horses, and meet me at the south gate in one hour." Orestes caught Pylades' eye and nodded to him, "Pylades, find the princess Hermoine and tell her what has happened here. With her permission I must leave Electra and Chrysothemis in her care until it is safe". The boy could command when he wanted to.

The hour passed while they got something to eat and a few supplies, agreeing that Arimnis would follow on the cart. They expected to be riding hard, and he would slow them down. When they arrived at the gate a crowd had gathered: young Spartans, shields and spears in hand, mounted on shaggy but sturdy horses.

Markus looked around; obviously Arimnis and Philip were missing from the group, but Kalliades and the other nine were with him. Orestes, Pylades and Castor joined them from a side street as they rode towards the waiting group of Spartans. Markus reined in just before them and asked the group in general, "What's all this?" Orestes seemed to have no greater knowledge of what was happening than he did.

One of the group broke from the others and rode towards them. "You are going to kill the man who sent the assassins?" he asked.

"With luck, we are," said Orestes, nodding.

The Spartan looked back at the group behind him. "They killed our friends, and when you are wed you will be our king. We want to ride with you, for vengeance and for our future king."

Orestes was stunned but grinning like a fool. He spoke in a voice pitched to carry. "I thank you. Now, let's ride."

CHAPTER TWENTY-SIX

AFTER SO LONG ON BOARD SHIP IT WAS GOOD TO GET OUT AND stretch your legs, but Romulus could feel the stiffness of the long hike settling in. and they still had to travel back to the ships. Autumn may well have set in, but the afternoon sunshine was stifling over a long walk.

He had been watching the hill grow closer over the last hour as he sweated; his legs had begun to burn almost immediately as the gradient increased. When they reached the base of the hill, it seemed to have doubled in size. Now it was taking all his concentration to place one foot in front of the other.

He looked across at Remus and Aeneas, frustrated to see that they did not seem to be experiencing any problems with the day's outing, but they had been keeping much more active than he had lately. Aeneas had had numerous hunting outings with Dido while they had stayed in Carthage, and Remus had been using his free time on land doing drills with what was left of his Myrmidons and had taken on the training of young Diomedes. He seemed to be trying to replace Patroclus.

The hill was steeper, rougher and scrubbier than it had looked from a distance; roots of trees caught his feet and rocks rolled away under his feet as he put weight on them. It was arable ground but not like the land he had left behind, though perhaps it had not yet been settled and farmed enough; that seemed likely from the land they had passed on their way here, which had a low level of population and only small farmsteads.

Aeneas was first to crest the hill and stood there like a man enjoying an afternoon stroll, spear grounded and staring out beyond. "That's more like it," he said.

Romulus was still struggling up the rough scree of the slope, wondering what was to be seen. Standing beside Aeneas, Remus lifted his water bag, pulled out the stopper, took a long drink and handed it to Aeneas. Romulus finally scrambled up beside them onto the broad open top of the hill and stood with his hands on his knees, breathing hard, until the water bag was held under his face. Aeneas shook it to get his attention, saying, "You need to take better care of yourself." He straightened and took the bag, tilting his head back to pour a stream of sour, warm, brackish water down his throat; nothing had ever tasted sweeter.

He lowered the bag, wiping his mouth on the back of his arm before he answered. "Someone had to take care of the administration side of things while you were away chasing pretty queens and you played with your toy soldiers; did you think the ships restocked themselves?" They laughed, but Romulus had only been half joking.

Then he looked at the view: houses, a lot of houses inside a large area enclosed by a wall. The hill they had just climbed gave him a direct view. From their vantage point, it suddenly became clear that they had entered a hilly area after the flat pastures they had passed since they'd left the sea. Perhaps they were the foothills of some distant mountain range, but all around them hills rolled and dipped into valleys. Who knew what was beyond that again?

There was a hill about a mile from where they stood, maybe

two when you took the valley between into account, where quite a sizable town had been built. A rough mixture of proper stone architecture interspersed with rougher wooden huts with thatched roofs. A hundred dwellings, maybe more; the hillside made it hard to judge. Smoke drifted lazily from a few roofs.

Excitement welled inside him, which he pushed down with some difficulty. He was naturally cautious, and if this trip had taught them anything it was that visitors were not always welcome. Some villages were so wild and savage that, given the chance, he was sure they would eat anyone they captured. Dido had warned them about outlying villages when they'd been in Carthage. Her exact words had been, "They kill foreigners and children as ritual sacrifice to their gods, but I'm sure they eat them afterwards because no bodies have ever turned up."

Those were backward, mud-built villages, he reminded himself. The stone-built houses here, though they were few and difficult to make out in any detail at this distance, suggested that these were a more civilised people. The need to find somewhere to shelter over the winter weighed heavily on his shoulders.

Handing the waterskin back to Remus, he moved forward. He had barely taken two steps when he felt a hand on his shoulder. "Is this wise?" asked Remus, unusually cautious, but Aeneas' face held a similar apprehension.

"Where are the villagers?" he asked, looking at the town. "In a settlement of that size, we should see some activity from here."

Remus was nodding agreement. "Something is strange; the city gates are open but there is no traffic. I think we should be wary, brother."

Romulus scolded himself for not noticing it. The town looked abandoned except for the wisps of smoke rising from a few roofs. "What choice do we have?" he asked the other two, with a shrug.

"We could return to the boats and maybe try a little further north," said Aeneas doubtfully.

Romulus could understand their reluctance. Their arrival had not been particularly welcome so far, with the exception of Carthage, who had secretly been planning to enslave them to power their ships. "Look, we have been searching for people, for a village where we might be accepted and could possibly settle; how are we going to do that if we avoid every town?" He looked from one to the other. "What makes you think that further north will be any better? Look at this land, Remus. It's like home; we know how to work with land like this."

"Fair enough." Remus exchanged a look with Aeneas, "But it's a long run back to the boats if we're wrong!" They both chuckled.

Romulus was laughing too. "Then pray that Tyche is in a favourable mood."

The hand was still on Romulus' shoulder but he moved on. Their reluctance was evident and he could measure their hesitation by how long it took till he heard the soft padding of their sandals following his as they moved out across the flat of the hill, carefully looking around. At least a full half mile of flat ground offered the most stunning views of the surrounding area.

The river sloped north around the hills, following the lazy pattern of the landscape between this and a much lower hill across the river. It disappeared somewhere between this lower hill and the inhabited one directly opposite. A lot of the landscape ahead was obscured by the rolling hills, the inhabited one having a slightly higher rise than the others, which gave it a better view of the surrounding countryside.

Although this provided a much better defensive position, it was also virtually hidden amid the other hills and almost impossible to see by accident unless you climbed the slopes; this confirmed Aeneas' suspicion that it wasn't an entirely friendly area since it warranted such fortifications.

However, even from this distance the stone buildings scattered around the town looked cultured enough to offer some hope of an educated civilisation here. Romulus commented silently in his own head that his point still stood: they must either find somewhere to shelter for the winter or risk a winter hiding from beach to beach, hoping to dodge between storms, as his people slowly gave up hope and strength and the risk of starving increased daily.

One risk increased another. A chance had to be taken, and it was theirs to take. Rough stone and gravel crunched underfoot as Romulus walked, creating an ominous hollow sound as he moved across the hilltop. More and more of the foothills opened up: the sheltered green of the lower section, with pens for animals below the town and sheep, goats and chickens patrolling the pastures, even an occasional cow. Still no human inhabitant was in sight. If the town had suffered an attack, then surely more of the houses would be billowing smoke? No raiders would have left the entire stock of animals freely roaming the countryside. Yet no children chased the chickens or sheep, no armour or spear points glinted above the palisade. No human movement was visible.

Remus moved up beside him, with Aeneas only a step behind; their hesitation was no longer apparent but Romulus knew they were still holding back. As they neared the edge of the hilltop, figures became visible down in the valley below; not just one or two, but what must be the entire population of the town they were looking at.

Centred in the crowd was a huge stone altar, where slick wet blood was visible even at this distance flowing over the edges, from the throat of a bull held by a priest, covered from head to foot in white bloodstained robes.

The ceremony was very familiar to anyone from Rhodes or Minoa, up through the Hellespont and across all Greece; so much so that the three friends stood in awe and worship of the gods. That proved their undoing. Forgetting to drop to the ground to watch discreetly, they were still standing in worship of the gods when a trumpet broke the silence of the crowd below.

Quick eyes flicking through the crowd, Romulus made out groups who were pointing towards them and shouting. Too late now to shrink back, he kept his back straight as a number of men mounted and broke off into groups of ten or twelve. Two of them moved as if they'd been born on a horse, approaching the flanks of the hill on which they stood, too impatient to wait for the larger group of warriors behind.

He could feel Remus and Aeneas fidgeting behind him, taking their aspis from their backs and fitting them on their arms, gripping their spears. Romulus did the same, looking west toward the river, watching the horses; he tried to judge their chances if they stood and fought or made for the river. The river would be their only option if it came to running; the horses would just run them down if they tried to stay on land.

Romulus had already made up his mind: running and fighting both equalled suicide with thirty experienced riders bearing down on their position, men who would obviously know the surrounding terrain better than he. He had cast the dice, and now it was time to see what Tyche offered.

"No sudden moves," he said to his companions.

"So we are just going to let them kill us without a fight?" cried Aeneas as the first group of riders crested the slope ahead of them.

"Fighting won't get us out of this, brother." Romulus threw him a withering look. "We might take a few, but they are thirty horsemen; it's better to take a chance on peace."

The horsemen did not come straight on but circled the group in a tight formation, spears pointed towards them as they circled, as if they were penning a bear. They slowed as the other groups crested the hill far behind; one man broke away and stopped outside the circling horses as signals were passed between the groups.

He was obviously the leader, judging by the barked order which brought the horsemen to a stop, all horses and spears pointing in towards the three companions with a gap left for the leader to approach.

"Bar-bar-bar," called the rough-clad leader in whatever barbarian tongue he spoke. Nobody moved a muscle and Romulus could feel the tension rising, like a bowstring pulled back to the ear, ready to be released.

"Bar-bar-bar," called the leader again, pointing his spear at the ground.

Romulus hesitated for only a second. It was useless to do anything else. Standing erect, spears pointed towards the sky and arms as open as he could make them to show he meant no harm, he leant down and called on Remus and Aeneas to do the same. "Lay down your spears."

"Are you mad, brother?" spat Remus. "They will skewer us. I will not go unarmed across the river Styx."

The venom in his voice was not lost on the locals, who were braced for a fight and watching Remus as if he were a vicious dog. Romulus' head snapped back to face him as he set his spears and aspis on the ground. "Do as I say. This is our only chance." In a voice calmer than he felt, he went on. "If they had wanted us dead, we would be dead already. Whatever is happening, this is our only chance at present."

Second which felt like hours passed by as indecision and anger warred on Remus' face. Romulus found his eyes flicking to where he had laid his spears, wondering if he could roll and come up with two if Remus did not see sense; one wrong move by him would see all three dead. The decision was made for him when Aeneas, quiet until now, laid down his aspis and spears alongside Romulus. With a grunt of frustration, making nervous horsemen twitch, Remus too put his arms in the growing bundle on the ground.

The atmosphere quickly changed when they had disarmed themselves. The leader of the horsemen barked another order, "Bar-bar-bar," and to the trio's relief the spears which had been pointed at them were raised and a gap opened up on the village side of the circle. As he pointed with his spear, the three friends realised that their immediate danger was over and they were to be escorted down the hill to where the rest of the village awaited them by the altar.

"I will fucking kill you if we are to be the next sacrifice, Romulus," grumbled Remus, still silently fuming.

"Oh, shut your mouth, Remus," he snapped back. "We're still alive." Ten minutes later, as they approached the altar still flanked by riders, the crowds separated for them to approach and even Romulus began to worry. They walked straight through to the centre of the crowd, heads held high, until they reached the priest, his white robes splashed liberally with scarlet from his sacrifice.

CHAPTER TWENTY-SEVEN

AEGISTHUS WAS ALREADY NERVOUS, ALL BUT TIPTOEING AROUND the stables. It was unusual for him; for the past four years he had been walking around the palace as if he owned the place, ordering servants around, beating men for not obeying fast enough. It was his word that had cast out Arimnis and Markus after many years of service, but now he stood in a dirty woollen chiton, casting nervous looks around.

It was fine, everything would be all right, he kept telling himself. Looking around, he could see only his own men, men who had served in his household for years; surely they would never betray him. He had been good to those men, but when the stakes are so high, whom do you trust? If he won today, he would take in one foul swoop what Agamemnon had spent a lifetime putting together.

The thought made him smile. Revenge would be his.

Cheering from the city down below snapped him out of his daydream, whipping his head in the direction of the gate then back towards the slouching figure of Banakles. With a leather apron on, his slouch was not as evident as usual. The man could blend in as a rough worker anywhere, and today the scout would be the stable master.

Aegisthus would be his assistant, looking rough and dishevelled. No one would pay a blind bit of notice to the servant, especially since Banakles had worked his magic on him; straw had been tossed through his rough hair and his chiton stained with horse manure.

When Banakles had rubbed some on his face, Aegisthus had protested that he was going too far; indeed, he could have sworn he'd detected the hint of a smile on Banakles' face as he'd smeared it on, but he was a spy by trade and swore blind that no one would get close enough to the source of the odour to recognise him. Aegisthus could not argue with the logic but he still had to breathe the putrid fumes, and as the temperature rose over the course of the day the fumes had been working their way further up his nose.

The cheering was gradually getting louder; from the direction and swell, he could tell that they would now be passing under the lion gate in the cyclopean wall. The city's main defence from invasion, these huge walls had protected the citadel from the time of the founding of Mycenae. The stones were huge, the size of houses, but they could not protect Agamemnon from what was already inside his walls. Aegisthus allowed himself a grim smile. Tonight the reign of Agamemnon would come to an end and Aegisthus would have his revenge.

The cheering continued to swell, rounding the curves of the path leading from the lion gate up to the palace proper. While he would have expected horses and fanfare, coming through the gate into the yard was a single horse. On its back was a woman, and Aegisthus stopped and stared, stunned, with the fork halfway through its task. Unkempt from what had obviously been a long and difficult journey, her exotic eastern beauty was still unmistakable as was her regal bearing. It was easily forgotten that the huge bear of a man almost overtopping her on horseback was the most important person in the group.

Agamemnon held the reins, easily controlling the horse who was skittish around the cheering crowd, attempting time and again to move away from his grip.

Aegisthus was brought out of his trance as Banakles' riding crop cracked his knuckles. "Come on, Empedocles, hold the horse for the lady!" The slight curve to Banakles' lips told Aegisthus that the man was enjoying taunting him in this position, but he had not used Aegisthus' real name and therefore had remained loyal. Aegisthus supposed that Banakles had no choice but to act in such a way with a moonstruck servant, so he decided to accept his behaviour.

"Yes, sir," said Aegisthus. "Sorry, lady," and he scurried forward to take the horse, head lowered and hair obscuring his face. He adopted a hunch and limp for the part he played, and was relieved when Agamemnon and the woman turned away from him with disgust on their faces at the smell emanating from him.

"Take the horse and rub him down." Agamemnon gave him no more attention than that before moving on, and Pylos went to intercept him, with Hycuse close behind carrying trays of drinks for their refreshment.

Risking a quick glance up at the balcony of the queen's apartments far up on the south side, around a curve in the room he could just make out the thunderous expression on Clytemnestra's face. He ducked back inside the stables to the sound of Banakles saying, "Stall number five, lad," while at the same time overhearing Pylos being obsequious to Agamemnon. "My lord, what an honour it is to welcome you home. The queen is making ready the feast to celebrate your arrival, my lord. If you would like to follow me, we can make our way to the banqueting hall, my lord." My lord, my lord, my bloody lord!

Aegisthus was sure the man was just trying to infuriate him over the role he had to play.

Dropping the horse into the stable with the real stable boy, Aegisthus was back in the shadow of the doorway in time to watch Agamemnon disappear through the main doorway, following Pylos, with the girl at his side. Trying to get an accurate headcount of his men was almost impossible, as they kept moving around the yard; some were getting a drink from Hycuse, who had remained outside when Agamemnon went in, and others were ducking their heads in troughs of water, trying to wash off the dirt from their journey. Those who worried him the most had gone straight to the armoury, inspecting knives and short xiphos swords and tucking some away. They had obviously lost their own when the ship had been damaged.

Still, after a few minutes he estimated that Banakles' scouts had been right; a few more or less would make little difference, but there were roughly fifty men here. Fifty men, some unfit, which meant that Aegisthus outnumbered them nearly two to one with only the men he had right here. It would be a massacre.

Discreetly he moved to the main gates. "Send word that the lion gate is to be sealed. If Nestor or any of his other ship's crews arrive tonight, they are to be kept in the lower city overnight. Also have word sent down to the city that every inn is to be at their disposal with as much wine as they want, courtesy of Agamemnon. That should keep them happy and out of action until this is over."

Hycuse nodded stiffly. "Of course, my lord, right away."

CHAPTER TWENTY-EIGHT

THE KNIFE WAS STILL DANGLING FROM HIS GORY HAND, DRIPPING blood onto the stone plinth surrounding the bloody altar. It was like a scene from a nightmare, one Romulus had seen many times before. The priest was like a spectre, but there were strong similarities to the rituals he had known growing up. Romulus struggled to control his breathing, to stand upright and not look away. He tried not to let his fear consume him as he was surrounded by strangers.

Battle he could face; a thousand slavering barbarians charging his battle line was something he had faced dozens of times but always armed, with a solid line of shields and his comrades by his sides. Here he had Remus and Aeneas at his back, but with no weapons he felt naked. They were surrounded by the buzzing of the native people, barking quietly in their barbarian language, "bar-bar-bar," from left and right. Most frightening of all was the silence from the figure they were approaching.

"Aeneas!" someone shouted from nearby; he couldn't make out from where. Maybe it was just one of their barbarian words that sounded like his friend's name.

"Aeneas, it is you!" Shocked, Romulus stood still. The priest suddenly turned back to the altar. When he swung around, the knife was no longer in his hands and he was sweeping the folds of clothes away from his face to reveal a huge grin. "Aeneas, what the hell are you doing here?" He pushed past Romulus, almost shoving others from his path in his haste to reach Aeneas.

Releasing a breath that he hadn't known he was holding, Romulus turned to look at an equally confused Remus as the priest stepped back from the now blood-smeared Aeneas, who was grinning as if he'd just win an Olympic race. "Evander!" said Aeneas. "Gods, is it really you?" He held the priest at arm's length, looking at him, apparently not noticing the blood he was getting all over himself. "What are you doing here?"

"Aeneas," said Remus, "you know one another, then?"

Romulus said nothing, still in shock from relief that they were not to be the next sacrifice.

"What am *I* doing here? What are *you* doing here, Aeneas? It's been years since I saw you." He ruffled Aeneas' hair as if he were still a child. "If you didn't look so much like your father did at your age, I probably wouldn't have recognised you."

Aeneas laughed and turned to the others. "This is Evander, a cousin on my father's side through Atlas, my great-uncle."

Romulus and Remus stood stunned to the spot, slowly releasing the breath they had been holding in anticipation of death while Aeneas told Evander about the war.

"Do you think I've been living under a stone, lad?" Evander laughed. "Everyone from the grey sea to the Indus knows about the war in Troy."

"But did you know it's over?" Aeneas shot back.

From the look on Evander's face, it was obvious that he hadn't heard this news. The shock rocked him on his heels; nobody had believed that war would ever end, since it had been going on for so long. An entire generation had been fed into that war.

"What happened?" It came out as a whisper. "Who finally won?" Like so many others, Evander could favour no particular outcome for the Trojan war; between generations of peace, the greatest city in the world had mixed bloodlines with those of Greece through marriages and treaties. "We left Pallantium rather than get drawn into that war, and we've been here ever since."

"Troy has fallen, Evander. We had left before its final fall, under orders from King Priam, but the tale has been haunting us across the sea." Aeneas looked down at his feet. No one liked talking about the fall and seldom had since their departure, but leaving before the fall reeked of cowardice, which they liked even less.

"Why would he send you away before the city was lost?" Evander looked at him with suspicion and something akin to contempt in his eyes. "Priam would have fought to the last to hold onto his city, to make the Greeks pay in blood for every stride they took into his land."

"You must trust me, Evander; we did not abandon our duty or take on this journey lightly. Priam was your cousin too, but to explain why I must first know that I can trust you."

"Trust me? You are still alive, are you not?" The implication that they might not trust him had angered him, but they risked the last of the people of Troy by telling him. "Tell me now why you abandoned Priam when he needed you, or you can leave our town right away."

Aeneas looked around, glancing first at his friends and then the surrounding crowd. "Alone," he said in low tones.

"What? Speak up, boy," thundered Evander.

"Is there somewhere we can speak alone?" he said, a little louder.

"No!" said Romulus. At the same time Remus elbowed him, whispering, "No, Aeneas, you can't tell him."

"You said it yourself, Romulus; it's time we took a chance." He looked back at Evander. "He is family; this could be our only chance." Neither man looked happy but they couldn't argue with his point. Evander didn't look happy or mollified either; his dark eyes bored into them as if trying to read their thoughts.

Eventually, however, he turned round and the crowd parted around him. He began walking towards the village on the hill and called over his shoulder, "We can talk at my house in the village." They hesitated and he stopped, looking back. "We can talk at my house, or you can begin making your way back to wherever you came from." He stood watching until Aeneas shrugged and followed, Romulus and Remus sullenly taking up the rear.

As they moved away the group of villagers were all eagerly talking amongst themselves, some in accented Greek and others in whatever barbarian tongue prevailed in this region. They began to break up and move away, casting furtive glances at the little procession making its way up the hill.

"Who are all these people, Evander, and how did you ever end up here?" Aeneas enquired as they moved away from the villagers and were finally walking alone.

Evander shrugged. "Mostly they are my own people. We knew that if we'd stayed in Arcadia we were going to get pulled into Agamemnon's war, so we came here. The others are a bit of a mixed bag, really, from a few of the tribes. They're mostly Latins. They are the dominant force in this area, from what I have gathered. Their king, Latinus, has become something of a friend; he is expected this week for Meditrinalia, their harvest festival." He smiled sideways at Aeneas. "If you're staying, you picked a good time to arrive: the feast of new wines."

"And the rest?" Aeneas didn't really care; he was just trying to lighten the mood, but information could always be useful.

"Ah," Evander waved a hand at them. "There are some Oscans, a few Etruscans and one or two Umbrians. The tribes are always at war over something, so there are always refugees. Fortunately for us, even those bigger tribes have smaller factions; there is often infighting between them, so they can never bring their full force to bear. Hence our little village has become something of a ..." he searched for the word, "neutral territory, I suppose. There have been a few peace talks while we have been here. They are treated like the Olympics at home."

"So you've had no trouble with the locals?" Romulus had been listening too.

"Nothing worth talking about until a few months ago," he replied, looking wistfully southwards.

"Why? What has been happening since then?" enquired Remus.

Evander looked round at them; they were just passing through the gate into the town and moving up the hill. "I think maybe it's time you gave me some answers before I answer any more of your questions, so let's wait till we get to the house." Aeneas walked straight on after him without a second thought but Romulus and Remus exchanged a quick glance, following a little behind.

It didn't take long from the gate; ten minutes later they were approaching a walled villa at the top of the hill. The house was a grand affair, built in the Greek villa style; colonnades marched around the small square garden with a pond in the centre and cloisters around the edge. It was larger than the surrounding houses by a fair margin and well pointed.

"My little piece of Greece in this land." Evander waved a hand around. "A sanctuary to keep homesickness at bay, you might say."

"It's beautiful," answered Aeneas, looking at a small statue in the centre of the pond. It was a miniature of Poseidon.

"That I brought with me from home," observed Evander. "It's

smaller than I would have liked, but they are difficult to transport. The locals are hard workers but they don't yet have the skills to create such things."

"What was going on down in the valley when we arrived?" Remus inquired.

Evander thought for a second before he replied. "The natives are quite primitive. They have impressive skill with gold and copper, and their metalwork is the equal of most of what you'd find in Greece. They made this." He bared his arm to demonstrate; on his upper bicep was a huge, intricately carved golden torc armband, made from hundreds of strands of gold twisted like a rope, with lion heads carved on both ends, facing each other.

"But they worship primitive gods, have that horrible barbaric language you heard and have no written language to speak of. They are, however, happy to learn and make good students. I have begun teaching them, and any who wish to stay in my village, proper religion and letters. In the valley just now, we were sacrificing on the altar of Hercules for a light winter."

They were interrupted as a door opened on the other side of the garden and a woman walked out. "Evander, you're back. And who are your guests?" Her dark eyes quickly took in the three travellers. "You should have said we were expecting company," she said, her eyes and face smiling.

"I wasn't," he replied. "Gentlemen, this is my wife, Carmenta. Carmenta dear, you remember Aeneas, Anchais' boy?"

"I don't believe I've had the pleasure," she replied, giving a small bow of her head in welcome.

"And his companions ... " He left the line hanging, and a pregnant silence filled the air as everyone looked at each other.

Remus was the first to break it. "This is Romulus, and I'm Remus."

Aeneas shook his head and blurted out, "No, they are Hector and Achilles."

If the silence before had been uncomfortable, this one was worse. Both Romulus and Remus looked physically pained and Evander wide-eyed and stunned. Only Carmenta seemed unaffected. "Well, it's lovely to meet you, Hector and Achilles."

It was as if she hadn't spoken or no one had heard her. Nobody reacted in the slightest. Eventually it was Aeneas who spoke, albeit rather nervously, to Romulus and Remus. "To lie now would destroy any possibility of trust. You know we have to take this chance."

"If it were just ourselves I would agree, Aeneas, but you risk everyone's lives," replied Romulus. "Well, it's too late now; the dice are rolled." He extended his hand to Evander. "Hector, son of Priam, formerly of Troy. My father spoke highly of you in days past, Evander. I hope we can still rely on your friendship."

Evander snapped out of the trance-like state he had been in. "Yes, I see it now; you are your father's son. I remember you from a visit to your father's court, many years ago. Much has changed since." He looked across at Achilles, extending his hand. "So that makes you Achilles of the Myrmidons?" Remus took his arm with a stiff nod. "What strange travelling companions," Evander said, almost to himself, shaking his head in disbelief.

He turned to his wife. "Dear, will you get us some wine and then leave us." He looked around the little group. "I believe we have a lot to talk about which should be kept quiet."

Carmenta disappeared beyond the door through which she had entered. "I think I need a seat," said Evander. He moved further into the garden where couches had been placed near the cloisters, and lowered himself on to one of them. Romulus and the others followed him. Moments later, Carmenta returned with wine and four cups before returning to the house.

"Will she keep this news to herself?" asked Romulus uneasily.

"Oh, you don't need to worry about her; she's Etruscan. I doubt if she even knows about the war in Troy."

"You married a local?" asked Aeneas.

"Yes, after my first wife died in giving birth to my twins, Pallas and Pallantia." Evander poured wine for them all, finished his own cup in one mouthful and refilled it. Remus took a swig and raised his eyebrows.

"A good wine."

"Thank you. It's from our own vineyard, just north of the city. One good thing about this country is that the vines and olives grow well in their soil." He took another mouthful before going on. "Now, tell me about Troy: what happened?"

The next few hours passed in a blur. They were only disturbed once when Carmenta brought a fresh jug of wine and bread, figs, olives and some meat. Each of them described what had happened in Troy from his own point of view, Evander occasionally interrupting to ask a question. It was an awkward experience for them all; they had rarely spoken at any length about what had happened, not wanting to relive the experiences which had defined their lives or think about all the people they had left behind and lost in the war. However, as the story poured out of them they each felt the weight they had been carrying ease a little.

"It was Achilles whom Agamemnon sent inside the horse with Ajax, but he and Odysseus had already warned Priam. Because he had lost the rest of his family to the war, Hecuba and Hector being the last survivors, Priam adopted Achilles in gratitude for his assistance and ordered him to take Hector and me to the ships Odysseus had waiting in the Hellespont," Aeneas said, finishing the tale.

"The city was just beginning to burn as we sailed away," said Remus. "I think the horse finally convinced Priam that Agamemnon would never leave until Troy fell, and while Agamemnon was continually bringing in fresh troops from Greece to replace the fallen, Troy's population continued to drop."

Evander had been silent throughout this final part, as was Romulus, who had spent much of his last month in Troy unconscious and recovering.. Talking over the fall of his home was not something he enjoyed, and his eyes rarely lifted from the silvery fish moving to and fro in the garden pond. Evander's eyes were fixed on him now.

"It has been many moons since I visited your father's court. Even then, Priam was known to be a good and fair king, but still a warrior king. Knowing that, I moved away rather than get dragged into a war against him. He would never have given up, but that's what this story describes." He put heavy emphasis on the word 'story' as if he didn't believe what he'd been told.

"It's no story but the simple truth. Far from giving up, I believe my father drew them into a trap in his city. Accepting something as inevitable is not giving up." Romulus shook his head in frustration, trying to explain what he meant. "He knew he would fall, but death was not far away for him anyway. He wanted his people, his city and his family to survive where he could not and knowing they could do so, he could give his all to obtaining victory in defeat; he destroyed his enemies as he had done in wars of old, knowing that we would carry on. I believe he destroyed their armies with his last breath, and the best I can do for him is to carry out his last wishes and build another city of his people from the ashes, and find allies to wreak revenge against those who came against him."

The garden was silent but for the cicadas calling from the trees. The wine jug was long since empty, and Remus was rolling his cup between his hands. Evander was deep in thought and turned to him. "And the supreme warrior in all Greece, Achilles - you just walked away and left the greatest battle history has ever known."

"If I ever had a part to play in that war, I had already played it," snapped Remus. He took a deep breath and went on. "Agamemnon was worse than he'd been when you knew him;

much worse. Odysseus said he had snapped; that he would never allow the host he had gathered to go home, even if he did win. I fought for Greece, and we could not defeat their walls. I gave ten years of my life to that war, and for what? I had always had a closer kinship with Hector than with some misguided warlord. Menelaus was dead; Helen, if she had ever been worth that war, would now be a fading flower: what were we fighting for? The honour of Greece? Trojans were Hellenes too. There was more honour in defending a friend." He patted Romulus' shoulder. "I think my mother knew that this was how it would end. She said that, if I went to this war, I would never return," He smiled.

As they sat there, the smell of woodsmoke began to carry on the breeze, cookfires lighting for the evening meals. Aeneas looked up beyond the walls surrounding Evander's house and for the first time realised how late it was getting. "Evander, I am afraid we have imposed on you for long enough. We must be going."

His voice was like a splash of cold water on the group. Evander's head snapped up to look at him. "Nonsense, you will stay and eat with me."

"I am afraid we must decline. Even leaving now, it will be dark before we reach our camp," Remus added.

"Then stay the night here," offered Evander.

Romulus rose slowly, like a man reluctant to leave. "No, Evander. Truly you are most kind, but we promised our people we would be back before dark, and they will already be watching for us and worrying. It took us fully four hours to get here."

"Where is your camp?"

"We are on the shores by our ships, where your river enters the sea."

Evander nodded. "To walk there would take you at least four hours. I have a small boat down by the river; rowing with the current, you should be there in under an hour." He looked around at the three friends. "I will send some food with you, and tomorrow you can bring your ships up the river. It's deep enough this far along, and you can camp outside the town for the present."

Their faces lit up at this offer. "That is very kind, Evander," said Aeneas.

"Then we can decide what is to be done," Evander went on. "Well, if you intend to return tonight then you really must go now. I agree that you should continue to hide your real names. If you are to stay with me, I could do without Agamemnon coming to look for you."

————

"Do you really intend to offer them sanctuary?" asked Carmenta when the little rowing boat was floating lazily down the river in the early dusk under a deep red sky, oars rising and falling with a gentle splash, "when we cant even guarantee that for our own people at the moment"

"Are you really so surprised that I would help out the children of an old friend and family member? This land gives us plenty to spare. It will be a lighter winter, for sure, but we can easily afford to be generous here." Evander didn't look at her as he spoke.

"I am surprised at you helping anyone, regardless of who they are, without some benefit in it for you," Carmenta replied coolly.

"Yes, well …" Evander took his eyes from the boat for a moment to look at his wife. She was studying his fine features, watching as his mind whirred with the ideas she knew were taking shape within. "The Umbrians and Oscans have been pushed north from the Greek settlements lately as they expanded. Latinus, for all his courage, may not be able to hold them back indefinitely. It will do no harm to have a large body of battle-hardened veterans of Troy as part of our settlement." He rubbed his chin in thought. "And if they are telling the truth, which I believe they are, a core of Myrmidons with Achilles himself leading them."

"So you believe that it was Achilles and Hector with him, then." Carmenta seemed genuinely surprised.

"That was definitely Hector. If I hadn't been paying more attention to Aeneas, I would have known him a dozen strides away; he is his father again, in more ways than one. I can't imagine why they would tell the truth about him and lie about Achilles." He strode back up the hill from the river with her in his shadow. Before he went through the gates, back into the populated area, he looked over his shoulder and said softly, "What I said to them goes for you too. No one is to know their real names; *no one*. They are Romulus and Remus."

She nodded silently in reply and passed through the gates.

CHAPTER TWENTY-NINE

Hooves drummed on the hard-packed earth, dust rising from the passage of so many riders. The rains from the storms of the past weeks had long since dried up, the stormy winter along the Aegean not yet in full flow.

Full of adrenalin as he was, Markus had checked Orestes' headlong charge for Mycenae, alternating between walking, trotting and cantering and never allowing him to release the horses into a full gallop.

"We have miles to go and few spare horses, Orestes," he had cautioned. "Even if a few of us could gallop our horses until they floundered and then changed to the spare mounts, from what you have told us we will need every man we can bring to bear. The time saved would probably make no difference, anyway."

Orestes had no choice but to accept the older man's wisdom on the matter, even going so far as to stop in the early afternoon for half an hour to allow the animals to eat and drink a little to keep up their strength. They had swallowed a few mouthfuls at the same time before remounting.

Early evening had arrived, the sky taking on a dusty hue

over the blue, but darkness was yet some hours off when they arrived at the pass through the hills entering the plains of Argos. On any other day, Orestes would have considered himself already home when he entered the plains. Visible from the citadel of Mycenae, these were the lands he had ridden and played in all his life, but today he could only think of the miles they had to cover before they passed through the lion gate.

Argos was almost impregnable, which was why their power base had been growing here for as long as it had. No enemy could come at Mycenae except through the plains of Argos, because of the surrounding hills and mountains. The plains also could only be entered through the passes in the surrounding hills with any sizable body of men, giving the people of Mycenae ample time to retreat behind the great cyclopean curtain walls which great Atreus had built for their defence.

That very source of their safety was now costing Orestes valuable time before returning to the city to warn his father of his betrayal.

Down onto the plains they rode. With good flat earth beneath his hooves, ground he knew well, he was sorely tempted to give the horse its head but again Markus held him back. The horses were already exhausted after eight hours of riding and the gallop could easily kill them. Not that the horse's life meant anything, weighed against warning his father, but with five miles to go a steady trot was still faster than he could run after eight hours in the saddle.

Orestes turned his horse toward Mycenae as he came out of the pass, Markus tight behind him, and began increasing their pace slightly on the flat. They had barely made it onto even land when a voice called out urgently, "Who's that?"

Orestes and Markus barely heard the words, but the urgency in the voice brought them to a stop and they turned in the saddle. Berisades, one of the Spartans who had followed Orestes, was gesturing urgently towards the sea. Following the direction of his hand, they could see sails on the water just rounding the headland, pointed very definitely towards the shelter of the bay of Argos. "Ships," replied Markus, pointing out the obvious.

"I can see that. Are they ours?" Orestes was already tired and his arse was on fire. He was in no mood to be polite.

"They are too far out. I can't make out the sails." Markus was leaning out of the saddle, as if that extra inch would give him the ability to see better.

"Traders sheltering for the night?" Orestes asked hopefully.

"Those are Greek biremes; few traders use them." Markus chewed his lip.

Antileon, still barely old enough to shave, piped up in a high-pitched voice. "Could they be ours? Ships coming back from Troy?"

"Possibly, but if what Orestes has told me is correct, they could just as easily be Aegisthus' people coming to reinforce his troops. I don't think that's a chance we want to take. If Agamemnon is already in the city, I think our best chance is to get to him first." He turned to look at Orestes; the final decision would be his. "We can join his men and try to oust Aegisthus before anyone comes to his aid."

There was no choice at all, really. "Ride on!" shouted Orestes, putting his heels to the horse.

———

ROUNDING the headland which sheltered Argos, the light but even wind had pulled them steadily onward. Today, though, that was not enough. Every man on board had their backs bent to the oars; ramming speed over the distance would kill the men but they could keep this up for a few hours.

Nestor had heard nothing from any of the missing ships since they'd been separated in the storm and found himself almost desperate for news of Agamemnon. He was not known to be the forgiving type, so reporting their survival was Nestor's first priority.

Even if Agamemnon had been lost in the storm, gods forbid, they would need to present themselves to the boy, Orestes, and bring news that Agamemnon was not among them. They would have to tell his son that he was missing, possibly dead in a shipwreck.

Taurion stood beside him, holding the second steering oar. One man could control both oars, but Nestor was a farmer's son. A wealthy one, too, and a captain in the army Agamemnon had gathered, but old habits die hard and he liked to have his hands busy; he liked to be working.

"What's that?" he asked Taurion. Younger than him by a good ten years, Taurion had sharp eyes. It was one of the reasons he was on the steering oar; it would not do to miss a rock sticking out of the water.

"What?" asked Taurion, scanning the horizon. He had been watching the waters and their distance to the other boats, so he could be forgiven for missing it.

"There." Nestor pointed to the edge of the plains and Taurion squinted into the distance. "In the shadows at the edge of the plain."

Seconds passed before Taurion replied, "Riders coming out of the pass."

"How many?"

"At this distance, I can't be sure. I can just make out the shape of the horses."

"Guess!" shouted Nestor, losing patience.

"Forty, or maybe as many as fifty?" Taurion said, clearly unsure of himself.

"Raiders?" Nestor mused. As unlikely as it seemed, it was always possible that someone would take advantage of the warriors' absence. Always better to be on the safe side, he decided, calling down to the rowing benches, "Ramming speed!"

The ship lurched as it picked up speed. It would be beached on the sand. They would never catch up with whoever it was, especially on foot before the city, but if the walls held them to the front there would be nowhere for them to retreat: no escape back to the mountain passes.

The ram rose out of the sea with the speed of their passage, churning through the water. With under fifty strides to go, Nestor called down the hatch again. "Ship oars!" As one the oars rose out of the water and hovered, two great banks of oars dripping like the legs of some huge beast before they were pulled inside the hull. The ship glided forward under the momentum they had built up.

Other men, the professional sailors, had already swarmed the rigging, pulling in the mainsail. They were holding onto ropes with their feet attached to the yardarm as their arms worked furiously, pulling in the sail and tying it fast. Not a second too soon, Nestor thought, watching them work as the ram raked up the shore and the bow buried itself in sand and shingle almost halfway along the keel. The ship lurched to a halt and the men on the rigging held on tight, arms wrapped around the big beams.

A ragged cheer erupted from the crew. For most of them, this was their first time home on the plains of Argos since setting out for the war in Troy. Nestor understood only too well what they were feeling, and would have liked nothing better than to get back to his house and hold his wife as he had when he'd been a younger man, but he couldn't afford them the time or luxury to enjoy it.

Taurion nudged him and pointed. "I think they've seen us; they are moving fast up the plains." Nestor saw, but he had never expected to be able to get to them before they reached

Mycenae; he could only hope the city held until they closed in, trapping the riders against the walls.

Again he shouted down into the hull. "Swords, shields and spears only. Form up on the beach now, you maggots. We need to move fast!"

CHAPTER THIRTY

THE TRIP PASSED SLOWLY AS THEY DRIFTED ALMOST SILENTLY ON the water. They had rowed out into the current of the river, but now Romulus simply steered the little boat and let the current carry it. Even at that, they were making good time in the fast-flowing water. The gentle lapping of the water on the hull could easily have lulled them into a doze after the day they'd had, but they were lost in their own worlds, each mulling over the same thoughts. Today's events had been unexpected.

It was Remus who eventually broke the silence. "Do you trust him?"

It was the same thing they had all been asking themselves, coming to the same conclusion for different reasons. Remus wanted to trust Evander because they were running out of options. Aeneas wanted to trust him because Evander had been a close friend of his father and he had known him as a child. Romulus trusted nobody; but they had to find somewhere, even for a short time.

"I do," said Aeneas hesitantly, "or at least I did. Many years have passed since I knew him and people change, but for the sake of our family ties I think we can trust him."

"It makes no difference, Remus. We'll just have to watch him for a while. At least we now have a chance of feeding and sheltering our people for a while." Romulus thought for a minute. "And if it turns out that he's not trustworthy, we might be in a position to take his little town from him before it becomes a problem."

Aeneas looked as if he wanted to argue, but even he knew that he could not guarantee Evander's reliability. Very little stays the same over ten years, but he hadn't joined the attack on Troy and that was something, at least.

The sun was continuing to drop in the western sky. As it dipped into the horizon the sky turned blood-red, colouring the bottom of the clouds hugging the sea in the distance.

"A bad omen," murmured Remus. "We should not have stayed so long."

"An old wives' tale," Romulus rebuked him. "We have enough real problems without worrying about the colour of the skies."

"Maybe, but blood has been spilled this night," said Remus, offering up a silent prayer that it was nothing to do with them.

With dark thoughts and silence for company, they drifted on down the river into the oncoming darkness. By the time the river began to open out where it reached the sea, night had completely surrounded them with darkness lit only by the stars far above, so it was with both nervousness and relief that they heard bows bending as bowstrings were drawn back and a challenge called out as they turned their boat to shore.

"Who goes there?" Euryalus called from the bank.

"Put the bow down, we surrender," Remus answered him, his voice dripping with sarcasm and humour. Achilles had always been good at breaking tension with his dry wit, and Nisus and Diomedes ran knee-deep into the water, laughing and dragging the little boat onto the bank.

"Thank the gods you're back! Some of the others were worried that something might have happened to you when you failed to return before dark." Euryalus gripped Romulus' arm and helped him balance as he climbed out of the boat.

"We were delayed, having lunch with an old friend," replied Aeneas and they laughed, thinking he was joking as Remus had been.

"Very funny," Nisus replied. "Where did you steal the boat? Is some poor fisherman going to starve now?"

Romulus was stretching his back after the cramped boat and looking around; he laughed, because they didn't believe Aeneas and he could understand it. He too would have been sceptical of the likelihood of meeting old friends so far from home. "What he says is true; we were having lunch with an old friend." He shook his head, looking at Remus. "The old saying is true: you travel to the other side of the world only to run into your neighbour."

Even with Hector's word adding weight to the story, they looked sceptical. "Who?" demanded Diomedes, his high-pitched voice incredulous.

"Oh, just some cousin of Aeneas," replied Remus. "He has some connection to your father's court too." This was addressed to Romulus.

"He did, but I'm not entirely sure what it was; you'll have to ask him when you see him again," admitted Romulus. "Before my time, I'm afraid."

"So you found somewhere, then?" Euryalus asked hopefully.

"Maybe," was Romulus' reply. "He will need watching for a while". He turned to lift his gear out of the little craft and started moving away. "Which way is the camp? I can't see a bloody thing in the dark."

Euryalus led them along, and Diomedes hared off ahead of them in his excitement.

"I'm glad to see you had a watch set, Euryalus. You've done well."

Euryalus blushed at this compliment from Romulus, though

his pink cheeks weren't visible in the dark. "Thanks," he muttered.

"You have people watching the water, too?" asked Aeneas. It was unlikely that anyone would be abroad on the water at night, but he was naturally cautious. After all, they had travelled by night away from Carthage.

"We had until dark," he replied. "As soon as it was night we doused all cooking fires, so the beach is dark."

"Good," he replied, thinking of Dido's death scene as they had sailed away from Carthage. "Very good."

The camp was a huge mass of bodies around where the ships had beached, but in darkness it was only visible as lumps on the ground spreading down towards the shore. That was good; the men had settled down to sleep. He would talk to them in the morning, thought Romulus, and they would need all the rest and strength they could get for the long row upriver.

He was pleased to find that Nisos had kept them some of the boar they had caught out hunting. They fell on their food with a hunger they had forgotten.

CHAPTER THIRTY-ONE

AGAMEMNON WALKED THROUGH THE CORRIDOR INTO HIS PALACE. He had not been here in ten years; even then he had only lived here for a few months or a year at a time, always on the way to his next battle, his next conquest. It raised the question of why he had fought so hard to win the palace in the first place, since it had never been more than a holiday villa between wars. He had no childhood memories of growing up here; his old nursemaid and a few loyal old warriors had carried Menelaus to safety the night his father had been murdered in these very halls. It was Sparta he remembered learning to fight, to ride and to rule. Every good memory had been forged there. And yet this was home, or would be.

He stopped following Pylos as he passed his throne room. There, raised on a platform, was the old wooden throne. It was made from rough natural wood, as if the tree had grown naturally into that shape, worn smooth through the generations of Atreus men who had made their proclamations from this very spot. He walked across the rough flag floor and ran his hand along the smooth arms.

His father Atreus had sat here. A good man by all accounts, a good king; murdered by Aegisthus in the prime of his life, by a man he thought of as his own son. Abandoned by Atreus' brother Thyestes, he had been raised as a brother to Agamemnon and Menelaus until one evening Thyestes returned, bent on killing Atreus and stealing the throne of Mycenae. Knowing he was his father, Aegisthus had opened the gates to him and his men in the dead of night and the city was lost before they even knew they were under attack.

Revenge was why Agamemnon had taken the city back, to avenge the death of his father, but the battle lust had taken him then. He had told himself he was doing it to safeguard the city for Orestes, to build the boy an empire which could not be taken the way his father's had been. Aegisthus was still alive, after all.

But that had not been the whole truth. He had lost his mind and his reason to battle lust; he could see that now and it gnawed at him. He had missed all this time he could have spent with his wife and children. He had missed watching Orestes growing up, becoming a man. The sinking of the ship and his own near death had shown him his own vulnerability: a battle over which he had no control, which his great strength and the size of his army could not defeat, showing him what was truly important for the first time in his life.

He could never get back the time, he thought, running his hand up the thick branches which formed the back of his throne, but he could try to make up for it. It was not too late to build a relationship with his children. Orestes and Electra were still here, he almost forgot Chrysothemis, only newly born when he left, she would be over ten now, and maybe there was even time to form a real relationship with Clytemnestra. She had been a good wife, giving him children and keeping his home safe for him.

"Chief?" called Polybius from the door. "Is everything all right?" Cassandra and Alkon were also in the doorway, watching him, and even Pylos had come back and was standing in the background.

"Yes, fine." He waved a hand at them. "It's been a while since I was here, and I was reminiscing," he said wistfully. "Ten years, and during that storm I didn't think we would ever see home again. I'm sure you can all find your own way to the hall, so go on and get some wine into you; you've earned it. I'm going to see where my family have got to. Pour me a cup and I'll be along shortly."

Cheers greeted him at the thought of the wine and they moved on down the corridor. Only Cassandra and Pylos remained, which he thought was for the best; the middle of a hall full of drunk soldiers was probably not the safest place for her. Better to keep her close until he decided what to do with her. If she still had her powers, she would be invaluable.

He picked up his hammer, still lying against the arm of his throne: a silent warning to anyone who had come while he was away and Clytemnestra ruled. The weapon was a promise that he would return; it demonstrated the weight of his authority.

It was a comforting weight in his hand. The solid unyielding stone on the end of the olive wood handle had settled many an argument for him, and even now he handled the huge hammer with the ease of familiarity, a weight most would struggle to bear.

It seemed childish now to have left it in his place at the throne so he settled it on his shoulder and walked to the doorway. "Lead on, Pylos," he said. "I would see my wife."

Pylos eyed the hammer with worry at Agamemnon's words, but did not question him and led the way down the hallway. Agamemnon smiled to himself as he realised how it must have looked to the new man he did not know. He felt a touch of sadness, realising that his old chamberlain, Arimnis, must have passed on while he'd been away.

The long corridor led past the hall where the sound of his

men drinking was already beginning to raise a clamour. The wine would flow freely long into the night. Passing the door, the waft of roasting boar reached his nostrils and he glanced inside to see the pig suspended over the fire, turning slowly on the spit. His stomach gave an ugly gurgle as he remembered how long it had been since his last proper meal.

Pylos continued on down the corridor and Agamemnon reluctantly walked past the door. There would be plenty to eat after he had seen Clytemnestra. Priorities, he told himself. This would be the beginning of the new Agamemnon, one who put his family first in all matters.

The corridor ended in a circular staircase leading to the upper level, which was mainly sleeping chambers. Following Pylos up the stairs past windows cut into the stone, Agamemnon looked out over the plains of Argos as the light dimmed in the skies. After so long away, for once the beauty of the land was not wasted on him. Movement caught his eyes and he saw horses galloping up the plains towards the coast. He remembered how he used to love to ride, though only the largest horses in his stable could carry him comfortably nowadays. He would ask Clytemnestra if she and the children would come riding with him. It would make a nice day out.

He pulled himself away from the window and carried on up the stairs. By the time he had reached the top, Pylos was standing in front of the door to Clytemnestra's chambers, ready to knock. "Ssh!" Agamemnon hissed urgently at the man, causing Pylos' head to spin towards him in surprise, his hand raised in the process of knocking. Agamemnon shook his head at him. "Wait, wait. Just give me a moment."

Pylos' hand dropped away from the door and he gave a gentle shrug, stepping back marginally from the door without saying a word. The depth of his feelings surprised Agamemnon. This would be the first time he had met Clytemnestra since the slap she had landed on his face ten years ago, after he had taken her daughter from her. He was nervous, a sensation new to him; he would have preferred to have charged the walls of Troy alone than walk through that door.

Suddenly he became very self-conscious, and the new chamberlain's presence became an irritation. He did not want anyone seeing him like this. Cassandra didn't count; she was his property, the spoils of war, no more than the armour he claimed from the battlefield. Apart from the obvious benefit to him of her gift of foresight, he would probably give her to Clytemnestra as a present. What more fitting gift to his wife than a former princess as her personal body slave? The thought of her face warmed him. How could she not appreciate such a gift?

"You can go," he said to Pylos. "I think I can find my own way to my wife's chambers in my own palace." Pylos looked uncomfortable to be dismissed in such a way and glanced nervously at the door. *He thinks Clytemnestra will accuse him of slacking in his duties*, thought Agamemnon, amused. The idea almost brought a smile to his lips. Pylos looked uncomfortably at the door to the chamber, but a glance at Agamemnon had him step away and move towards the stairs they had ascended moments before.

With slow steps, Agamemnon made his way over until he was standing in front of the door. The pause before he raised his hand to knock was barely perceptible but it was there. The thud of his big knuckles on the door would make it obvious to Clytemnestra that it was not the little chamberlain knocking for admission.

The sounds on the other side of the door ceased. There was a momentary pause, then the sound of steps came to his ears as someone approached the door from the other side. The door crept open and a younger face appeared, obviously the maid. He saw her nervous apprehension without surprise; all any of them knew of him were the stories from ten years before of his drunkenness and temper. He could not blame them for being worried.

The door opened slowly. Agamemnon raised his hand flat against the wood and pushed it wide. His eyes locked on Clytemnestra across the room and the world froze: he remembered he had married this woman for more than just a treaty between cities, Menelaus' marriage would have sufficed for that, and all the years since faded into nothing.

"You can go," he said, without taking his eyes off Clytemnestra, but it was obvious he was addressing the maid. Again there was apprehension in the air. Without even looking at her, it was obvious that her head had turned to Clytemnestra, looking for permission to leave. At a barely perceptible nod from the lady, the maid scurried out of the room, circling around Agamemnon.

He stepped into the room, closing the door behind himself, leaving Cassandra alone to wait in the corridor beyond. Dropping the hammer from his shoulder, he set the head on the ground with the handle leaning against the wall, Clytemnestra's eyes following the movement of the great hammer then returning to his face. Her emotions were visible: confusion, anger, frustration, all the things he had expected. A maelstrom of emotions filled the space between them.

He took a step towards her. "Clytemnestra," he tried to say, but the word stuck in his thick throat as her hand dropped to the bronze jug on the table beside the bed and sent it flying towards his head.

"You bastard!" she screamed as the two bronze cups followed, then the polished tray they had been sitting on. The jug hit the wall behind his head, but the cups hit the forearms he had brought up to defend his face, the heavy tray spinning into his unprotected midriff driving the wind from his chest. He jumped out of the way as the chamber pot followed, moving further into the room towards her.

She had just picked up a fine pottery flowerpot filled with soil and lavender as he reached her, causing the pot to drop out of her hands and crash unceremoniously to the floor. It broke on his foot as he wrapped both his big arms around her, pulling her tight against him. Fists pumping against his chest, she repeated, "She was my daughter!" as tears streamed down her face, ruining her perfect kohled eyes as the expensive dark make-up streaked down her cheeks.

"Hush," he whispered into her hair. "I know. I'm sorry," again and again. The grief he had ignored and held in check for ten years of war, grief he had forgotten he held at all, bubbled to the surface in longing for the favourite daughter he had sacrificed in order to make the trip to Troy. She continued thumping his chest until she went limp, weeping.

He held her for several long moments, her tears and kohl soaking into his already filthy chiton and the skin beneath. When the sobbing had reduced to trembling, he whispered so that only she could hear, "Iphigenia is not dead."

Shock stilled her as she tried to comprehend what he had said. He held her as she pulled back to look into his face in abject confusion. Her hand shot up from between his arms, hitting the side of his face, as she looked at him in disgust, "Don't you dare lie to me," she screamed, spittle flying from her mouth in her vehemence.

"I'm not," he whispered. "It's true." Hope warred with despair in her eyes. "The priest did demand that she be sacrificed, but when I looked into her eyes, my baby girl's eyes, I couldn't do it. The priest said there was more than one way to sacrifice her to Artemis, that she would accept her as a priestess in her temple in Athens. He said that Artemis would accept this as long as we told no one and didn't attempt to make contact."

She slapped him again, harder this time, fire burning deep within her blotchy kohl-smudged eyes, giving her a demonic look. Again she slapped him, with her other hand this time, across the other cheek. Face burning from the blows of a woman trained in combat, Agamemnon's hands dropped away from her and he took a step back. What was wrong with the woman? He had just told her that her child, long thought dead, was alive and instead of being grateful, she was slapping him harder than before.

"You knew this!" she screamed at him. "Ten years you knew, and yet you let me suffer!" Again her hand shot out, taking him in the face, his own hand involuntarily rising to the burning red handprint. Her voice dropped to a dangerous whisper. "You let me believe you had killed our baby by your own hand, and all the time you knew!"

"She is alive," he said again. "If I had said anything, she wouldn't be."

"I lost my daughter to feed your pride," she said, thumping him in the chest, "so that you could wage another of your wars."

"I was defending my brother's honour, and creating a safer kingdom for our children to grow up in," he muttered. The oft-repeated lie he had persuaded himself to believe for so many years rang hollow in his own ears in the face of her onslaught. His voice went icy cold; faced with an uncomfortable truth, his old anger bubbled towards the surface, forcing the lie. "I wanted to give Orestes an empire that could not be taken from him as easily as my father's was."

Again her hand swung for his face. This time, though, the heat was in his blood; rage at himself for the truth in her accusations and at her for making them. His hand came up like lightning, catching her wrist, and with a snarl he turned her and threw her backwards. She landed with a thump beside the bed and he turned to storm out the door.

"Wait!" she whimpered from the floor. "Wait."

He stopped with his hand gripping the handle of the door, shoulders rising and falling with his deep breaths as he struggled to control his temper. He had never struck her and didn't want to start now, but if he stayed here with her in this mood, he couldn't guarantee that he wouldn't.

"I didn't intend it to go like this," she said. "I had meant to welcome you back properly, but I miss her so much."

"What I did, I did for the good of the kingdom," he said without turning around, his hand on the door. "And I found a way to keep her alive."

"I know," said Clytemnestra. "Stay, at least until you have cleaned away the dirt of your travels before returning to the feast. See, I have had the copper bath brought up here and filled for you. When you go back to the feast you can look presentable to your men again, as a king should."

Agamemnon turned his head and saw the steaming bath near the open doors to the balcony. His shoulders slumped; how long had it been since he had washed properly? The anger leached out of him like the steam from the bath. She was trying, after all.

CHAPTER THIRTY-TWO

THE CITY WAS DESCENDING INTO NIGHT WITH DARKNESS COMING on quickly. The streets were deserted, lights springing to life in many windows. It was into this silent evening that the passage of a large group of horsemen brought people to their doors to witness the arrival of Orestes, at the head of a mixture of Mycenaeans and Spartans on horses sweating and blowing past their homes on their way to the citadel.

The hard-packed dirt road, hemmed in on both sides by the stone houses of Mycenae and leading up towards the citadel atop the hill, caused the passage of many hooves to echo up into an otherwise quiet night, startling the few people who remained on the streets at that hour as they jumped for cover from the press of men, arms and horseflesh.

Rounding a corner in the road brought the lion gate into view, the great lions carved in relief on the huge capstones above the thick gate. It was closed, not surprisingly; once darkness had descended, the citadel was usually sealed. Orestes nearly stumbled as he jumped down from his horse onto legs stiff from hours spent in the saddle; he limped up to the gates, trying to work the feeling back into his legs.

Behind him the others were dismounting as well, a little more calmly; they knew it would take some time to get the gate open, but wanted their legs well stretched in case they were called into action.

The thick planks thudded as he hammered on them. "Open the bloody gates!" he yelled and hammered again. Time seemed to be suspended; after the headlong dash from Sparta, it was difficult to slow down again. He wanted to charge up the path, but there was no way in except by the gates. Eventually, after what seemed like an age, a head appeared above the wall.

"The gates are closed for the night," someone called down. "Come back tomorrow."

Looking up into the glaring light of the torch held by the sentry, Orestes recognised Perseus peering down at him. "Perseus, it's me, Orestes. Open the gates; I have to see my mother," he called up. Perseus was a young guardsman, one of those brought in since Aegisthus had started spending time here; although Orestes liked the man and had even drunk with him once, he would not trust his loyalty to Agamemnon's house.

There was muttering up on the walkway. Orestes heard his name mentioned in hushed tones and felt a chill run down his spine. Perseus called back down, "Orestes, is it really you? We had heard ... "

"Yes, it's me, Perseus. Now open the bloody gates or I'll have your head!" yelled Orestes.

"I'm afraid we are under strict instructions not to open the gate tonight," called Perseus. Markus was now at Orestes'side, pulling his arm. "Who is that with you?" asked Perseus.

"It's happening tonight!" Markus whispered urgently. "That's why they won't let us in."

"It's Castor, my escort," Orestes called up, looking at Markus and hoping the torch had blinded the guard's night vision to all the other men further back. He called up, "You must have realised when you got those orders that they didn't apply to me."

Again there was whispering on the walkway. Markus, still at his side, whispered too low for anyone else to hear, "They thought you were dead. If they open the gate they will try to kill you, thinking that they're doing Aegisthus a favour. Be ready." Orestes nodded. It sounded as if an argument was happening up on the walkway, but eventually Perseus' head appeared above the wall again.

"Okay," he called down, "but we can only allow you to enter alone. Your escort will have to find somewhere in the city for the night."

"Agreed," called Orestes. Then he whispered to Markus, who was gesturing silently to the others to get back. "How many?"

"I could only hear two, but there could be a third. Given what's happening in the palace, I can't imagine them leaving any more men down here tonight; they will trust in the walls to offer security." Markus' thinking made sense and, as they heard the locking bar being moved from the door, Orestes indicated that Markus should hide in the lee of the doorway.

The wood of the gate creaked as light spilled through the gap into the night beyond, lighting Orestes' face in the darkness. They parted just enough to let him through and Orestes moved towards the gates in the shadow of the wall, his body shielding Markus. He dropped his hands to either side, with a hand on his dagger on one side and the hilt of his sword on the other, holding them against his thigh to prevent them catching on the gate as he slipped through sideways.

As he passed through the gate, the head of Markus' spear passed in the shadow of his back and took the first guard holding the gate in the throat. Orestes, blinded by the light of the burning torch, threw himself backwards, hitting the gate and throwing it wide as he drew his dagger and dragged awkwardly at the sword hilt on the other side. Luck saved him twice; he stumbled on a loose cobble and fell against the gate, just as a spear from the second guard passed over his left shoulder where his head had been, and he landed hard on the ground, the edge of his sword only grazing his hip as it hung half-sheathed.

Markus was through the gap behind him in a heartbeat. The second guard was still trying to free his spearhead from where it had buried itself in the wood after missing Orestes' head. Markus' kopis smashed through the spear shaft, showering Orestes in splinters, but the loss of the spear gave Markus a second's respite; he brought his sword up to block a second spear from the last guardsman as the first went for his sword. Orestes stumbled to his feet in time to stop the first slash with his dagger, before abandoning the attempt to free his sword and diving at the guard dagger first, aiming for his neck.

The guard rocked back against the inside wall, managing to knock wide the killing blow of the knife to bury it in his shoulder, and suddenly the two were rolling on the hard rocks, each trying to bring their weapon to bear while holding off their opponent. The guard's arm, weakened after being stabbed in the shoulder, proved to be his undoing; as Orestes twisted the knife, he let out a scream. Orestes ripped out the knife and thrust deep into the muscle and cartilage of his neck, and the scream transformed into a soft gurgle as he choked on his own blood, sword dropping away from his fingers as he clutched at his ruined throat.

Orestes hunched over him, holding the knife and dragging breath into his burning lungs as he heard more men, his own, pass through the open gates. Putting his hand on the dead man's chest, he pushed himself to his feet and turned to Markus, who had finished off his own opponent. "Are you all right?" asked Markus, also trying to control his breathing.

"I think so," replied Orestes, wiping his knife on the dead man's cloak as he checked himself for injury. "What now?"

"The palace," said Markus between breaths. "We have to find Agamemnon. Go, quickly!"

Orestes nodded and led his surviving companions and the Spartans towards the palace. Markus watched him like a proud father, before lifting his hand from his waist to look at the coating of blood from his stomach. He shook his head slowly and stumbled after Orestes towards the palace.

CHAPTER THIRTY-THREE

THE BANQUETING HALL WAS NOT EVEN HALF FULL AS AEGISTHUS poked his head around the door to the servant's entrance, concealed behind one of the long wall hangings which softened the hard stone walls all around the sides. These hanging tapestries of past battles and victories, and the fires glowing at either side of the hall, together added warmth and comfort to the otherwise austere room.

Agamemnon's men had wasted no time settling in and the wine was flowing freely. They were a dirty and ragged group who had dragged themselves, injured and bleeding, across half the Peloponnese.

Food, wine, and celebrating having made it home when so many had not, was of more concern to the men in front of him than changing clothing and bandages after their journey. Weapons had mostly been left outside in the yard. Even for his own men, it would have been considered rude to come armed to the feast in their lord's banqueting hall. It was an old custom, which Aegisthus thought was probably designed to reduce the chances of fatal fights breaking out among armed drunk revellers, but this evening it suited his purpose perfectly.

As the servants circulated in the hall, filling cups and carrying plates of food to the men, Aegisthus looked left and right. Along the walls, using mostly leather armour for fear of the noise of metal against stone, his men were moving into place slowly behind the cover of the wall hangings.

Carrying swords and knives only, still sheathed, with the hilts wrapped in cloth against unintended noise, they slid slowly down the full length of the hall. The slight noises they made were easily concealed under the revelry of Agamemnon's men, talking, singing and banging cups or plates on the table. Aegisthus almost felt sorry for them; almost, but not quite.

———

AGAMEMNON LAY BACK in the large bath. He had never felt comfortable in the bronze tub. He was too big for it, his legs bent almost double with his scarred hairy knees sticking up when he tried to lie back. The heat felt unnatural and tingled his skin; give him a nice cool stream any day.

Well, if it kept Clytemnestra happy to bathe him, he thought, it's a small price to pay; it would be over soon and he could get downstairs with his men and look like he had the right to command them, freshly groomed and clothed with his immaculate lady wife by his side.

Clytemnestra poured a bowl of water over his head. The sudden wash of water brought back his brush with death on the ship and he grabbed the sides of the tub, flinching, almost pulling himself out in a fit of panic. He saw again the main mast snapping, dragging men away into the dark, the murky waters closing over their heads, the waves crashing against the sides of his galley, tilting it up onto its side and frothing violently into his face.

Clytemnestra was calmly humming a tune he remembered her singing to Orestes when he was a child, and that kept him from tumbling out of the bath onto the cold stone floor. Her tune soothed away the nightmare as her hands smoothed his tangled mass of hair. A bone comb began slowly to work at the knots in his hair as he lay there, listening to her hum.

"Where is Orestes?" he asked, his head resting over the edge of the bath. "Is he not around to welcome his father home?" He laughed.

"He should be back tomorrow or the next day," Clytemnestra replied, interrupting her humming. "When I heard you were on your way, I sent him to Sparta to meet his betrothed so that we can arrange the wedding as soon as possible and bring stability to the land. It can be a joint celebration: their wedding and your return after victory over Troy."

Agamemnon grunted and Clytemnestra continued combing his hair, gently easing the knots and twigs acquired from so many nights sleeping out in the open. Agamemnon felt disappointed but didn't let it show; if Clytemnestra was willing to make the effort and let them move on, it was the least he could do. Ordinarily the chores she was performing now, helping him bathe and making him presentable to his people, would have been the task of a household slave. That she was taking it upon herself, lowering herself to performing a slave's chores in order to be close to him, said more than words ever could.

The excitement at the thought of seeing his son, however, was almost more than he could take: to see what kind of man the child he had left behind had become, to hear tales of his training, to see him practice his arms.

He opened his eyes slightly as the brushing of his beard ceased, and his eyes flickered to the door far off to his right, to the hammer he had left lying there: the hammer he had left beside his throne as a reminder to anyone who might attempt to occupy it that he would be back. There was gold inlay detailed around the head, its only adornment. It was a worker's hammer, not a pretty thing; it was a weapon, and he wondered again about Orestes. Would the boy be able to wield such a weapon? Only the biggest, strongest Greeks could do so. Even Menelaus, his brother, had chosen sword and spear instead of carrying the great heavy hammer into battle.

The cold touch of bronze on his throat brought him back to the present with a jolt but Clytemnestra placed a calming hand on his forehead, easing his head back gently to expose his bare neck. He tensed and felt his hands gripping tightly to the smooth copper sides of the bath.

"Easy, husband, "whispered Clytemnestra gently. "We must tidy up some of this mess." The cool, smooth blade scraped along the line of his throat, slicing hairs in its passage. Agamemnon had never allowed a slave to do this for him; trusting someone with a knife at your throat was not something that came naturally to any man, and a king had to be more careful than most.

But this was his wife. He forced himself to relax his grip on the bath, forced his head to extend back against the edge, and forced himself to close his eyes and relax the muscles of his neck against the blade which swept along it.

This was his wife, he thought again; if she had wanted him dead, his throat would already be lying open beneath her.

CHAPTER THIRTY-FOUR

AEGISTHUS CLIMBED THE TWISTING COLD STONE STAIRCASE. HIS men were ready in place for his signal. He hated taking the backstairs, the servants' entrances, but he knew that neither Agamemnon nor his men would barely realise they existed, let alone use them; and if one did happen along, he could pass himself off as a servant for a few minutes since he managed to wash off the manure in the horse trough and pulled on a clean chiton.

Failing that, he was fairly sure he could silence them before they could raise the alarm. There was a party going on downstairs, after all. That would drown out most sounds.

Reaching the landing of the staircase, he moved along the empty grey corridor till he reached the right door. Putting a hand to the thick wood he eased the latch gently, careful not to make a sound, and pushed the door on well-greased hinges. He had checked the door earlier to make sure it wouldn't make a sound, and hung new tapestries around what he had already come to think of as his room.

Aegisthus had to duck his head through the door. He had made up his mind to have it built up and sealed when he took over, so that it could never be used against him in a similar fashion. Soft leather sandals whispered across the stone as he worked his way to the edge of the tapestry and eased an eye to the frayed hole he had created. An awful waste of a new tapestry, creating that hole, but when you were playing for kingdoms the value of a tapestry was negligible.

Putting one eye to the hole he had created revealed the whole of the room to him. Clytemnestra had told him earlier of her plan and there she was, one hand on Agamemnon's forehead with the beautifully crafted knife at his throat. He still thought that she should finish it at this stage.

She had made the point that he might still have enough strength to kill her before he lost enough blood to fall unconscious, but that would just have saved Aegisthus a job later on. The thought was a grim one; he had enjoyed her body, but with the two of them and Orestes all gone he could seize control and marry the beautiful young Hermione, thereby taking Menelaus' kingdom too. His revenge would be complete against the sons of Atreus.

The curse on their family would finally be broken, with nobody left to avenge them. His line could continue to rule in peace for years to come. His name would be remembered down through the years as the man who had defeated Agamemnon, the conqueror of Troy. He could decide later how the story was told.

Slow methodical strokes of the knife along Agamemnon's throat was like a balm to his mind; this game would soon be over. He could almost see the blood running in rivulets down his great body into the water he lay in, the look of horror on his face as he realised his time had come. Aegisthus wanted him to know before he died that his line would end with him, but that would have to wait until the knife was out of Clytemnestra's hand. She loved the boy. He knew that at least part of her affection was due to Agamemnon's sacrifice of Iphigenia. The loss of one making her relationship with the others even deeper.

He might keep Electra or Chrysothemis alive afterwards, in case Hermione didn't produce an heir, but unless the child was his they would never be allowed to bear children. He would not take the risk of one returning some day to claim vengeance against him. No loose ends, he thought. The curse would end tonight.

He watched as Clytemnestra rinsed the loose hairs from Agamemnon's neck and then took the knife to his cheeks, cleaning the rough stray hairs while leaving his beard intact. She slowly worked oil into his beard, easing out the natural curls on his chin, and finally he was ready.

Aegisthus was frustrated, his eye stuck to the hole in the tapestry, watching Agamemnon receive this treatment. She had explained everything to him, but he still couldn't see the need to bathe him to such a degree just to watch him die.

He stood up in the bath, water cascading down his hairy body. Even past his prime, his body heavier than it used to be, he was still an impressive man. Clytemnestra moved towards him with a long white towel. Watching her wipe him down brought a wave of jealousy to Aegisthus. Even planning to kill her, her still thought of her as his. Soon ...

————

CLYTEMNESTRA RINSED the last of the hair from Agamemnon. She worked the citrus-scented olive oil into his hair and beard and declared him ready.

"I had a new chiton made for the occasion," she told him. "Tyrian purple, the very best. It cost almost as much as your armour, but you will look as regal as you should and it will also be suitable for a royal wedding, if you don't ruin it tonight."

She stood back, holding it up for him to see, and indeed it

was a garment fit for a king, gold-trimmed and elegant. He looked across to where she held it, the light from the candles making it sparkle. He reached out a hand to touch the cloth and she pulled it away, just out of his reach.

"Not with your wet hands," she laughed and threw it on the bed. "You had better come out of there before you wrinkle up."

Agamemnon stood up in the bath and she lifted a towel and moved towards him, wrapping the towel around him. She patted it against his chest and back, drying the water from his skin, rubbing it against the rough hair of his chest to draw out the moisture.

Agamemnon, arms tangled in the towel, wrapped his arms around her and drew him in close, pressing her to his chest through the blanket. She could feel his excitement through the towel as he kissed her neck, her hair falling across his face, and in that moment she could remember how she had felt all those years ago when they had first met and she had fallen in love with him. The gentle strength of his arms tightened around her and she giggled, pushing him away with an effort.

"Not now; your men are waiting for you downstairs." The mixture of emotions she felt were confusing her. She wanted to believe that the man before her had changed, and it was only with an effort of will that she reminded herself that it was he who had cost her Iphigenia. She had another man who loved her and who would never have sacrificed their daughter in his pursuit of glory.

"Screw the men," said Agamemnon. "They've probably forgotten me already in their revelry." His voice was husky with unconcealed desire.

"No," she said again, her voice hardening. "There will be plenty of time for that later. Now you must honour the men who fought for you." She turned away, walking back towards the bed and his chiton. "Dry yourself and put on your new chiton."

Agamemnon dried himself on the towel and stepped out of the tub, feet dripping onto the rough woollen rug. Clytemnestra lifted the chiton off the bed and opened the bottom, as Agamemnon took it from her and slipped the garment over his head.

CHAPTER THIRTY-FIVE

EVANDER AND CARMENTA WERE SETTLING IN FOR THE NIGHT; lamps had been turned down and the grounds were in darkness. Sitting in their private gardens with a glass of wine, they talked over the day's events and what it could mean for the future of their little town. Suddenly there was a commotion at their gate.

Evander rose to find out what was happening, and an entourage came towards him. Panicking at first, it took him a second in the dim light to make out the familiar shape of Latinus. The king of the Latins was of an age with Evander, but the constant state of turmoil in Italia had kept the man strong, if heavily scarred. A large, vulture-like nose dominated his face, a characteristic common to many of the locals, if not quite so marked. Evander remembered joking with a friend when they had first arrived on these shores that this was the purpose of the open-faced helmets favoured by the tribes.

"My lord," said Evander, surprised. "We had not expected you for another four days. What brings you to my door at this hour?"

"Turnus," spat Latinus. "Always bloody Turnus." He wiped a hand across his face and sent his guard away before moving to one of the benches in the garden. It was only then that Evander saw Amata.

"Carmenta," he called to his wife, "Amata looks tired from her travels. Would you take her inside to freshen up and make her comfortable? Please send a servant with wine for our guest; we shall stay here and talk for a while."

"Certainly, husband." Carmenta, the perfect hostess, was already moving to Amata's side to greet the lady.

When the door had closed and silence had returned to the walled sanctuary, Evander turned back to the king, but even alone he kept his voice low. "Tell me what happened, Latinus." He took a quick drink of his wine, giving himself a second to think, very aware that he should do so before Carmenta returned with wine for his guest. "Did he turn down the offer of Livinia? The betrothal ceremony should not be over for at least another two days."

Even while saying it, he knew he was wrong. He had met Livinia and no man would turn her down, especially when she came with a potential future kingdom: the price for peace. His daughter's hand weighed heavily on Latinus' heart.

"He accepted," growled Latinus. "But he has no intention of honouring the terms of the treaty, or of waiting to inherit the throne." He wiped a hand over his face, covered in sweat from travelling in the warm evening. "His actions spoke louder than his words ever could. The man doesn't want peace, he wants war. He thirsts for it!"

"Then why agree to the proposal at all?" asked Evander, though he could guess.

"Legitimacy." The door to the main house opened and they remained silent while servants brought water and towels for Latinus to refresh himself, and another cup with a jug of wine, some cheese and figs with whatever bread was left in the kitchen. When the servants had returned to the house and they were once again alone, Latinus continued.

"He wants her to make his claim to Latium legitimate before the gods after he defeats us and kills me." Latinus looked down at his hands, clasped in his lap. "I had thought that this marriage might save my people more war, but it looks as if I have only delayed it and given him another reason to finish me in the process."

Evander thought about it. This did not bode well for him any more than it did for Latinus. Tarnus had made his feelings about the little colony clear enough. They were here only under Latinus' protection; no welcome would be extended if Latinus fell.

"Are you sure about this? It would be a big risk for him to take; wars can go both ways." Evander had to ask; if there was a way of ending this without prolonging the war they had to grasp at it. However, it was obvious even to him that if the war continued, Latium would fall. The numbers against Latinus were overwhelming.

Latinus laughed, a deep, rolling, belly-laugh that held no mirth; his bitterness swept through it. "Mezentius was with the dog," he growled. "The Etruscans who left with him have joined the bloody Ratuli." He paused, gulping down the cup of wine in one swallow. When he continued, his tone was more measured. "Remember what it took to send him into exile? No, that was before your time. My marriage to Amata depended on our helping them to remove him."

He leaned down, elbows on his knees, his head bowed below hunched shoulders and Evander had never seen the man look so beaten, even after a particularly vicious battle. Latinus turned his head without raising it to look at Evander before he went on, "He didn't just kill, Evander, he tortured; men, women, children. He enjoyed it; he looked for fights. And this is who Tarnus keeps company with! Mezentius has wanted revenge ever since, and after us he will use the Etruscans again to seize power and take back his kingdom."

They sat in silence, the song of the cicadas screeching and chirping a strange counterpoint to the silence that reigned between them. Evander was deep in thought.

"What if Lavinia doesn't marry him?" he said eventually.

"Then he would likely be at our gates before the next moon." Latinus shook his head. "We would fall within another month. Even without the arrival of Mezentius, we would struggle to hold out."

"If you don't call off the wedding, how long could you delay Tarnus?" Evander's mind was spinning. The timing was too convenient to be coincidental; did the gods have a hand in this?

"We might delay it for four months, perhaps six if we invented some story." He shrugged his huge shoulders and the movement dragged them down further. "What does it matter? The result would be the same. It's better to face your fears without putting off the evil day. We will make him pay a bloody price for it, though."

"No, wait," Evander interrupted. "Give me a moment." He raised a hand as if to physically prevent Latinus from interrupting his thoughts. Latinus sat in silence, patiently watching him as he dragged his ragged thoughts into line. Eventually he dropped his hand and looked at Latinus in the dim light of the garden. "What if I could offer you men?"

"Pah!" sputtered Latinus. "While I appreciate the offer, Evander, we both know that your people are of no use in war. They're not fighters. You said it yourself, they're mostly farmers. You were leading them away from war when you came here."

"No, no," Evander replied. "Not my people; well, not just my people." He grinned at Latinus. "What if I could give you warriors?" He took a drink from his cup. "What if I could give you the very embodiment of Mars himself?" He laughed.

Latinus looked across at him in confusion and not a little

fear. "Do you mean to call on this Hercules you pray to? Did you not say that he went mad and killed his own people?"

"No, it's not Hercules, though if all I've heard is true it might as well be." Evander drained the last of his wine and picked up the jug, filling both his and Latinus' cups to the brim before he went on. "I had some visitors today." He watched Latinus closely for a reaction. "Refugees from the war in Troy."

Latinus' eyebrows rose. "Mercy! But what use are a few war-worn refugees? They lost, remember."

"But we are not facing the entire might of the Greek world, Latinus. These men are veterans, and I know some of them. They are not just refugees, my friend, but some of the greatest heroes and warriors the world has ever known. I don't know how many yet, but they include some of Troy's finest warriors, along with their Dardanian allies and maybe, just maybe, a small number of Myrmidons."

Latinus sat stunned, staring at Evander, his mouth hanging open in a vacant expression. "How?"

"According to them, Priam sent them away before the city fell to save what he could of his people. Then he sacrificed himself and all those who would stay with him to delay or destroy the Greek army, giving them time to slip away."

"And they just left him there to die?" Shock and anger warred in Latinus at this news. He found it shameful that such men would abandon a leader who was prepared to do that for them. "What use are they to us if they run from a fight?"

"They say that he gave them no choice. He ordered them away. It was what he wanted."

"Do you know them? Can they be trusted?" asked Latinus.

"I imagine they are asking themselves the very same question about us, Latinus." Evander looked off into the garden, as if searching the darkness, and took a drink of wine. "I think that if we can offer them a home they will fight for it, for a place where they might save the remnants of their city, their people. Can I trust you not to tell anyone if I reveal who they really are, and not to tell them that you're aware of their real identities?"

"Of course," answered Latinus, "but why the need for such secrecy?"

"Because of who they are, Latinus. If word were to get out, we would have more to worry about than Tarnus; the whole of Greece might well descend and destroy us all."

Now Latinus was beginning to look almost as worried as Evander had been before revealing the secret. "Who are they, Evander? What have you brought on us, and what promises have you made to them?"

"I have promised them nothing, Latinus, believe me. I said they could stay here for the week, until you arrived for the festival, and they could then petition you to be allowed to stay. I told them it was not my choice to make." Evander took a deep breath and looked directly at Latinus. "As to who they are - they are travelling under the names Aeneas, Romulus and Remus. For Aeneas of the Dardanians, this is his real name; but Romulus of Troy is Hector and Remus is Achilles, leader of the Myrmidons."

"Oh great and powerful Dia and Discordia!" Evander was taken aback; it was the first time he had heard Latinus use the names of his native gods and that was the measure of his shock. "How many?"

"That I don't know yet, Latinus. Their ships should make it up the river sometime tomorrow, and then you can meet them for yourself. My advice, for what it's worth, is to make them feel welcome, offer them a home; it's what they're searching for. Whatever you do, avoid talking about Tarnus or the problems with the Ratuli until they're settled in. Don't cancel the wedding, but cut off all contact with Tarnus other than that." He spread his hands. "A lot can happen in six months; maybe we will be ready when he comes."

Latinus sat in deep thought. Of course, he knew who they were. Greek traders were not common in these remote parts, so far from the great settlements of southern Italia, but even here word had travelled of the prowess of Achilles on the battlefield, of the strength of Hector, of his daring counter-raid on the Greek ships where he burned and burned until only Ajax stood between him and burning the Greek fleet, and even the great monster Ajax had taken an injury in stopping him.

"Achilles is Greek," he said at last.

"He turned. When Menelaus died and there was no longer any reason for the war except the megalomania of Agamemnon, Achilles' loyalty to his childhood friend prevailed over his loyalty to a war-crazed madman," replied Evander.

Latinus nodded, and a tiny flicker of hope ignited in his gut.

CHAPTER THIRTY-SIX

"Looks like Agamemnon has found someone more interesting to celebrate with than his men." Alkon nudged Menander. The big man laughed then coughed painfully as he nursed his rib, still healing from the shipwreck. The break was healing well but he was still badly bruised, the side of his almost square face gone a sickly yellow. He slapped Alkon with the back of his arm as if the pain were his fault.

Alkon gazed around the table, taking his first real opportunity to appreciate how lucky he had been to come out of the wreck virtually unscathed. The fact that he was still alive was miraculous in itself when the wreck had taken so many. The table, less than a quarter full with another two behind lying empty, was grim testament to how few had made it back.

Their own ship had lost three-quarters of her men, but there were more out there. There had to be, hadn't there? Poseidon couldn't have been so spiteful. The gods were said to respect bravery and cunning, skill at war, and had they not just defeated the greatest city in the world?

As if echoing his thoughts, he looked down the table at Polybius who was looking back. They had been the closest to

Agamemnon on the walk home, as they were the least injured of
their party. They had led, and very often helped to carry, some
of the worst injured. As the journey continued more had recovered or needed less help, which made their jobs easier, but in
the meantime they had fallen into a semi-leadership role
amongst the men. They were respected.

Polybius nodded to him and Alkon nodded back then rose,
mug of wine in hand, and thumped the table for silence. Slowly
voices dropped away, those who hadn't noticed being hushed
and nudged to silence by the men beside them.

"While we wait for Agamemnon to ah … finish" a cheer went
up at this with a round of laughter going around the table. He
smiled broadly at the men who were raising their mugs and
swigging their wine in toast to their lord, and the noise died
down again allowing him to continue. "I would just like to say a
few words."

He looked around at the expectant faces. "The last time we
were here, we filled this room to the rafters with cheering and
celebration. We were on our way to bring Troy to heel for the
insult they dealt us when they took Helen from Menelaus."
More cheering, but it died down quickly and he continued.
"This room is now nearly empty. Many of those who left with
us may even now be making their way back, but a lot of empty
chairs will remain."

This took the wind out of them. The men looked around, as
if noticing the empty seats for the first time. Sadness filled their
faces as they remembered missing friends and brothers.
"Tonight we celebrate winning the greatest war in history, but
let us not forget the cost. Let us remember all those who will
never make it back safely. To those who are not coming home!"
He raised his cup, a gesture which was repeated around the
room.

The door behind him leading to the main hall burst open
and a man appeared, the groom who had taken the few horses

they'd had when they arrived, which they had taken from bandits. He stood there staring at them with the dopey slouch that had marked him out so clearly. What had the chamberlain called the man? "Banakles?" he called to the servant, who was holding his xiphos exposed at waist height and breathing hard.

"Now!" shouted the man. His hand shot out and gripped the edge of the door frame to steady himself as a spear point burst from his throat. The xiphos dropped from numb fingers as his hand went to his neck in a vain attempt to stop the bleeding, then the spear disappeared backwards and blood spurted in a red wave from the wound, soaking Banakles' front. He fell forward to reveal grim faces pushing their way into the hall.

Even as he fell, the tapestries along the wall began to ripple with movement as they were pushed forward and away from men standing behind. Dozens of men pushed past the tapestries along the walls, as if they had been there all along. A noise caught Alkon's hearing and he turned to see the same happening along the wall behind the table: long-bladed knives and kopis blades wielded by men who were pushing tapestries aside in their rush to get at them. Antileon fell forward onto a plate of food as Alkon opened his mouth to scream a warning.

Men crowded through the doorway, men came from behind tapestries all around, and they all seemed intent on his men, who were sitting unarmed and half drunk at the table. Chaos reigned. Alkon took in the room at a glance, reaching his decision. Two rows of tables separated him and his men from the wall and door. It wasn't much but it gave him a few seconds. Those behind the table were the more immediate threat.

"With me!" he screamed at his stunned men. With no weapons at hand, to go straight hand-to-hand meant death, but if he did nothing, his men on the other side of the table would be cut down in seconds. He could see them fight valiantly with anything to hand as cups were lifted. Battle-hardened from ten years in Troy, no one was lying down for the murderous assassins coming at them.

Those who had reacted with him were following his lead. They grabbed the edge of the table at which they'd been sitting and flipped it on its side; lifting it like a shield they ran at the wall, crushing everyone on that side of the table against the wall with the force of an armoured charge. Swords became useless as bodies and arms were pinned to the wall. Eating knives, broken mugs, chairs - anything at hand instantly became a weapon as those pinned down were ruthlessly dispatched in a blur of blood.

Even drinking and unarmed, these were hardly defenceless children. The battle-hardened veterans of a dozen wars relished the smell of blood, encouraged by what they'd drunk. They dropped the table. Those of Agamemnon's own men who had become trapped behind the table with their assailants were stunned from hitting the wall with such force, but it had saved a few of their lives.

Alkon grabbed a sword which had fallen from one of the enemy's dead fingers, finishing off one who had escaped the ram. He had barely time to register the sickening sight of so many of his own men who, minutes before, had been relaxing in safety, enjoying the fruits of ten long years of war, now lying in pools of their own blood with stab wounds and ripped throats.

He turned quickly to assess the next threat, now armed. The scene was a mass of chaos and confusion.

THE COURTYARD WAS silent as Orestes made his way through. The palace was well lit; the soft golden light of lamps and candles made the curtains glow and noises could be heard reverberating through the windows, more life than the palace had seen in some time. Out here, all seemed quiet; still he padded softly into the square, eyes raking the shadows as more bodies piled into the yard behind him.

Kalliades pushed in at his elbow, shield at his side as he watched the area. "See anything?"

"All seems quiet," Orestes replied and moved further into the square. He could feel Kalliades at his side all the way, and Castor had taken up a position on his other side. The thought that they were trying to shield him brought comfort, but there was no place for that here. In the confines of the palace, when battle was joined it would be every man for himself, with no space to form shield walls.

From the stable across the yard a man took off, running towards the doorway of the palace. The movement caught Orestes' eye and he was after the man like a hound catching the scent of game. His sudden rush outstripped his companions as he made to intercept the man, but two more bodies rushed out of the darkness. The first spear hit his shield with enough force to rip it clear from his arm; a broad, leaf-bladed boar spear designed for taking down much larger prey, not the slimmer war spears he carried himself.

The impact saved him, though, as it threw him out of the way of the second spear which whispered past his ear, sending the long hair blowing from the back of his head. Only the arrival of Kalliades saved him from a second blow as Kalliades swung his kopis, severing the first man's arm and sweeping the point into the leg of the second on the backswing.

Agamemnon's men weren't like those of Aegisthus. Aegisthus' men were well trained and drilled in weapons; they looked wonderful on the training yard and would terrify the untrained. Markus, however, had trained Agamemnon's men for war. They knew they didn't have to kill the enemy right away, but they would not be fighting again tonight. These were tested warriors, these were killers of men.

Kalliades helped Orestes back to his feet and handed him his shield which Orestes accepted, a little embarrassed for having been caught out in the first place, but Kalliades just smiled and indicated silently that Orestes should lead.

The man they were following looked old and overweight but moved with a speed that surprised them, darting through the door and down the hallway. Orestes flew after him into the dimly-lit corridor which was still considerably brighter than the yard they had just left. The thump of his feet was soon joined by those of his companions, echoing round the narrow hall.

Just ahead, approaching the banqueting hall, was the man who had run from them in the yard. Feet pounding on the hard-stone floor, matching his heartbeat, Orestes raced after him. The man burst through the door into the hall, sword and knife out in his hands, shouting something Orestes couldn't make out, but he now recognised the man as one of Aegisthus' most trusted and drove his spear deep into the man's back, the momentum of his sprint pushing it straight through and out the other side as he slammed into his back with his shield braced in front of him.

The abrupt halt in the doorway almost sent him on his face to the floor; stopping with his spear almost pulled from his grip, he set his feet and pulled it out as the man sprawled to the floor.

Right away Orestes could feel the crowd gathering at his back, pressing him forward. Glancing into the room over the body, he saw men sitting at the long table eating, cups and joints of meat in hand; they stopped and looked up at the disturbance.

The sudden intrusion might have brought an abrupt silence to the room, but at the same time that he burst through the door, men in light armour with drawn weapons began to break from cover behind the wall hangings all around the room. Their presence at the door provided a distraction which gave the assailants an advantage; even as Orestes was jostled into the room by his own men, he saw men at the table who were staring at him in shock being butchered from behind.

His first instinct was to rush to their aid, as his men were piling into the room beside him, but that would leave his back exposed to those along the wall to his right. As luck would have it, the decision was taken out of his hands as he realised that not everyone at the table was drunk. Someone quickly took charge, he couldn't see who; they upended the table they were sitting at and used it as a battering ram against their attackers; it caught some of their own surviving men on that side of the table, but they would all have died if nothing had been done.

Kalliades was ordering his men in their corner of the room. Orestes decided to take the enemies along this wall before they could clear the tables between them and the battling revellers, obviously Agamemnon's men, though he couldn't see his father amongst them. Orestes hoped he wasn't already a corpse cooling on the floor.

"Mycenae!" he roared, and along his line he heard calls of "Sparta!" taken up by some of his followers.

Aegisthus's assassins had been expecting no resistance. The strung-out line, some still disentangling themselves from the wall hangings, were in ones and twos along this wall. Orestes missed the first two completely, as Kalliades' spear took one dead in the eye and Levidis took the other with a ragged tear ripping open his throat.

Orestes' spear broke in the next man who, armed only with swords and knives, couldn't get close enough to take a proper swing at him. Dropping what remained of his spear took valuable seconds; as he ripped his ornate kopis from its sheath at his waist, he fell behind the flow of bodies as everyone wanted to bloody their blades. The Spartans were especially vicious, taking their vengeance on anyone they could blame for their friends who had been murdered in Sparta when Orestes had been targeted. Levidis, the largest Spartan or indeed man whom Orestes had ever seen, bodily lifted him back, bringing his own spear in to impale the man aiming for Orestes.

Levidis seemed to be the leader of those Spartans who had followed Orestes, and he could clearly see why. The man was not merely strong, he was ridiculously fast and could read the movements of a battle at a glance.

As they had cleared one side of the room, the men sitting at the table had killed those hidden along the opposite wall, though with much higher casualties as they'd been taken by surprise while feasting unarmed. Only a dozen enemy along the third side of the room remained standing as Levidis called a halt.

"Drop your weapons," he shouted to the remainder of those who had appeared from behind the curtain. Hesitation met him. One of his own Spartans moved towards them, leading with his spear. Levidis swung his own spear sideways, the shaft catching the man in a glancing blow on the side of the head. "I told you to halt!" he growled at the man before turning his attention back to Aegisthus' assassins, dropping his voice and repeating, "I told you, drop your weapons."

They had backed into a corner of the room and huddled together. Without armour or shields, there was no way they could win this fight. A spear rattled to the ground, followed by another, and suddenly they were all throwing down their weapons under Levidis' glare.

When it was clear that they were no longer a threat, the big head swung towards Agamemnon's men who were watching what was happening wearily, like cornered animals. Clutching the weapons they had taken from their fallen adversaries, unlike Aegisthus' thugs these men wouldn't be cowed with threats. Wine-fogged eyes were taking everything in, desperately trying to figure out what was happening and who was trying to kill them when they couldn't tell friend from foe.

One man took a hesitant step forward from the group. Orestes thought he recognised the man, but it had been so long that he wasn't sure. "Who are you," called the man, "who brings death to my lord's house?"

Rather than being afraid of dying, this man looked angry. No one from this group was throwing down their weapons. The very air in the room sparked with tension. Orestes felt like an observer, as if he were watching a play on stage. The surviving twenty or so of those who had arrived with Agamemnon looked ready to charge to a glorious death, a futile death in confused combat against men there to save them from Aegisthus' soldiers. They would be doing the traitor's work for him.

Strange the things that work through your head at times like that. With all their lives on the line, inside those split seconds a question formed in Orestes' mind: was Aegisthus a traitor? He had never sworn loyalty to Agamemnon, had very openly been his sworn enemy almost his entire life. Well, that was a thought for another time; he pushed it away.

Just when it seemed that this must surely end in more bloodshed, Levidis, spear and shield unmoving, swung his head back to Orestes with irritated impatience on his face. He felt Kalliades' big hand on his back, pushing him forward to the front of their group, and reality snapped back into place as he realised they had all been waiting for him to speak.

Kalliades came forward beside him and ground the butt of his spear on the rough stone floor. The Spartans did not relax a muscle but Orestes sheathed his sword, trying to calm the situation. He released the breath he realised he had been holding and inhaled deeply. "I am Orestes, son of Agamemnon of Mycenae," he said aloud, louder than necessary but he was still regaining control of his nerves.

He could see the surprise in the face of the leader of the group, whose eyes flickered with recognition to Kalliades at his side. "Is this true, Kalliades?" he asked, ignoring Orestes.

Kalliades nodded his head, watching the room for any movement.

"And this?" A second man waved his sword around the room in anger. "Is this the welcome we can expect in our own home?" he roared.

Kalliades opened his mouth for the first time. "Polybius, calm yourself and listen to the boy."

Orestes looked him over, taking in his scarred flesh and fresh blood in a glance. "We have been betrayed," he said. "While I was in Sparta arranging my wedding, an attempt was made on my life by agents of Aegisthus." He pointed to the unarmed men in the other corner. "Upon realising who was behind it, we knew that he intended to end the line of Agamemnon upon his return. These are our friends." Indicating those behind him, he went on. "Once again Sparta has come to our aid in our time of greatest need."

Orestes looked around the group of Agamemnon's men, who were now eyeing Aegisthus' men with open hostility. "Where is my father?"

The first man who had spoken to him, Alkon, he vaguely remembered although he was now much older. He seemed one of the calmest of the group and most in control, and it was he who replied. "Your father is safe, lad. He is upstairs spending some time with your mother."

The world around Orestes seemed to slow and stop as he heard those words.

CHAPTER THIRTY-SEVEN

His head went into the top of his beautiful purple chiton, the wool fine and soft against his skin. It truly was a garment fit for a king. Personally, he was not fond of that colour, but it had been chosen so that he should be perceived as regal and it was a gift from his beautiful wife; perhaps the first step towards rebuilding their relationship.

The top was caught on something; he couldn't seem to find the opening for his head. He probed gently with his hands; the opening had to be here somewhere, and it wouldn't do to rip his gift before he'd even worn it. The fit was tight for pushing his arms up but he managed to get his hands alongside his head to search for the opening.

It was no good; he would have to take it off and examine it.

A sudden stabbing pain in his back caused all his muscles to tense at once. His arms went rigid, pushing against the unyielding material.

Confused, he knew he was under attack; he had sustained enough wounds to recognise the feeling of cold metal piercing his flesh. Warm blood spouted from his back as the blade was withdrawn. He sucked in a breath at the pain.

All senses heightened from the attack, he could make out battle noises echoing through the stone wall from what had recently been a party. Then everything was blacked out again as he felt a second stab, lower this time, near the kidney. A scream ripped its way from his throat, muffled by the material,

"Help!" he tried to scream. "We are under attack!" The knife punched into him again and he fell to his knees, still desperately clawing at the cloth, his great strength reduced to nothing against the soft material which was now his prison.

On his knees, the knife punched into him again, on the shoulder from above this time; it must have cut some of the stitching because, as his body contracted with the pain, he could hear ripping and the cloth fell back from his face.

Sucking a huge breath into his gasping mouth, like a drowning man breaking the surface of water, as the knife was once again pulled out he fell forward. He rolled onto his side, arms still trapped, held tight against his body inside the chiton but he could finally see behind him. His disbelieving eyes fell on Clytemnestra, who stood there holding a small bloody kopis, her hands and arms covered in glistening blood - his blood.

"Why?" he called in desperation, feeling his lifeblood leaking out and pooling on the ground around him.

"Why?" she screamed, tears flooding from her eyes. "You sacrificed my daughter, my firstborn, and you ask why!" Then from behind her stepped a man he had never expected to see again.

The sight of Aegisthus, his most bitter enemy, a man he should have hunted down and finished many years ago, fired what little blood he had left and he struggled again against the chiton but to no more effect than before. As Aegisthus leaned over Clytemnestra's shoulder, grinning, to kiss her lightly on the cheek, he finally understood.

All fight went out of Agamemnon and he flopped back, exhausted. He knew now he had lost.

"I'm glad I arrived in time. I wanted you to know it was I," drawled Aegisthus, sounding almost bored as he reached around Clytemnestra to take the knife from her shaking hands.

Agamemnon stared at Clytemnestra, tears stinging his eyes at the betrayal and the defeat. "What about the boy?" he asked. "At least tell me he is safe."

"I have already told you," she said. "I sent him to Sparta to arrange the wedding, and to keep him safe and out of the way until this was over."

The noise of battle had died and the palace seemed eerily quiet; only Agamemnon's gasping breath and Aegisthus' laughter broke the silence. "Your boy is dead by now," Aegisthus said, barely controlling his laughter. "I sent men to Sparta with him."

Clytemnestra's head swung round in shock. "But you said …" was all she managed to get out as the knife he had taken from her only a moment before sliced through her throat.

"I said a lot of things," Aegisthus sneered as the blood choked off her words. Shock, betrayal and terror flashed across her face. The front of her peplos was soaked with blood; in seconds she could feel it running down her legs as her hands scrambled frantically at her throat in a vain attempt to staunch the flow.

Aegisthus wiped the knife on the back of her gown and, as weakness caused her knees to give way, he shoved her forward so that she landed across Agamemnon's bleeding body.

"You killed my father!" Aegisthus snarled. "Your father killed my brothers. Did you really think I would forget that and just move on?" He was almost shouting now. He stopped to gather his breath and suddenly tilted his head to the side, a grin replacing the snarl on his face. "Do you hear that?" he asked?

All Agamemnon could hear was silence.

"The battle is over." That was it; in his own slow dying and the murder of his wife, Agamemnon had forgotten all about the sounds of battle he had heard. "My men have just slaughtered the last of your troops, Agamemnon. No one is coming to save you." He laughed again.

Agamemnon felt his slow breath rasp over lips wet with blood. Even if someone was coming, it was too late for him. He had seen enough wounds to know that; the blood in his mouth was bubbling up from his lungs.

"I'm glad I was here to witness that exchange, however," he said, looking thoughtfully at Agamemnon. "Iphigenia is in Athens, you say? With Electra and Chrysothemis in sparta still within reach, I may have to send a little visitor to Athens. If I end your line now, I can be sure no one is coming back to avenge you."

Agamemnon made one last Herculean effort to rip the chiton, which was now wet and sticky with his congealing blood. A low growl in his throat was all he could manage, because this was not the story of Hercules. Exhausted, he flopped back. His eyes opened wide, his jaw went slack. His spirit fled.

———

ALONE AND FORGOTTEN, Cassandra huddled in the hallway outside the door. Shouts leaked round the wooden frame. Agamemnon had barely gone through the door, had probably not even embraced his wife, before the sounds of argument had begun.

She could understand the woman's feelings; he had effectively abandoned her for ten years. Some of it made little sense to her, though; he was apparently being accused of having sacrificed their child to appease the gods.

She shuffled closer to the door, curiosity getting the better of her. Father had always said she was too nosey for her own good; that why he had sent her to be a priestess of Apollo. She could still hear Priam's voice: "No man will want a wife interfering in his business; better you should learn to weave."

The voices were clearer now; he had not sacrificed his daughter, but sent her into an exiled priesthood in Athens. The details make the story, she always found. The voices died down then, making hearing difficult. Agamemnon's heavy footsteps were approaching the door and she retreated quickly back to where he'd left her, in the middle of the hallway. Just before he reached the door, there was some mumbled speech on the other side and the footsteps stopped.

A few moments more and silence had descended on the room. The footsteps could be heard moving away from the door, not as heavily as before. Whatever argument they had been having was over, or put aside for another time.

Time slowed now as she waited. Was this to be her life now, waiting on these people in a strange and frightening land? She supposed that, when she'd been trained as a slave, it wouldn't be very different from her life serving as a priestess of Apollo: waiting on supplicants, cleaning the temple, making the sacrifices. But there she had been a respected figure, both as a daughter of the king and a servant of their patron God. She had been almost untouchable.

In the quiet of the hall, she passed the time as she had so often before, quietly singing the hymns to Apollo. She was constantly waiting for a servant or member of the household to arrive, demanding to know who she was and why she was loitering alone outside their queen's bedroom door, but she did not know what else to do until Agamemnon returned to instruct her about her duties.

If she listened carefully, she could hear the sounds of merrymaking from downstairs. Agamemnon's men were celebrating their return and the noise was audible through layers of stone and wood, but from the room ahead of her there was almost no sound. Moments passed, dripping through syrup.

Noise erupted up the stairs. Someone had opened the door to the celebrations, and the noise of men cheering rolled up the hallway punctuated by a shout, then a scream of pain. The sound of clashing weapons followed close on its heel.

Cassandra's eyes shot open at the sounds. The war in Troy was still all too clear in her mind. The memory of all those she had lost was still raw and terror clawed at her chest, tightening her throat. Everything that had happened since then had been like a waking nightmare, but while Agamemnon believed her to be an oracle of Apollo she had some vestige of control. Knowing she was going to be a slave, she had warned Agamemnon that they would be safe as long as they were together. Better to be a slave in his palace than in some shepherd's hut, and everyone, even these Greek barbarians, knew that oracles were inviolate; to abuse them would cost you their power.

So Agamemnon had kept her close, even allowing her a certain freedom that the other slaves didn't enjoy because the implications of her prediction were that she would not be safe away from him. When the other slaves had been packed like stock in the cargo holds of the ships she had shared his cabin, living like a princess. With Troy gone, it was the closest she could ever hope to get to regaining her position.

Then the ship had crashed during the storm, but she could see in Agamemnon's eyes that he held her responsible for their survival upon waking up on the shore. He had treated her like a little sister, or a daughter, and when she was being raped there was genuine fear and anger in his eyes. He had not yet managed to bring himself to ask if her powers were gone, but the assault had brought home with pain and blood the knowledge that Troy was gone. With her father and brothers dead, she would never again feel safe.

Backing across the hallway till her back was against cold stone, she pressed herself against it. Her eyes never left the stairs at the end of the hallway; it was her fingers that found the recessed niche in the wall as she pulled herself deeper into the shadow, trying to make herself disappear.

If time had seemed slow before, now it seemed to stop entirely. If it weren't for the clash of bronze ringing like a deep bell and the screams of men, she might not have realised it was moving at all.

After what felt like an age the noise stopped, and only then did she remember to breathe again. White fingers clutched the edge of the stone as she peered from the darkness into the shadow-flickering, torch-lit hallway, every creak of wood in the old building sending shivers up her spine.

A noise from behind the door indicated life in the room beyond, but other than that she could have been alone in the palace. Surely Agamemnon had heard the noise of battle from downstairs. She couldn't imagine him just sitting there, enjoying the company of his wife, with whatever was going on. She had seen him during the battle of Troy and knew that his temper alone would send him charging into the fray, even if all seemed lost.

She waited, expecting him to come barrelling through the door like the force of nature he was. She waited and she waited.

When finally she heard the sound of steps moving in the stairwell, many feet, though not heavily armoured, she already knew that something was wrong. It looked as if a change of ownership was the best she had to look forward to.

She pushed herself back into the niche, trying to make herself smaller, trying to make herself disappear beside the statue which already stood there, clinging to the feet of some long-dead ancestor.

The footsteps of many men finally topped the stairs, spilling men onto the hallway. A young man led the way, followed by one of the largest men she had ever seen. Swords in hand, blood dripping to the floor unheeded as they walked along the hall, their eyes were focused on the door directly across from Cassandra, and she pushed herself further into the shadows.

Their focus and the darkness saved her from being discovered as the younger man stopped just before the door. There was a second of impatient confusion among the men behind as him as he looked at the door, taking a visibly deep breath.

He looked up at the big man standing beside him. This man was only slightly older, maybe twenty-two, but he had already begun to go bald on top and had decided to shave it all so clean that it shone with damp sweat in the torchlight. His thick black beard more than made up for the lack of hair on top.

Despite the big man's size, it was immediately obvious that the smaller, younger man was in charge, which could only mean one thing, she hoped: this was Agamemnon's son. He had talked about the boy a lot on the trip home. Cassandra knew he'd been keen to see what the young man had become, but she doubted if dripping in blood was what he'd had in mind.

He nodded to the bigger man without even trying the handle. Immediately a huge foot lifted and crashed into the door. It didn't stand a chance; the sound of ripping hinges and splintering wood accompanied the crash of the door into the wall.

"And here are my men …" the voice stopped as the big man walked through the door, warily followed by the one she assumed to be Orestes. "But you're dead!"

It was a voice she didn't recognise. It certainly wasn't Agamemnon's, but she hadn't seen anyone else go in.

"Not exactly, Aegisthus. Your men failed." Orestes' voice echoed off the stone into the hall. "They killed a few of our friends, however, and paid for their mistake." There was a pause. "Father!" Between the legs crowding the door, a red pool of blood appeared.

———

THE DOOR burst inwards in a spray of splinters, Levidis' heavily-muscled legs making short work of the timber. Without waiting he had stepped through, sword leading as his big head swung from side to side, surveying the entire room for danger before he moved aside to let Orestes in.

Orestes' eyes immediately locked with those of Aegisthus as the man spoke in confident tones. "And here are my men …" he stopped abruptly as Orestes stepped through the door. In seconds his whole demeanour had changed, the colour drained from his face as he exclaimed, "But you're dead!"

"Not exactly, Aegisthus. Your men failed," replied Orestos. "They killed a few of our friends, however, and paid for their mistake." The venom left his voice as his eyes slid from Aegisthus to his parents, lying dead in a pool of blood between them. "Father!" he said, his voice echoing through the room. His eyes blurred with tears. For so long, all he'd had was a memory of his father and the dream of his coming home and removing the hate-filled Aegisthus, and now Aegisthus had taken even that from him.

Anger swelled in his chest and burned through his veins. His mother lay almost on top of Agamemnon, her arm on the calf of his leg, stretched out as if reaching toward him. Orestes knew she had probably had some part in his father's death, but a part of him hoped that her outstretched arm indicated a change of heart, that she had been trying to get to him, rather than the way she happened to have fallen when Aegisthus cut her down.

The bloody dagger was still clutched in his hand, no longer a proud declaration of his actions but more of an unnecessary indictment. He backed away from the corpses, one slow step at a time.

Orestes lifted the point of his xiphos, pointing it at Aegisthus. "You …" was all he could utter around the lump in his throat, but it was enough for Aegisthus who turned on his heel, quickly making for the servant's door at the end of the room.

Before he reached the door, the rattling of bronze against stone sounded from beyond the curtain. Aegisthus stopped short as a hand ripped down the wall hanging, unveiling Kalliades and Markus leading half a dozen of Agamemnon's surviving men.

"I know the servants' pathways as well as you, Aegisthus," growled Orestes. "I played in them as a child. Remember?"

Seeing the walls close in around him, Aegisthus glanced around desperately for some way out of the rapidly-filling room. Orestes sheathed the sword he had been carrying and picked up his father's hammer, which was still standing beside the door where Agamemnon had left it. The weight of it no longer surprised him; it had spent most of his lifetime sitting beside his fathers' throne and he had played with it many times as he grew. He turned the head over in his hands, looking at the intricate carvings inlaid with bronze, and moved his gaze to Aegisthus.

Aegisthus pulled his own kopis from its sheath and held it out in front of himself, pointing it at Orestes. Orestes looked coldly back at him and moved forward. Aegisthus made one wild swipe for the stomach, which Orestes easily blocked with the hammer's shaft, but it was a feint and Aegisthus swept the knife around, going straight for the younger man's throat.

Orestes had trained under Markus, who had made him watch other men's fights. This had included Aegisthus training his own men in the yard, and Orestes had expected the feint; it was something he did constantly with the new recruits to make them fear him. Orestes didn't fear him. He was too angry to feel fear and, in the same movement, he blocked the kopis and brought the head of the hammer down hard, connecting with Aegisthus' wrist. The crack of stone against bone hung in the air, and the knife clattered to the ground from his useless fingers as he moaned in pain.

Pulling his injured arm towards his body, Aegisthus swung again with his kopis but Levidis' blade caught it mid-air, holding it there with little effort as Orestes brought the hammer back in an upward swing, catching Aegisthus a crushing blow to the stomach and up to his sternum. More than just knocking the wind out of him, the blow caused serious internal damage; Aegisthus folded around the hammer and blood spewed from his mouth as he coughed and choked.

Orestes stood over him for only a second before raising the hammer again and bringing it down on his head, driving him into the ground and opening his head like an over-ripe pomegranate.

He stood over the body for a minute, looking down at the mess he had made of the other man. Aegisthus had certainly deserved it, but it didn't make Orestes feel any better; his parents were still dead. As if in a dream, he let the handle of the hammer slip through his fingers to drop to the ground by the body of Aegisthus, and turned back to his parents. Kneeling beside their bodies, he finally began to cry and his youth returned. No longer the raging warrior, the child wept for his dead parents.

Men came forward to give him a consoling pat on the back. Markus squeezed his shoulder, though his grip was weak, and beside him Kalliades gripped his shoulders for a brief second.

Suddenly Nestor was there in the doorway, fully armed and ready for battle. "What has happened here?" he bellowed from the door. Behind him his men, similarly arrayed, filled the hallway outside.

Kalliades told him. "Agamemnon is dead?" Nestor said quietly, the colour draining from his face.

"He is," replied Kalliades.

"And who is this boy?" asked Nestor.

"Agamemnon's son, Orestes," said Kalliades. "He killed the traitor by his own hand and avenged his father."

"So what happens now?" asked Nestor.

"What do you mean, what happens now? We have funeral games for all the dead."

"You know what I mean," said Nestor. "The king is dead, but there must be a king." Suddenly the tension was back in the air. Everyone in the room knew the weakened situation of Orestes at that moment; the new arrivals would probably follow Nestor if he decided to make a play for the throne, and Orestes' men had already been through a battle and were bloody and tired.

Through the haze of grief Orestes heard the words, and the meaning too. He pushed himself to his feet. Even at this tender age, he already had his father's bearing. He wore his tears proudly, making no attempt to wipe them away from his red eyes as he faced Nestor.

It was again Levidis who came to Orestes' rescue. Stepping forward, towering over everyone in the room, he stood facing Nestor and one pace to the side of Orestes. Slowly he drew his great oversized xiphos from its sheath and caught Orestes' eye. Orestes drew a deep breath and held it, as he felt all the men in the room deciding which way the dice would be cast.

Watching Levidis, Orestes saw the big man cast a glance back at some of the other Spartans he had in the room and hold it for a second. Orestes had no idea what passed between them in that glance but, as Levidis nodded deliberately, some agreement was made. As if in a practiced reflex the big man dropped to one knee, keeping Nestor in focus from the corner of his eye, and reversed the blade in his hand, offering it hilt first to Orestes.

"Sparta stands with Orestes. I offer you my blade." Still getting over the loss of most of his family in one evening, Orestes wavered with shock at the gesture. Steadying his feet, he reached out a tentative hand, touched the hilt with his fingertips and nodded his thanks.

Nestor watched events unfold with a calm, hawk-like glare on his face. He moved his gaze around the room, finally settling on Markus. "And you, Markus?" he asked. "I assume that you still control the household guard, though how you let this happen I will never understand. Where does the house of Markus and the royal guard stand?"

Markus was leaning against the wall at the foot of the bed, but upon being addressed he stood straighter in the flickering light of the bedroom. "I am afraid, Nestor, that Clytemnestra saw fit to remove me from my position." Nestor showed a reaction for the first time, a deep frown creasing his sun-browned forehead. "She removed all the guards who had held position under Agamemnon, replacing them with men loyal to Aegisthus."

"But you know I did not want that, that you will be immediately reinstated … " Orestes interrupted, but Markus held up a hand to cut him off.

"Almost all the men who were discharged have stayed with me," he went on. "Our intention was to remain loyal to Agamemnon and try to warn him of the danger upon his return. Until our dismissal I watched this young man grow, and believe him to be as good a leader for our people as Agamemnon was, if not better." He gave Nestor a hard look. "The house of Markus, and the royal guard, will stand with Orestes."

Orestes almost gasped with relief. He turned his head to Nestor, who still stood in the doorway. Orestes knew that Nestor had already worked out that he had the numbers to overpower the Spartans, Markus' men and the remaining troops Agamemnon had brought back. Markus moved forward to stand at Orestes' other shoulder, opposite Levidis.

Nestor drew his sword and dropped to one knee, offering the hilt. "My apologies, lord. I was always loyal to the house of

Atreus, and meant only to ensure that everyone else was of the same mind."

Orestes sagged then, and Levidis' arm steadied him as the exertions of the last day caught up with him. He regained his feet and took a steadying breath, reaching out to touch Nestor's hilt. Turning to Markus, he took his hand in thanks. "You will, of course, return as head of the guard?" he said.

Markus winced through gritted teeth. "I fear it would be a short serving of office," he replied as Orestes noticed the stickiness on his hand. Looking him over, Orestes noticed for the first time the paleness of his skin. He backed away a step and saw the blood trailing down Markus' leg. His dark tunic and breastplate had hidden the wound well in the light, but when he put his hand to his side it came away slick with blood. "Fetch a doctor!" screamed Orestes, catching Markus as his legs finally gave way.

"I'm afraid it's too late for that, my boy," muttered Markus as Orestes placed him gently on the floor and men crowded forward to see. "If there were ever a chance of saving me, that time has passed."

"No," sobbed Orestes. "I can't lose you too."

"I have done my duty and seen you to the seat of Atreus," gasped Markus as they stripped away his breastplate. "The rest depends on you." He raised a blood-soaked hand, cupping Orestes' cheek and smearing it red. "Your father would have been proud to see you this day."

"No!" cried Orestos, but Markus' hand dropped away and went slack as his eyes glazed over, staring into the near distance.

CHAPTER THIRTY-EIGHT

Morning dawned dry and hazy but the autumn chill was evident in the air. All that was missing was the light sprinkling of frost which must now be only a few days away. It was that, as much as anything else, which made up their minds for them.

Hunting teams had brought in meat while they had been away the previous day, but staples like grain, olives, and even grapes were running precariously low, so that even if they found somewhere else quiet and relatively uninhabited, gathering food at this time of year was going to be a problem. Evander had at least offered some succour and would open whatever food stores they had from the previous season to tide them over.

"Anyway," said Remus, "if things don't work out well there or we get a bad feeling about Evander, we can do again what we did in Carthage and just sail away. The river will carry us to sea quietly at night."

Romulus nodded, but as usual he had to be the cautious one.

"Everyone who can walk should do so," Romulus called out to grumbled acceptance from those clearing up the beach of their belongings. "Only one bank of rowers on each ship. Keep them as light as possible. We don't know if there are any sand-banks in the river."

This made practical sense, but they had also decided to leave the damaged hull on the beach for the present. They might send a team back to repair it when they had settled into Pallantium, Evander unimaginatively having named it after his own home in Arcadia. That already meant two hundred people walking, so they might as well make it fair and keep their surviving ships safe. All their possessions were packed up and stowed on board, so people would only need to carry themselves.

The sun was only just releasing its hold on the lip of the world when they were dousing fires and pushing the ships off the beach to circle round and enter the river mouth. They would try to find somewhere convenient along the way to swap rowers for some of those following in their wake along the riverbank.

Around halfway to noon that became possible, when a large sandy bank opened up at the side of the river, sufficient to dock two boats at a time. Those walking broke out some food and drank from the river, filling their skins as they did so. Even with the days cooling, the exertions of the walk were already building up sweat and hunger on many.

It was a few hours after noon when their destination came in sight. Again the town itself was hidden from view so that no one but Romulus, Remus and Aeneas knew they were finally approaching their destination; complaining had begun as people asked for another break.

Aeneas had gone aboard the lead ship during the midmorning break to guide the boats up the river.

"You know we should have just taken Carthage before their navy returned," Remus said for the hundredth time since they had sailed from the city. "Ready-built palaces, that harbour ..." he whistled through clenched teeth. "We could have lived like kings and taken over the trade with the Phoenicians."

"And I've told you to stop saying things like that in front of our people," Romulus barked at him. This conversation was nothing new, but he worried that word of it would get back to Aeneas. "What would you have done when their navy returned? And what about Queen Dido?"

"Hah! The navy wouldn't have stood a chance if we'd finished the harbour defences. And Dido ... well, Aeneas could have kept her as a pet if he wanted."

"You saw what she did on the beach!" exclaimed Romulus. "Do you really think she would have stood aside if we had taken her city?" He shook his head at Remus' foolishness. "Besides, it would have broken guest laws; it would have been dishonourable."

"Pah!" spat Remus. "Guest laws indeed! I have lived as a mercenary since I left my father's halls, and silly rules like that were left by the wayside long ago. And what difference would it have made if we'd killed Dido? It's not as if things would have turned out any differently."

"Yes, but that was by her own hand, Remus. Can you imagine Aeneas forgiving us if we'd had a hand in it? He already blames himself for what happened to her. He hasn't been the same since we left that beach." Romulus looked at the ground remembering the scene.

"He would have got over it. That boy falls in love more often than I sharpen my sword, I swear." Remus laughed at his own joke but Romulus didn't join in.

"Look, we did leave, so please stop saying things like that where it might get back to him. He is hurting; whether it was a passing fling or not, he feels it and he is your friend as well." Romulus looked across at his friend. "Whatever about the laws of hospitality, I know you haven't given up on the laws of friendship." He clapped Remus on the shoulder. "Otherwise you would be sitting in Agamemnon's hall, drinking his wine and celebrating right now, instead of walking through these gods-forsaken fields."

"Hah!" barked Remus. "Maybe I just hated Agamemnon more than you, eh?" He grinned. "Didn't think of that, did you?"

Romulus threw his arm around his friend and they laughed together in the late autumn sunshine while the past months and years faded away. They were children again, playing and joking together.

A call from the ship brought them out of their revelry, and they looked up to see Aeneas gesticulating excitedly from the deck of the lead ship. Looking where he was pointing, they saw only the hill they had ascended the previous day but, as they rounded the base of the hill, Aeneas was already pulling the she-wolf up the stony beach a little down from the jetty they had set out from the night before. They could now see what he had been pointing at: half the town stood down by the shoreline, ready to welcome them.

In front was Evander, but beside him stood another man; taller and broader than Aeneas' cousin, he carried himself upright to the point of being haughty. As Aeneas disembarked, Evander moved forward to embrace him. Evan at a distance Romulus could recognise that his manner towards the other man was slightly subservient, and he was now introducing Aeneas to his companion.

Neither Evander nor the other man had noticed them yet, and Aeneas had obviously had no opportunity to tell them that they were coming over land; this gave Romulus some slight advantage, as he watched Aeneas bow deeply over the larger man's hand. The man immediately removed his hand and grabbed Aeneas by the shoulders, standing him up straight and embracing him as Evander had before him.

It was a small thing, but Romulus knew what the bow meant: this was the king Evander had told them about the previous night, the king they hadn't been expecting for nearly another week. It was probably better that he was here for their arrival rather than returning to find an extra thousand people living on his land without his permission.

Aeneas was released from the hug and some conversation ensued, during which he began gesturing towards Romulus and Remus as they approached across the plain between the river and the hill. The king turned around with Aeneas and Evander trailing in his wake, noticed them for the first time and strode across the grass towards them.

Evander called something to the villagers as he moved away from them, at which they began to approach the men disembarking from the ships, with baskets of freshly-baked bread and platters of meat to distribute among the refugees.

As the king approached, Romulus turned to Remus and muttered, "Watch your mouth here; be very careful what you say."

"I'm not stupid," replied Remus in exasperation, and then the two groups met. The crowd behind paused, no doubt wondering what was happening. For a second they stood, looking at each other, sizing each other up as one would before a fight. The smile on the king's face didn't quite reach his eyes; he was nervous about this meeting as well.

Romulus couldn't say he blamed the man, with a thousand new arrivals on his soil. He might rule Latium, however large that was; Romulus still didn't know. From what he'd seen the previous day, however, Evander's group and Romulus' own people together meant that those of Hellenic origin now outnumbered the natives in Pallantium, which was by no means a small town. Evander had been there for years already, and Romulus didn't know where Evander's loyalty lay; he didn't want to have to depend on it if trouble arose.

As Evander and Aeneas drew level with the king, he glanced at each of them in turn. "Evander," he said, loudly enough to carry, "would you introduce our guests?"

"Of course." Evander shuffled forward between the two parties but over to the side, as if dealing with a formal parley. "King Latinus of Latium, might I introduce Romulus and Remus?" He looked between Romulus and Remus, asking permission with his eyes, Romulus nodded soberly. Evander lowered his voice so it would not carry beyond their small group. "Formerly Prince Hector of Troy and Prince Achilles, leader of the Myrmidons."

The lack of reaction from Latinus told Romulus that Evander had already informed him of their former identities, and therefore he had been correct to let Evander name them. When you come looking for assistance, it's rarely a good idea to begin with a lie.

Evander raised his voice again as he continued. "Romulus and Remus, I present to you Latinus, the king of Latium."

"An honour ... um," Romulus hesitated, but Latinus stepped in, obviously having experienced the same situation when Evander had originally arrived.

"Just Latinus, please. We don't stand on ceremony here as much you Hellenes. My position is more ..." he struggled for a word; his Greek was good but among themselves they apparently had a title for him which didn't translate well. Eventually he settled for an explanation. "I am the first among equals. I lead my people."

Romulus nodded his understanding and Latinus went on. "Evander here has told me of your situation, and we are happy to provide shelter and perhaps even a new home for you and your people." He said this loudly enough for all to hear, and a cheer broke out behind Romulus among his band of refugees. It made him uncomfortable, though he could not say why.

Latinus then directly addressed the band of footsore refugees. "Come, my friends. Food has been prepared in anticipation of your arrival. We shall make it a festive gathering. Come!" He gestured to them in a warm, friendly manner and the bravest of the refugees began to file past, until suddenly it was like being in the middle of a river of people, flowing past them to reach the local people who had food waiting.

"Now, my new friends," said Latinus when everyone else had moved on. "If you would care to join me at Evander's house, we have much to talk about." He took a deep breath before going on in the halting, broken Greek of one still learning the tongue. "You are of course welcome to stay here, but you have been honest with me, at great risk to yourselves, so I owe you honesty in return. Things are not as simple here as they may appear."

Evander was frowning, lines creasing his forehead as he looked at Latinus

———

DINNER WAS SIMPLE BUT DELICIOUS. As much roast meat as they could possibly eat: venison, boar, and some especially good fowl which Romulus had particularly missed since they'd run out of it in Troy four years into the siege. Only the occasional few managed to get smuggled through the Greek lines; attempts had been made to breed from these, but inevitably the eggs or bird would disappear so the numbers never rose.

These were accompanied by olives, grapes, flatbreads and what passed for wine here; after the spiciness of the North African fare and their time at sea, it was a bounty they could only have dreamed of.

They sat in the ornate gardens of what was, in effect, a palace in the middle of a village. It was Evander's home, but there was no question that Latinus was their host for the evening, ordering Evander's servants around and making sure everyone had anything they might want. Their wives had joined them for the meal, but when it was over Latinus dismissed the ladies and servants to the main house while the men remained reclining on couches, doing so with a grace that Romulus found surprising in a barbarian, even a barbarian king. Three large firepits kept the chill away as night drew in on a late autumn evening.

When they had all settled down, Latinus sat rolling his cup in his hands, thinking about how to begin. "Latium accepted Evander here and gave him land on which to live and farm. His group has been here for about ten years now, mixing with the locals. There have been more marriages than I could count, and children of two worlds abound from those unions. This town of Pallantium has grown and prospered in that time."

Romulus and Remus looked over at Evander, who was looking down into his cup of wine, nodding thoughtfully. Latinus went on. "You may ask yourselves why we accept foreigners to our land and share so willingly what we have. I know that many of the other tribes around have wondered at it."

Romulus nodded. He had been wondering too; there had to be some catch to this generosity.

"You see," said Latinus in a serious tone, "a lot of this has been my daughter's idea. The younger generation often see things that my old eyes might miss. These people whom we accept are the reason that this town and my lands are prospering. They have brought new techniques of working metals, and new ideas. They have greased the wheels of commerce and what is now being made in Pallantium has been selling all over Italia; there is demand for everything from their pottery to the bronze they are making with tin from these very lands, which is stronger and more pure than any we have had before."

He looked up at the sky as he spoke, thinking about how to continue. "Of course, there is always a cost. Not all the tribes of Italia are quite so welcoming; they see what is happening on Sicilia. The rumour is that there are more Greeks there now than in all of Greece. They have begun pushing further into Italia, taking the land from the tribes already there. They win the battles with their … fancy armour and their bronze shields, against tribes without either. The tribes don't stand a chance."

He took a mouthful of wine and rolled it around in his mouth before swallowing. "As those tribes lose ground to the Greek forces, they are being pushed further and further north. This creates pressure, like a fermenting cask of wine, and the pressure pushes along the next tribe, and so on. We have been lucky: the improved armour and weapons which Evander's smiths have been able to produce have given us a decisive advantage so far, but the Rutuli, one of the largest and strongest tribes around, have been pushing us for a few seasons now. We are roughly equal in number. I have been trying to unite some of the tribes, to form an alliance that could put a stop to the constant pushing from the south. We are happy to integrate people with us, but not to have our lands taken away. Unless we can unite they will keep rolling over us, one at a time. The Rutuli's continual attacks are a drain on our resources which we could do without, so I have been away trying to negotiate a truce with their king."

Remus was impatient. "From your face, I would say that it didn't go well."

Latinus looked at him and snorted a laugh into his wine. "It went about as well as I might have expected: he accepted my offer of marriage to my daughter to unite our tribes in a common purpose."

"Then what's the problem?" asked Romulus.

Latinus looked into his empty wine cup. "The problem is that he has no intention of honouring the peace. He will take my daughter to humiliate me, and her, and will attack us anyway."

Romulus frowned. "How do you know this?"

"Because he has found himself a new ally," said Latinus gravely. "A man whom I helped the Etruscans remove from the king's seat for his excessive cruelty. He has joined Tarnus just

244

to get revenge against me and my Etruscan queen. And if they win … well, keep your ships stocked and ready to sail at a moment's notice, because even if he doesn't want to take everything from me, he detests anything even remotely Hellenic."

Romulus and Remus looked at Evander, who nodded, then at each other in silence.

Evander spoke. "Sometimes it feels as if the whole world is going to hell. We left Arcadia behind so that we wouldn't get dragged into the Trojan war, and now Greece has caused war to break out across Italia as well." He shook his head and drained his wine before retrieving the jug to fill all their cups.

Aeneas was on the couch beside Evander. He didn't talk as much as he used to, but now he spoke up for the first time all evening. "If matters lie as you say, then you cannot allow this marriage."

Latinus glanced at Evander and shrugged. "What choice do I have? I have to do what I can to save as many of my people as possible. Even if it only delays an attack, it will give us more time to prepare."

"If you know already that he doesn't intend to honour the agreement and is likely to hurt or debase your daughter, you can't let that happen," insisted Aeneas.

"I am not just thinking about myself." Latinus looked defeated. "My daughter knows the responsibility of royalty, and it's not just our people anymore; Tarnus has made it very clear he will wipe out all the Greeks I have allowed to settle here under my protection. Those he allows to survive he will keep as slaves, to continue making bronze and trade goods." He shook his head sadly. "I will do what I can to prevent that."

Aeneas was looking at Romulus and Remus. "Are we some helpless children to be kept safe behind our mother's peplos? Here we have somewhere we could have a home and a king who is willing to sacrifice his own daughter to keep his people safe, but he shouldn't have to. If our warriors are added to his and fight with him, we could prevail."

Romulus looked annoyed at Aeneas' interruption, but also worried; Remus appeared to be amused, as if the idea excited him somewhat. "Aeneas," said Romulus rebukingly, "we should talk about this among ourselves." He waved a hand at the glowing red star in the sky which hadn't left since the night of Troy's fall; Latinus noticed the gesture and glanced at Evander, who gave a slight shrug to show it meant nothing to him. Romulus went on. "My father, may he have peace, gave his life and his city, gave hundreds of her sons so that we should save this remnant of Troy; to rebuild, not to throw away the few we have on the next battle that comes along."

"Your father gave his life to save his son and the last of his people, but they will have to fight for a place in this world of war and chaos, Hector." The use of his old name indicated the depth of Aeneas' feeling. "She is a royal princess, destined for a life no better than that of a slave. Remember your sister who was taken when Agamemnon sacked the temple of Apollo: would you so quickly throw her away?"

Romulus' anger roared to life and he was on his feet in a heartbeat. "Don't you dare say that to me, Aeneas," he roared, pointing his finger. "Every battle, every time I charged their line, I wanted to bring her back."

Aeneas was on his feet now too, and from the shelter of the colonnaded atrium servants could be seen, peering out fearfully at the fight brewing in the garden. Aeneas was leaning forward towards Romulus, and Evander got to his feet to try to calm matters as Aeneas rebuked Romulus. "And yet you would ask Latinus to sacrifice his daughter to the same fate? Do you think that is why your father saved you, to hide from danger?"

Remus spoke quietly, but his voice caught the others by surprise for the calm and amusement it held. "Of course, there is a way we can all win." They turned to him questioningly.

"They don't know we are here, which gives us the advantage. They don't know our numbers. Let it play out as if the marriage is going to take place at the spring festival, then refuse at the last minute. Latinus meets Tarnus' army head-on, knowing he has them outnumbered" - his smile broadened - "then, when Tarnus is fully engaged, we take him in the flank and destroy him."

Latinus sat quietly watching them. Except for Aeneas' outburst, they were reacting as Evander had anticipated; they were planning the campaign themselves.

"It's still a huge risk." Romulus sighed, unwilling to commit to anything.

"Then we do everything we can to increase our odds," answered Remus. "Delaying until spring gives us time to prepare."

"We should build a proper wall to defend the town." Romulus sat down heavily, frowning in thought. "That makes it much easier to defend."

This idea worried Latinus. "That is all right here," he said heavily, "but my lands cover more than just these hills. I will have to ride out and meet him in battle if we do this. I must defend my land and people; it is they who are farming the land and feeding my towns."

"He is right," said Aeneas. "By the end, Troy was almost starving for the lack of food and supplies."

"And we learned a lot from that failure." Romulus spoke thoughtfully, chin in his hand, looking at the ground. "We would need to defend a larger area, not just the hill of Pallantium; maybe the entire valley where we originally met Evander at the altar of Hercules."

"Building on hillside will be nearly impossible." Aeneas scoffed at the idea. "We would need to encircle all the hills."

"Well," said Remus, smiling, "It would give us land to feed those inside the walls. And we could even grow grapes for wine on the hills."

"As I said," interjected Latinus, losing his patience, "I will need to ride out. I have more to worry about than just your colony."

"Yes," replied Romulus, "but this is about being prepared. It gives us somewhere to fall back to and regroup if we lose. It keeps the women and children safe so the men can concentrate on the fight."

"You would know all about hiding behind walls," Remus goaded him. Romulus frowned at him but didn't rise to the bait.

"And who will be defending these walls if the men are out fighting?" asked Latinus.

Silence fell as they thought. "Diomedes is always looking for more responsibility," mused Aeneas. "The lad's coming along well."

"It would keep him out of the way for a while," laughed Romulus. "The boy's a dead shot with that bow; we could put him in charge of training the old and the children, those who can't fight: a sort of city militia."

"If he is as good as you say, we could use him as a skirmisher," put in Latinus. "We send some of the young ahead of the main body to harass the enemy, draw them into battle with the main line." He looked from one to the other.

"You put your young in the front line?" said Romulus in disgust.

"No, they harass the enemy from a distance. We use archers and slingers. If the enemy try to engage, they pull back behind the main body; the danger is minimal. Besides, it distracts the enemy; keeps them looking forward while you get into position hidden on their flank." Latinus shrugged. "It has been common practice here for years. It gives the young a chance to prove themselves and get a taste of warfare, so that they are ready when the time comes for them to join the battle lines."

"I like it," said Remus, grinning. "Obviously only those of a certain age, which leaves the old and injured as the city militia."

Romulus was frowning still; putting their youth in harm's way did not sit well with him. "They will be doing the same thing themselves, Romulus, so at the very least it will keep them from hitting our main body," urged Latinus.

"The experience will stand to him." Remus turned to Romulus. "You and I were already through our training and on our way to battle at his age."

"Those were different times," Romulus rebuked him. "The whole world was going to war somewhere then. The kids today are different; they're softer."

"Bollocks," said Aeneas. "The only way for them to be ready is to do it, like we did. This could actually be better; they toughen up in training and get first-hand experience with minimal risk. We got the training and were thrown under a mule cart, straight into the line in our first battle. I was there too, remember."

Romulus frowned at the memory but couldn't argue the point. They had shed a lot of blood together before growing into what they had become.

Remus added, "Besides, it's probably safer than Troy was. The whole world is still going to war somewhere, Romulus, or maybe it's just all turning to shit."

Romulus drained his cup and nodded sadly, looking at the ground between his knees. Finally he spoke. "Fair enough, but if we're going to do this, we do it right. There will be no rest for anyone until then; there's too much to do. We will be taking the entire population," he looked over at Evander as he spoke, "including your people, Evander, split into two groups. I will take one group in the morning. This wall must be started, and there's not much time." He looked across at Remus. "You will take the other, Remus, and do what you do best: teach them to kill. At lunchtime we will switch groups; that way everyone gets trained and everyone gets callouses carrying rocks."

Latinus looked at them, shocked, and shook his head. "I'm glad it's coming into winter and there are no crops in the fields."

Romulus didn't relax his expression. This was now a business, and it was the business he had been born into: preparing for war. He looked at Latinus sternly. "It would be better if you brought your men here to train with them also, so we can fight as one unit."

Latinus laughed but nodded. "Your wish is my command, my lord."

CHAPTER THIRTY-NINE

WEEKS HAD PASSED AND IT FELT AS IF IT WERE STILL THAT SAME night. Orestes was stunned, unable to accept he was now alone. For so long he had waited for his father to return, thinking that when he came back everything would be right again, everything would be as it should be, and now it never would.

Orestes had relied on the belief that his father's return would rid the land of the disease that was Aegisthus. His father was a hero of legend, spoken of in every town and village in Mycenae, who had returned from exile in Sparta with his brother to rid the land of the tyrant Thyestes. He still couldn't fully grasp that it was himself, Orestes, enraged by the death of his parents, who had finally killed Aegisthus.

The man had been at the palace for years, so long that Orestes still thought of him as the person he had been when he'd first arrived and Orestes had been smaller. Looking up at that face had seemed a huge height for an eight-year-old, and he had never before realised that he had grown to an equal height.

And then Markus: poor, beloved, loyal Markus who had taught him how to hold a sword. Losing him also had been almost too much, and even now the loss tore at his heart; more so than that of his parents. The man had been a father figure to Orestes when his own sire had gone to war; he had been a mentor, a hero and a friend. Today of all days, he felt the loss bitterly.

He lifted his cup of wine to another round of applause, another toast from another dignitary come to pay their respects to his marriage, but he heard none of it. He placed his hand under that of Hermione, lifted it to his mouth and kissed the back. They married as equals, both orphans now.

When everyone had turned back to their food and wine and the music had once again begun to drum out a beat, he squeezed her hand and rose from the table. He moved towards the door, where he was intercepted by Kalliades. Orestes had reinstated all the old guard and put Kalliades in charge in Markus' stead. He was determined to live up to the standards Markus had set. "Peace, man," said Orestes, trying his best to sound cheerful. "I'm only going to take a piss."

"I'll come with you," said Kalliades. The guard were turned out as if on parade; they would celebrate with Orestes tomorrow when the official wedding party was over and it was just themselves, but now they were on duty and sober.

"No, thank you," said Orestes, patting him on the shoulder. "I need a breath of air and some solitude."

"But it might not be safe," argued Kalliades. "We still don't know if we got all the traitors' men."

Orestes shrugged, "Even if we didn't, he is dead so what use would it be to them to kill me now? Please sit with my wife while I am out; she is just as alone as I am in this crowd."

Kalliades didn't look happy but he did as he was asked, nodding to the other guards as the door opened and closed behind Orestes.

Orestes used the latrine, but when he was finished he didn't return to the hall; instead he made his way to the stables, and from there up the narrow stone steps to the wall of the citadel. There he sat down, dangling his legs over the edge of the wall. He tilted his head back, looking up at the curtain of stars drawn across the night, breathing in the cold winter air. There would be snow before the year was out; he could smell it.

How often had he sat here over the years, just looking out over his city as it dropped away down the mountainside? Even in the dark, this early at night he could make out the streets which curled with the natural turns of the hilly land by the lights in the windows of the houses that lined it. He had grown up knowing that one day it would all be his to rule, yet as far as he could see that had done nothing to prepare him for this day.

A shadow appeared at the top of the stairs, moving with a silent grace. Orestes reached for his belt knife, the only weapon close to hand, and had it half drawn before a voice he recognised cut the night.

"Oh, my apologies. I hadn't realised anyone was up here," said Levidis, his disappointment evident though he obviously had no idea whom he was addressing.

"It's fine," Orestes said lightly. He had wanted to speak to Levidis since that night of violence, but various duties had prevented him; organising the funerals, the wedding and dealing with petitions to the new king had taken all his time. "Sit with me, if you don't mind my company," he joked.

Levidis was taken aback. "My lord, I would be honoured if I am not disturbing you."

"Not at all. Sit down." Orestes patted the wall beside him. "I'm afraid I forgot to bring cushions and the stone is a little cold, but I have always felt the view was worth it. Don't you think so?"

"Indeed, my lord," said Levidis, looking out towards the sea where the moon was only beginning to rise, the reflection shimmering on the waves still visible miles away.

"I have not forgotten how often you have already saved my

life," said Orestes. "At least while we are alone, please call me Orestes as you did while we were drinking in Sparta. That feels like a lifetime ago."

Levidis laughed at the memory. "Orestes, then."

They sat quietly in companionable silence for a few minutes before Orestes spoke again. "Why did you do it?"

"Do what?" asked Levidis hesitantly.

"When it looked as if Nestor meant to take the throne, you pledged your loyalty to me." He looked across, but in the darkness he couldn't see the other man's face. "Even with all our men Nestor could probably have cut his way through to the throne, but you risked your life yet again for a man who would marry the woman that a blind man can see you're in love with."

The silence went from comfortable to uncomfortable in the length of a sentence. Just when Orestes thought that Levidis wasn't going to answer, he did.

"I grew up watching Hermione," he said hesitantly. "I was occasionally set to minding her as she played with my little sister as children. My family is noble, probably next in line after hers." Orestes could feel his discomfort. "Yes, I love her, though I never realised it until she was betrothed to you." He took a deep breath, "But she loves you. In all the time I have known her, I have never seen her as happy as she was when she met you. If she is happy and the union keeps peace in our land, how could I come between you?"

Orestes placed a hand on his shoulder. "I will take care of her, Levidis."

"You had better," he replied. In a lighter tone, he added, "Besides, my family have watched others fall from grace through disloyalty, and before I left my mother warned me to watch over you. She is a hard woman. Her words were, 'Come back with your shield or on it.'"

Orestes burst out laughing and Levidis joined in.

When they had managed to control themselves, Orestes

turned to Levidis. "You were the first to swear allegiance to me. I will have need of such loyalty in the days to come. Mycenae will be the first city of Greece, and I will rule it. Sparta is now also mine through marriage. I cannot be in two places at once. I have thought hard about this for weeks, and I think it would be wise for Sparta to have two kings ruling together, working with one another, so that it still has a leader when I cannot be there."

"Your idea has merit," replied Levidis, "but two rulers can cause conflict."

"Which is just why it must be someone I can trust completely, and you would be answerable only to me," Orestes said flatly.

"My lord," gasped Levidis, "surely there is someone more suitable."

"No. From this day forth, Sparta will benefit from the wisdom and protection of two kings so it will never be left without a ruler, and you are the only choice I can make. I feel closer to you than to any other since the death of my parents. I think fighting together, side by side, formed a bond; I feel as if we were now brothers." Orestes' mind was made up but Levidis still sat in stunned silence. "It is also my intention to give the control of Aegisthus' city to Nestor for his loyalty. Argos shall be his under Mycenae; let him guard our approach from the sea."

Orestes rose. "We are missing too long from the celebrations. It is my wedding, after all. Can you bear to sit through it, brother?"

"I can, my lord." He took Orestes' outstretched arm and allowed himself to be lifted to his feet.

At the bottom of the stairs they turned back towards the palace. A cloaked, hooded figure carrying a torch moved towards them. For the second time that night Orestes flinched, but, before he could move a hand towards his knife, Levidis had already moved him aside to block him with his own body. The figure stopped before them.

A slim hand moved the hood of the cloak back from the head to reveal beautiful dark features surrounded in hair so black that it disappeared into the night. Orestes recognised her vaguely from around the palace but couldn't place who she was.

"I would have words with the king," she said. Even in a strange accent, the high-pitched voice had an intoxicating, exotic quality, along with the air of one who expected to be obeyed without question.

"Who are you?" growled Levidis. With one hand on his knife, he glanced back at Orestes.

"I am Cassandra." She inclined her head. "Formerly a princess of Troy and loyal priestess of the great Apollo, I was brought here by your noble father, Agamemnon."

"So you are a slave, demanding to speak to the king," barked Levidis, ignoring all her airs and fancy titles.

"I am one who humbly brings a wedding gift for the king," she said.

"Easy, Levidis." Orestes put a placating hand on the man's arm. "What gift could a slave possibly have for a king?" asked Orestes. "Surely you have no love for those who killed your people and enslaved you."

"Your father never treated me as a slave," replied Cassandra. "He continued to allow me to serve my master Apollo for the gifts I have from him. Your father was one of the few people who believed in them."

"And what might those be?" sneered Levidis.

"Do not mock the gods, Spartan," she replied. To Orestes she said, "In his wisdom, the god Apollo has given me the gift of sight, of reading the future. This is the gift which I offer to you."

"Really?" Orestes didn't believe in oracles and readers, or even the gods if he was being honest with himself, but he was intrigued. "And what has the god seen in my future?"

"One of the many possible futures." Cassandra bowed her head again. "The god has asked me to carry a message. He asks that I tell you, as a wedding gift from Apollo himself, that Iphigenia is not dead. You can find her and unite what is left of your family. She is being held as a priestess by the goddess Artemis in Athens."

EPILOGUE

NEARLY TWO YEARS AFTER LEAVING TROY, ODYSSEUS HAD ALMOST given up on ever finding them. He spent every day in a debate with himself: was it time to give up? Had they been dashed against the shore somewhere or crushed in a storm? Had they found somewhere far away and lived the peaceful lives of farmers?

Somehow he found it hard to imagine Achilles pushing a plough behind an ox. Hector could probably settle down running a town, but as much as Achilles wanted to believe that he could live in peace without hurting anyone, Odysseus knew that the boy had been born for war. That was why he'd been so shocked by the peaceful silence everywhere he docked.

Then today, running before a spring squall, he had spotted a ship on the beach: a Greek ship. His breath caught; he would know that ship anywhere. It was the Syren, one of the ships he had managed to hide away for them to make their escape from the Hellespont. They had to put in here to hide out from the storm anyway, so he drove the prow of his ship onto the rough stone beach and jumped ashore with a rope, preparing to pull it further up the shore as his crew jumped from their rowing benches to join him to get a closer look.

As his men prepared shelter on the beach he scouted the shore, finding the ship empty, stripped of everything. The reason they had abandoned it was clear; he could see where the timbers had been damaged, and he had spent long enough at sea to know exactly how much water that would let in.

The surrounding area told him nothing except that they had been here. He would need to search further and talk to the locals when the weather settled. A few days ashore would do all the men some good.

———

"THE BLOODY NERVE!" Pyrrhus thundered. "Who do they bloody think they are?"

Philoctetes sat with his head in his hands, his bloodshot eyes staring at the floor. This was not how he had intended to spend his hangover. Every yell from the enraged spoilt child send shards of glass slicing through his delicate head.

The woman with whom Pyrrhus had spent the night tried to calm him with gentle cooing noises, stroking his chest, but he split her lip with a back-handed slap that sent her sprawling to the floor to curl up in a whimpering ball.

"Calm down, Neoptolemus," pleaded Philoctetes. "They probably didn't know about the promises Agamemnon made when he summoned you to Troy. The messenger said that Agamemnon had been murdered the very night he arrived home; he probably didn't have a chance to tell them that he'd arranged for you to marry Hermione."

"Even if you are right, we weren't even sent official word of his death. Surely Odysseus would have told them when he returned that we were here." Pyrrhus fumed. "They have forgotten about us, Philoctetes. We have been abandoned here."

"Abandoned?" repeated Philoctetes. "Pray that we have been, Neoptolemus." He waved a hand around him. "Look around you; we live like kings here. You took the largest palace in all Epirus; you keep a stable of fifty women and seem intent to repopulate the area by yourself." He shook his head. "There is no one here to challenge us. If they have forgotten us, that's all to the good. We can rule here unopposed and enjoy life without living under any other king."

Pyrrhus paced the floor, chewing over what had been said. "No," he growled. "No, I cannot let this insult to my honour go unanswered. The gods hear promises, Philoctetes, and I was promised Hermione. I will take her. I will bring her back here. She will be my first wife and live here with me."

"If you go, Pyrrhus, you go alone," sighed Philoctetes. "I will not risk the life I have hear, with as many women as I want, for one girl." Rising, he made his way to the door. "I hope you can let this go, lad." He looked sadly at the girl lying in a ball on the floor. "If not, try not to kill any of the girls before you go. She is carrying another of your children." The door closed silently behind him.

ACKNOWLEDGMENTS

Huge thanks are due to Shawn T. King, whose cover art probably encouraged you to buy this book, and to Nils and all the Fantasy Hive team for hosting the official cover reveal.

I would also like to thank my Editor, Elaine Kennedy, for her work on both this book and The Fall of The Phoenix. She is the reason you can understand what I was trying to write. (Any mistakes in acknowledgements are my own).

Also thanks are due, in huge part to Mr. Ben Galley, please take a bow. Towards the end of getting this book ready, Ben was taking time out of his already busy writing schedule to walk me through the basics of how to, when it came to self publishing. Much appreciated mate.

Christian Cameron and A.M.Steiner, who gave me advice and encouragement especially when I was lucky enough to meet them at Worldcon.

Angus Watson and \SJA turney who are even now reading this

and Eric Sparks and James Simonds who acted as beta readers for me, they read they earlier versions so you didn't have to. Thanks for your help lads.

And to everyone in the wider community for support, the writing community really are an awesome community to be part of.

And to everyone who reads this book. Thank you

Lightning Source UK Ltd.
Milton Keynes UK
UKHW010936140921
390557UK00001B/206